The Witness Tree

The Witness Tree

The Witness Tree

By Terri Morrison Kaiser

The Witness Tree

The Witness Tree

ACKNOWLEDGEMENTS
The road to publication for this book was long with unending twists and turns, and many helpful souls along the way. First off, I want to thank the members of the Third Story Writers Guild at the Park Falls Public Library for the countless hours they listened to my ideas, critiqued my re-writes, and their generous advice: Karen Dums, Anna Maria Hansen, Peg Zaemisch, Mary Lobermeier, Scott Schmidt, Lisa Cook, Rebecca Kasowicz, Dawn LeDuc and Roz Gelina. Thank you to my beta readers: Betti Michalski, Kathi Franke, Mary Peters, Catherine Schmidt, Jean Fischer, Rebecca Furtak, Sandi Bucheger, Jacci Wirsing, and Holly Kaiser. Price County Sheriff, Brian Schmidt, for advice on crime scene procedures and lingo. Thank you to my mother, Arlene Morrison, for being one of my readers and more importantly, for introducing me to a love of books. To my sons, Bill and Tom, my son-in-law, Kris, and grandchildren Anna, Jack and Lauren—you inspire me every day. I cannot say thank you enough to my dear friend, editor, and birthday buddy, Barbara Lobermeier, for the countless hours of advice and support. And thank you to my husband, Tom, for all your patience as I pursue this passion of mine (and for the title.)

The Witness Tree

With gratitude for the strength shown me by my grandmothers, with love and admiration:
Stella Padour Morrison and
Frances Huml Loula Prezak

The Witness Tree

PROLOGUE

They called it the Witness Tree. Nigh on a hundred years ago, four landowners came together seeking a common boundary of their properties after Old Man Kennedy's cows strayed one too many times. The men agreed that this tree, with roots deep and hungry along the Redemption River, was the nearest they would come to a common bearing marker without a surveyor to make it official.

As basswoods go, this was a prime specimen. Mother Earth had planted it in a peaceful glen along the river where it grew stalwart and true. At ninety feet tall, and a trunk over four feet wide, it held a respectable girth. In spring, leaves the pattern of hearts cut with ragged-edged shears pushed forth from sturdy branches followed by buttery-white blossoms in June.

Over time, its gray bark furrowed like the face of a withered old man watching seasons drift slowly by. Then one, treacherous night, a violent storm churned over the land. It began a raucous tug of war, the wind whipping and twisting the bulk until, with one murderous blast, the top gave way and hurtled through the night, leaving the trunk leaning at an angle like a weary sundial.

With the passage of time, exposure to the elements hollowed the trunk giving small creatures, bugs and things that slithered a fine home for anything worth hiding.

The end of the Witness Tree's time by the Redemption was a curious thing, indeed. A small boy, no bigger than a twig, climbed the summit and the whole of it crashed to the earth. No one was prepared for what spilled from the hollow center, 'cept maybe the spirit of the poor soul left to rot inside.

The Witness Tree

CHAPTER 1

Esther Foley

It was July, nineteen hundred and forty-four, and the summer day promised to be hotter than a pistol. These tiny farms tucked into the north woods of Wisconsin had enjoyed a bountiful growing season. The measure of a good corn crop, 'knee high by the fourth of July,' held true and then some. The farmers were blessed. Well, most of them.

And me, I was curled in a ball on a bed of fern along the banks of the Redemption River where it cut through our back forty. It's where I spent a fitful night. Me and my two children.

Morning sun warmed my cheek, and I knew it was high time to be moseying on back, but I didn't want to open my eyeballs yet. It was soothing to listen to the river slap the rocky shore and burble through the rapids. Wasn't a better song in the world.

It was now Sunday, the twenty-third. Most of the families in Peeksville were sitting in pews dressed in their Sunday best, praying for God knows what: a good crop, healthy children, forgiveness of their sins? I suppose then they hope like hell it comes true. I wonder, do those people really sin enough to call for a church visit on such a sweltering day? The idea of those starchy outfits and the sweat trickling down their backs, all the while listening to a preacher tell 'em how to live, as if they couldn't figure that out on their own.

Although maybe, I coulda used a bit of advice from a higher power those twelve years ago as I'd certainly mucked things up by marrying Harlon Foley, even though it really weren't my doing. Wasn't fair, but I guess, what is? It was a shotgun wedding, and my Ma was the one holding the shotgun.

I hadn't yet opened my eyes, but I knew change was in the air. I felt it. My dearest friend Ruby teased me about my intuition. I never thought much of it. It didn't keep me from marrying Harlon, so what good was it? Guess my rebellious streak over-rode it for a time.

It was pathetic and humiliating, to be sure, to find yourself sleeping among the nightbirds and the worms, but Harlon gave us no choice. He had been flat-out drunk again and chased us from our warm beds to the barn then threatened to burn it down. It was then we snuck out the back and ran through the black night across our field, through a stretch of woods and then just into the neighbor's land. I coulda kept running all night, until Harlon was nothing but a bad dream, but the children were exhausted. The night was warm, so we lay among the fern, making a game of sleeping under the stars like cowboys.

Luddie didn't buy it. He was too old for that sort of thing, but Helen did, or so I hoped. Although Helen wasn't much for make-believe.

In the past we woulda made beds in the hay mow and I woulda told stories of my growing up years until they fell asleep. In the morning we'd traipse on back to the house for breakfast while Harlon slept it off.

My tolerance with him weren't what it used to be, and I about had my fill of it all. Plans were flitting through my brain like leaves in a tempest. I weren't sure what I was gonna do, but something was gonna come to me. It had to.

I stretched and straightened my legs. My denim pants, stained with grass and the rich forest soil, exposed my ankles now dotted with mosquito bites. A tiny black ant tickled its way over my wrist. I smooshed it with the pad of my thumb and flicked it off with a bit of triumph.

Checking our surroundings, we'd crossed into the neighbor's land in the night. I knew this by the Witness Tree that served as a bearing mark between our property and theirs. It was behind us when it shoulda been to the north if we'd stayed true to the path. The night was black as tar under the cover of the forest, and I couldn't see a thing.

Rising up on an elbow, I looked over my shoulder.

The children, Luddie and Helen, stirred only a tidge, crooked arms for pillows. My two perfect angels.

The overalls covering Luddie's skinny body bore the spoilings of a restless night, dirt smudged here and there, a stick in his sandy hair. He worried so about me, about Helen, about the farm and the animals. Too much for a boy of eleven.

Helen's blond curls fanned out from her little heart-shaped face, long eyelashes over cheeks rosy in slumber. At six years old, it was easy to see she'd be a beauty one day. It could easily be said that my Helen would rule the world when she was older, or her corner of it anyways.

Beyond the rise farther down the river, lay a pasture where the neighbor's cows fed and farther still, their white two-story farmhouse flanked by a small white barn and a lopsided garage.

The Witness Tree

The old Kennedy farm. Rumor in town held that a new owner purchased the place last month, although I ain't seen any sign of 'im yet.

A shadow passed overhead, and I ducked out of instinct. I braced and trained my ears for sound, but all I heard was the whispered gossip of the leaves and the distant, lonesome song of a robin. Nothing human.

Carefully, I ventured to look up as a crow was perched on top of the Witness Tree, staring down at me with judgment in its black old eyes.

"Go on. Get gone," I said as loud as I dared. Damn bird dared look on me like I was nothing but trash. Well, I couldn't argue any with my current circumstance, now could I?

The crow opened its razor beak and let out a 'caw' that broke the stillness saying 'take that' before it took flight. I never did like crows.

I sat up and crossed my legs. My hands were a God-awful mess. Dirt rimmed my short fingernails, and my palms were all calloused from farm work. I dusted them off and shook my shoulder-length hair free from being plastered to my head. I weren't no beauty by the standards of the day, no sleek curls sitting pretty on my neck or piled over my forehead, no red lipstick, or blushing cheeks. No. My dish-water colored hair hung in frizzy corkscrews to my shoulders and I could never do nothing with 'em.

A slight breeze kicked up and felt good. Soon, we'd be needing to start the short walk back to our little farm in the valley. Harlon would be sleeping it off for a while yet, but the pigs needed slopping, chickens fed, eggs gathered, and the cows to be milked. There weren't never an end to the work.

The chickens had been laying poorly of late. If only those bunch a feathers knew how I counted on the profits of their production for my secret fund. My freedom fund. Just a little

4

longer and I just might have enough squirreled away. Then, well I hadn't thought that far ahead yet.

I turned to face my children who still slept soundly. That's when the true sum of the situation hit me. It was like a sledgehammer right to my heart. Children should never have to live like this—fearful of their father, led to sleep outside by their mother with no covering, no pillow. Maybe I shoulda doubled back to the farm later that night, but what if Harlon made good on those threats? Maybe I shoulda went to the neighbor and called the sheriff, but then everyone would know. I couldn't stand it. I'd made my bed and I was lying in it. Just like Ma had told me I had to.

A tear leaked down my cheek and dripped onto the front of my sleeveless blouse. Another followed that one and then another. I slapped them off my cheeks. Tears never solved a damn thing, but this, this was as low as I ever planned to go.

All of a sudden, a voice mingled with that of the rustling leaves. I turned this way and that. I couldn't see the source.

There it was again. Somewhere beyond the bend of the river. A muffled voice carried on down by the morning breeze.

I stretched my neck, straining to hear more. It was a man's voice, deep, yet, pleasing somehow.

"Here girl. Come, Winifred." The voice was so faint, I wasn't certain I'd heard right.

I stole a glance back at the children, then carefully followed the path along the shore, keeping my head low. I crept through a stand of evergreen and knelt behind a large boulder.

"Come here, Winnie."

And then, he stepped out into the glen. Tall and slender, with hair the color of rusty water, sun glinting off his wire-rimmed glasses. He had on a white shirt tucked into brown pants, suspenders over his shoulders to hold it all in place, and work boots crunching over the ground. He held a stick in one hand.

A dog ran to his side. A golden retriever. A beautiful dog. Made me think of our old Petey back at the farm. That poor mutt was knocking at death's door just waiting to get in.

The man spoke to his dog and tossed the stick into the trees. The dog bounded off and returned with the prize. His master gave him a gentle nuzzle and a pat.

This had to be the new neighbor.

Ida Valentine said she heard a single man with a mysterious past bought the farm. She warned me to be on the lookout for anything suspicious. Ida said word around Peeksville was that he dodged all questions about family and past occupations, but then, the Kennedy's said his money spent as good as the next. Harlon said Ida didn't know her arse from a hole in the ground. On that, I hated to admit, my husband was probably right.

I watched as the man played fetch with the dog. He'd throw that stick with his long arm and the dog would move as quick and fluid as the rapids of the Redemption. After a few minutes, the dog found something of interest in the woods and the man stood and watched with his hands on his hips.

He angled his weight against a maple and stared off toward the other side of the river. Whether he was looking at something in particular or lost in thought, I couldn't tell. Then he turned his head in my direction and I about had a fright. I ducked down behind the boulder again then cautiously peeked out. He couldn't see me, and I was grateful.

Then he did something curious. He started to recite poetry. Why, I hadn't heard anything like that in ages. I knew I had heard those words before, probably in the few short years I'd been in school reading every book I could get my hands on, but I could not place the poet. As he spoke, I tipped my ear to listen.

The Witness Tree

But our love it was stronger by far than the love
Of those who were older than we-
Of many far wiser than we-
And neither the angels in Heaven above
Nor the demons down under the sea
Can ever dissever my soul from the soul
Of the beautiful Annabel Lee,

With a turn of his head the words drifted off and I couldn't catch the last of it. And then, it was as if his whole countenance changed. His shoulders slumped like he held wet sacks of laundry, and his head bent in a downward angle. It was as if a fit of melancholy grabbed holda him and wouldn't let go.

I don't know why, but I felt sorry for him. He looked to have a heavy burden upon his soul. Maybe the whole mystery around him was something sad, something terrible. I'd have to tell Ida to watch her mouth.

Just then from behind, I sensed a stirring in the way a mother would and hurried to return, careful to keep my head low so as not to alert the poet at the river.

Helen scratched at her cheek. Then the bluest of eyes opened to the morning light.

"Mama?" The girl had a dark streak on her chin.

I spit on my thumb, wiped it away and whispered. "Mornin', deary."

"We slept outside all night. I didn't like it very well." Helen's brows knit like little worms and her lips drew up in a perfect bow.

Guilt pricked my heart. I put a finger to Helen's lips. "Shh."

"Why do I have to be quiet?" While cute as a button, this daughter of mine questioned everything. She'd narrow her eyes, furrowed her brow, and scrunched her little nose as she analyzed each situation. It was kinda tiring at times. This girl was an old

7

soul stuffed into the body of a petite sprite of a child.

I lowered my face until we were nose to nose, forehead to forehead.

"We don't want to wake the baby bunnies now, do we?" Helen shook her head and rubbed her eyes. "I saw the mama hop on through here just a minute ago."

I touched Luddie's arm. "Luddie my boy, rise and shine." With a finger I pushed the hair from his forehead.

Luddie opened his green eyes and did a quick check of his surroundings. He pulled his skinny body up, pulled in his shoulders and rubbed his eyes with the backs of dirty hands. Luddie had never given me an inch of trouble, ever.

"Well, if you two aren't the dirtiest cowboys on the ranch." I grinned, trying to lighten the sorry situation.

"Time to get back now." To Luddie I said, "Check the hen house. I'll scramble some eggs."

Helen said, "I'm dirty, Mama," and brushed at her overalls. "This wasn't a very good idea."

"Shush. We'll clean you up good as new. Now, Luddie, take your sister and get those eggs. I'll be right behind you."

"Yes, Ma," he said keeping his eyes to the ground below him. "Do ya think he's up yet?"

"Goodness, no. You'll be fine. I'll be there shortly."

I glanced back toward the clearing. "I'm goin' to check on somethin'." My curiosity was running higher than the Redemption in spring.

The children stared at me.

"Now go on. I'll be right there." I shooed at them and watched as Luddie took Helen by the hand and led her back along the path.

I waited only a few seconds then went ahead in the opposite direction. As I neared the bend, I hid behind the boulder again and peered around to see the man was still there, still lost in his thoughts, the dog nowhere to be seen. The poet turned in my direction, and I quickly ducked from sight. With my heart banging and my breath holding in my chest, I waited, afraid to move for fear he'd see. What a stupid thing to have gone back.

Then it happened.

The dog came from nowhere and ran right toward me, ears pricked, wet tongue hanging out the side.

Fretfully, I didn't move a muscle as the dog sniffed, came closer, sniffed some more, and then backed away.

And then it barked. I was so frightened, I backed away, but my ankle caught, and I fell back onto the ground.

It was then the man saw me through the trees. Our eyes met for a brief, strange moment. It was a moment that seemed to carry a deep connection, like a tether from one soul to the other. My sister Hattie would have said that was utter nonsense, but sister Violet would have described it as kismet. I wasn't really sure, but Vee was always one to find magic and romance wherever she looked. Silly girl.

I quick pulled my gaze from his. Would he call the authorities? After all, I was trespassing, had gone way beyond the Witness Tree, and for all he knew, I was trying to steal or harm his property in some way.

The dog advanced on me, barking as it did so. The man called, "Winifred, it's all right. Winifred, come."

Desperately, I scratched for purchase among the forest grasses and fern, my heart thumping wildly. I pulled myself up and ran as fast as my legs could go.

"Wait," he called after me. "Are you hurt? Can I help you?"

I just kept running. It was all I knew to do.

CHAPTER 2

Helen Foley

"Hmph," I had given my best stink-eye to the enormous zucchini plant in the middle of the vegetable garden as I crossed the yard. I'd watered and fertilized, cajoled even, but all it managed to produce was two piddly vegetables for my trouble.

"Slacker." Benevolence was never my strong suit.

The hollyhocks *tsk, tsked,* and shared my disgust.

Our growing season was about over here in northern Wisconsin, and I was left feeling short-changed by that lazy zucchini plant, promising bounty with its many golden blooms. *Liar.* The yellow squash right next was going to keep me busy harvesting in the next week for its large plant had six new sprouts just in the last day. The green beans and lettuce were done a while ago now, as were the

The Witness Tree

green peppers, their carcasses lay in the compost bin. The tomatoes
were being slow to ripen this year, but once they did, the shelves in
the basement would be heavy with canned tomato juice and
spaghetti sauce, maybe some chili.

Anyway, it was my flowers that need attention that day.

My ramshackle garden shed was the previous owners 'she-
shed', whatever in hell that meant. Such frivolousness. The shed
was a pleasing shade of rusty red with white trim now after I
covered the horrendous baby blue. A green flower box hung under
the one paned glass window spilling over with trailing geraniums
in pretty pink. That's where I spent most of my time until winter
sealed me up inside. I pushed back the barn style door with what
muscles I still had at seventy-eight and the tired groan of the door
likened to what my joints experience every time I moved.

Inside, the shed was nothing fancy. The shelves were lined with
empty pots, my favorite of which were the clay for there was
something satisfying about the simplicity and the fact that they are
of the earth themselves. Although, whatever I plant in them were
thirstier than all the others as the clay soaked in the moisture so
quick. Baskets of all kinds hung from nails up above that generally
snagged my halo of white hair if I forget to duck. Toward the back,
next to my beat-up orange tiller. the rakes, hoes and shovels were
lined up like soldiers waiting to go to war against the weeds. Can't
remember when I bought the tiller. Must be an antique by now,
like me, but ran like a top, also like me I liked to think. Well,
except for the aches and pains of age.

I rooted around the various pots looking for my favorite
trowel—the one with the sturdy yellow and black handle that fit so
well in my bony hand. Finally, I found it in a rusted metal bucket
in the corner and returned to the flower beds.

The lilies had dropped their blooms with the cold nights, so I
had planted mums in orange and yellow, rust, and white to keep

11

the bed in color.

It's all a fine distraction to while away the time until I was able to leave this life behind. My usefulness was finished for anything but the gardens, and all that remained was a haunting feeling that my life was running on empty. I feared the day the gardens got to be too much and nothing else remained.

"How are you holding up?" I cradled a spikey, white bloom in the deep lines of my hand. The tips were nipped in the frosty night and left the whole plant looking a bit bedraggled.

"Getting tough to keep up appearances, isn't it? I know how you feel."

Yes, yes, they replied.

When I bought this little house in Peeksville three years ago, first thing I did was hire carpenters to put a nice tall fence around the backyard to guard my privacy. I needed a smaller house, a manageable piece of ground, but I did not need neighbors. I hadn't wanted the responsibility of the farm any longer.

My mother held onto it for some reason, refusing to sell when all the work fell upon her shoulders. Of course, Luddie and I did what we could, but it was a hard life. Mama had a fierce hold on that piece of ground and after everyone went and died on me, I suppose pride prevented me from letting it go. I had to prove I could do it all. And why? It served no one.

I sat back on my heels and stretched. I was proud of what I'd accomplished in my little yard. I'd put the vegetable garden in the middle of the yard, with flower beds along the fence on two sides. The south side was shielded by the small garage where I planted snow-on-the-mountain and fiddlehead fern. The back fence was graced with sun-loving flower beds like zinnias and balloon flower, hollyhocks and coreopsis, silver mound and dahlias, to name a few. Not to mention the bulbs of tulip and daffodil that popped up here and there in the spring.

12

The Witness Tree

Along the back of the house is where I put the peony bushes and lilies from starts I brought from the farm. On the north side were variations of hosta that thrived in the shade of a big maple tree like lazy girls just in from the sun. Out in the front yard I had a row of phlox, purple and white, with tiger lilies thrown in here and there. On a windy day, they all flounced about so nice.

Oh, and I can't forget about the lilac bush that I planted in the corner of the backyard. It was also a traveler from the farm. It gave me fits at first, but finally took off. Many years ago, my mother took a cutting from the original plant that grew at the neighbor's place up the road. It seemed to hold a special meaning for her, so I felt I had to bring a portion with me.

The gardens, after all, were where I felt closest to my mother.

The black-eyed Susans, the mums, and the marigolds thrived mightily in mid-September as they always did. Everything else was holding on by a thread. When we get that first frost, which wouldn't be long, the colors fade, and the greenery darken as it all would bow and curl back into the earth.

From behind the fence and across the alley, the Meyer's rock-and-roll had drifted over from their open window. Such a pain in the neck. Unfortunately, sound was not something I could block with a fence. Not sure what was the name of the song, but 'I can't get no satisfaction?' Really?

To the north, the Ryerson children were squealing in the back yard. Must be some sort of game. Thanks to the fence, they'd have to keep it on their side. If not, they'd be sorry.

Some days I wondered at the wisdom that made me think I should move into town. After I sold the hardware store, the farm kept me good and busy, but I couldn't keep up, no matter how hard I tried, and I'd be damned if I'd ask anyone. Besides, being at the farm every day, all day, allowed too many images and voices to fog my brain and keep me up at night. It was time to leave it to

13

someone else.

If only I didn't have to deal with neighbors and could spend my days blissfully lost in broccoli, blooms, and butterflies, so much so, there'd be no room to think of anything else.

At that time of year, it was a bit more difficult to kneel and lift and bend after a summertime of doing just that. My inspiration— one glance out the kitchen window at the swath of color that adorned the yard, when the phlox thrived, the lilies danced, the hollyhocks trumpeted, and the bee balm dazzled. Just like children. Lots of work, and for the most part, lots of reward if everything turned out all right. Of course, I only had the burden of raising Ivy, and that had been challenge enough, thank you very much.

Flowers behaved better than children. They understood me, listened to me and offered comfort when no one else did. And I swear, they spoke to me.

From the street, my little yellow house with white trim and green shutters, had the appearance of a happy little cottage. Appearances were important after all. Not that the farm had been a showstopper by any means, but this place was mine alone, the only thing that had ever truly been mine, except my memories and my secrets.

A sudden breeze caused the blooms to bow and twist in an explosion of color, whispering *'hush, hush'*. The crimson dahlias I'd been weeding gathered close as though to whisper a piece of gossip.

I looked at my hands. In some places a person couldn't tell the difference between the dirt and the age spots. I savored the organic feel of my fingers working the rich, aromatic soil. Hard to believe those old hands were the same with which I worked the gardens at the farm with my mother so many years ago.

Wiping my gnarled, work-worn hands on the grass, I pushed up and brushed the grime from my blue linen pants. A strand of long, white hair fell from the twist at the back of my head, and I used my wrist to push it away, trying to hook it on an ear and not get dirt all over.

It was nearly time to start the cabbage rolls. You see, my mother's recipe had been niggling at me all morning. Esther Foley hadn't been a fancy cook, but by God, she created the most wonderful meals with what she had at hand.

The garden gate creaked and startled me. *Who the hell would dare?*

"Miss Foley, you out there?" A deep male voice called.

If it was Norm or Pam Oakley looking for their cat again, I'd give them what for, I certainly would.

"Miss . . . oh, there you are." It was Reed Bolton, all gussied up in his deputy finest making him look tall and very important. He'd been one of Ivy's friends from school, in her class since kindergarten.

Reed's mother, Aggie, knocked on my door once asking me to join her church group. I hadn't even bothered to be nice when I shut the door in her face. Why in the world would she think I'd want to do that?

Reed got me back for my rudeness to his mother. At least that's how I felt. He had the nerve to stop me for a broken tail-light only a month later. I hadn't appreciated that one bit. Although he only gave me a warning, It was beyond humiliating to have been stopped on the side of the highway, a mere mile from town. He could have simply called me on the phone to inform me of the problem and saved the embarrassment. *Little shit.* Still, I suppose, he could have given me a ticket.

"What?" I gave him my best glare.

"Hello, Miss Foley." The downturn of his mouth worried me, and he looked awfully pale.

His thin lips stretched into a smile that quickly faded.

15

"How are you?" Reed clasp his hands before him.

"I am just fine," I gripped the garden trowel in my hands. Trouble was coming.

"Something has happened, Miss Foley. Do you want to have a seat?" He motioned toward the small bistro table and two chairs under the enormous mock orange bush in the southwest corner of the yard.

"I do not." I stiffened, waiting for whatever was to come. I'd become very good at that over the years—readying for bad news. The flowers stretched to hear.

Reed stepped forward, his blue eyes piercing. "I don't know how to tell you this. Please sit. It might make this easier for you."

The hostas began to quake as I felt my throat closing off.

"I will not sit down. Is it Ivy? An accident? I haven't seen the girl in a coon's age. Just tell me."

"Remains have been found at your old farm this morning. It appears they were hidden inside of a hollowed basswood in the back forty," Reed said and waited for my reaction.

I stared at the mole on his right cheek, just under his eye. If it was orange, it would look just like a ladybug.

When I failed to respond he continued. "I'm talking about the farm where you grew up out on Thornapple Road, now owned by Joe and Carrie Jennings."

The trowel landed at my feet, my lungs refused to expand, and all reason seeped from my brain. I willed my knees to keep me upright.

I grabbed hold of a thick lilac branch and held on. I was afraid I might vomit and simply focused on a sparrow scratching under the bush. Breathe, just breathe.

Reed continued to explain. The Jennings boy, Dylan, crawled up a dead, hollow tree on the property that then fell over, and wouldn't you know, a skeletal foot dropped out the bottom. The kid

16

was terrified of course, and their parents immediately called the sheriff's office.

Images long locked away circled, pointed fingers, taunted without mercy. I closed my eyes, holding the lids tight, but the faces of a night long forgotten, of Mama and Luddie, my father and...and two faces I didn't recognize. Or was it one? I couldn't bring the memory close enough to see. And the sounds, oh the sounds of that night, came roaring back in a muddled mixture of what, I wasn't certain. All of it breathed cold upon my skin. My poor old heart thumped and sweat gathered on my upper lip. I tried to swallow but couldn't.

"Miss Foley, do you understand what I'm telling you?" Reed spoke slowly as though speaking to a child. He bent for the trowel and handed it back to me.

"Of course, I do." I grabbed the trowel and gripped it so hard I feared the bones in my hand would come apart.

Honestly, at that age, a person shouldn't have to deal with such an awful shock, or any shock at all.

"I know this is not what you expected. After all, you spent most of your life on that farm. This can't be easy to hear." Reed touched my arm. I brushed him away. "Are you sure you heard me right, and understand what's happened?"

"I'm not deaf. Just old." My shoulders slumped with the weight of it all. "Just too damn old." My heart ached for my mother with a fierceness I hadn't known possible. 'It'll be fine, deary,' Mama would say, 'it'll be fine'. Well, it wasn't going to be fine. Someone was dead, and on what had been our property.

"Helen, do you have any idea whose body could be in that tree?" Reed hovered close as though I might keel over. "Whatever happened appears to have taken place a long time ago. That's why I'm here. This is not a crime that happened recently. Think back. You've seen a lot of history at the farm, this whole area. Why, I'm sure you must be a treasure-trove of information by now."

A massive stroke right then would have been my saving grace. I felt numb, my head spinning.

"Not the information you're looking for," I said. "You can trust me on that."

Reed took off his hat and scratched his head. "Seriously, Miss Foley, we need your help. Your parents, Harlon and Esther Foley, do you remember anything they might have said over the years? Rumors, stories? Anything you might remember would be useful. No matter how small."

"I don't know anything that would help you. My family are all gone, I have no one other than Ivy, and she certainly wouldn't know anything." I brought a wobbly fist to my mouth, then shook my head. The young man was simply doing his job. I took a breath and calmed myself. "What's with this Miss Foley? My name is Helen."

"Alright, Helen." His smile was gentle, reassuring.

"Now, go bother someone else." I shooed him away with my hand and turned back toward the garden, steeling my body against the current of fear coursing through me.

Breathe, just breathe, said the tiger lilies as they fluffed their foliage and beckoned me to come sit.

"Well, I … will you call me if you think of something? Anything? Please, Helen?"

"Playing goose chase with you is a waste of my time and yours," I said over my shoulder. "I don't have the answers you're looking for. Go play cop somewhere else." I knelt onto the grass and resumed my work.

From behind, I knew he hadn't left. *Dammit all to hell.*

Reed was standing over me. "Someone in the area knows something. I'd guarantee it."

"I don't care about any damned old tree." I refused to look up

18

from my work. "And I could give a rats ass about anybody stuck inside. It's no one that I know, and yes, it's a terrible tragedy for someone, but not me. I'm just sorry it was found on my property. What *was* my property. But I certainly don't know anything. And don't you be thinking that I do."

"You're upset. Can I get you a glass of water?"

I stabbed the trowel into the dirt. To hell with the cabbage rolls I'd wanted. My appetite had flown south.

I tried to snap off a spent mum with my thumb and forefinger, but my hand was shaking so, the deadhead wouldn't release.

Reed dropped down onto the grass alongside me. "Helen, this is your home we're talking about. Someone has lost one of their own. Please give this some thought."

"You're wasting precious time here." I tried the dead blossom again, but the stem turned rubbery. In frustration I grabbed the limp stalk and plucked the whole plant from the dirt, its roots reaching for its home. "Now look what I've done!"

"People are going to be deeply disturbed by this. It's my job to find answers and give reassurance."

"I can't help you. You're going to have to come up with more than me to solve this. By the way, what will you do?"

"We'll start a study of the whole area looking at missing persons cases, branching out into surrounding counties and states. As we speak, the area out there is being cordoned off and a grid pattern search will begin as soon as possible. We need something, anything, to point us in a direction."

I began to rock back and forth, trying to stem my nerves. It was an old habit when stressed. I still held the murdered mum.

"Do they know? Peeksville?" I asked.

"Not yet. We...I came straight to you. Of course, there are those people that watch every move we make, so it's probably out there by now."

19

The Witness Tree

I shook the soil from the mum's roots. "I wouldn't worry about that too much. Like you said, this...this skeleton you found in the Witness Tree will soon be ancient history when the next piece of gossip comes along. Then the good people of Peeksville can focus on something new, and you can go back to traffic stops."

Reed leaned into me and quietly said, "I never said anything about it being a Witness Tree. You know what tree I'm talking about, don't you?"

"I don't know why I said that." And that was the truth. I wasn't certain where my brain had connected the body found in the basswood to the hollowed-out tree back by the river, the one we called the Witness Tree. There were a lot of basswoods on the property, and surely there were more than one that were hollow. But how was I going to convince him of that now?

I swallowed the hard knot in my throat, but it only settled as a tight ball in my chest. I wiped the sweat on my upper lip with the back of my hand.

"There had to be a reason." Reed raised one eyebrow as he studied me.

"It's the only hollow tree I had seen on the farm. It being the bearing marker for the property, of course, I'd think of that one first. So, you're telling me that's the one?"

"I am." He was looking at me as though he'd caught me in a lie and I resented it.

"As a kid, Ivy crawled up that tree, and I gave her the dickens over it. The damn thing was ready to fall at any time back then. Can't imagine how rotten it is now." I curved my fingers into the grass and held on.

"Interesting thing—there's a carving on one side. I removed some of the moss to find a heart with an R and a B carved into the middle. Do you know anything about that?"

Yes, I had noticed that over the years and wondered about it, even asked my mother about it, but she denied any knowledge.

The blood pounded in my brain with a thump, thump, thump. I threw the dead mum to the back of the garden where it lay, my victim. "I had seen it, but those initials didn't mean a thing to me. I thought they'd been there since before my parents bought the place, or maybe some young people trespassed at some point. You know, I don't appreciate you coming to my house as if I would know anything about this...this crime." I brushed the dirt from my hands. "I'm sure the neighbors are having a good chuckle seeing a squad car in my yard."

"You never struck me as someone who cares what anyone thinks."

"Well, you don't know me as well as you thought." Oh, how I wished I wouldn't have blurted that out.

Reed's previously kind face now reminded me of the neighbor's dog. It was a rottweiler or some such. It had eyes that could look right through a person, see every nook and cranny, and not buy one bit of bullshit handed out.

"Are you sure none of this sparks a memory of something you may have heard in the past?"

"This is foolishness!" I wanted this to stop. "How would you feel if something like this was found where you spent your whole life? If I knew there was a dead body, why would I take Ivy back there on walks or to swim in the river? What kind of sick person would do that? Is that what you think of me?" I struggled to keep control. My stomach turned at the thought of Ivy and I spending time at the river, just underneath what had been someone's tomb.

"Calm down, Helen. I didn't mean to upset you so. You shouldn't be alone. I could call Ivy for you, if you'd like. What's her number?" He stood and pulled out his cell.

"Absolutely not. I bet you'd like that. A reason to call Ivy. Don't think I don't remember you sniffing around her in high school." It felt good to turn the tables on him, even if just a little.

"How is Ivy?"

"Still resenting the hell out of me for not supporting her marriage." I raised my hand to him, and he helped me to my feet. "I did the best I could with her, but that girl...I don't think she will ever forgive the world for taking her parents—my sister, Annabelle, and her husband—in that car crash. Only five years old, no parents, and stuck with me. I admit, I was ill-equipped to be a parent, but she didn't make it any easier. She and that lazy husband of hers live in Amery now with their two kids. I don't see her much."

"That's too bad, Helen. I'm sure you gave her the best life you could."

"Oh, I don't know about that. Anyway, I don't know about anybody stuck in a tree and I resent that you think I do."

"Just doing my job. The sooner we can get this mystery solved, the better for everyone. I had hoped you'd have some insight, that's all."

"You're going to give me a coronary with all this. Go. Just leave me be." I flapped my hand at him in a wobbly dismissal.

"We'll talk." Reed nodded, replaced his hat, patted my shoulder, and left.

The garden gate whined as Reed closed it behind him. A rush of despair hit me, and I steadied my knees to keep from tipping over.

I'd only been a child after all. How was I to know? Could I be so lucky that the remains could be some other poor soul? The odds, I was sure, were not in my favor.

I balled my fists and put them to my closed eyes to prevent any tears from leaking through.

"No, no, no. This can't be. It can't." I looked to the hard, gray sky above. I wanted to scream with all I had in me, 'This isn't fair. I was only six-years old. I didn't know.' Those damn dirty bones were going to ruin everything.

Hush, hush, said the black-eyed Susans. "Go to hell," I said.

CHAPTER 3

Esther

Harlon's rusty Ford pickup rumbled over the gravel road, the tires sending up great windrows of dust spiraling in their wake. Harlon was in a hurry to get into town and back again. Impatient as always.

I sat on the towel covering the grimy cloth seat to keep my green going-to-town dress clean, not that it was fancy by any means, but its always nice to show up in clean clothes. I had one hand bracing the dash, the other on the open window, my legs, all nicked-up from picking blackberries, straddled the stack of eggs on

24

the floor cushioned with an old blanket.

Harlon abruptly maneuvered around a pothole, knocking me sideways into the door. A yelp from the truck-bed and a cry of "Mama" sent my head out the window, wind whipping my hair like a tempest as we flew over the country road.

"What's the matter?" I yelled into the wind.

Helen's blond head popped into view, braids dancing all wild, "Mama, Luddie hit his head and he's bleeding," she yelled as loud as she could.

"Luddie, you all right?" When he didn't answer, I pulled on the sleeve of Harlon's flannel shirt. "Stop the truck. Luddie's hurt."

"Can't be that bad." He kept his squinty eyes on the road, chewing on a toothpick. How I wanted to shove it into the back of his throat and watch him squeal.

I looked through the back window. Helen sat back so I could see Luddie. He had a gash over his right eye and blood trickling down the side of his face. "I'm okay," the boy said, although I couldn't hear him, and he wiped at the red with the palm of his hand, then onto his pants.

"Pull over, he's hurt," I said more forcefully, giving Harlon a nudge with my elbow.

"No."

Normally, I held my tongue, but I couldn't stop it. "I said, pull over."

"Goddamn it." Harlon's face creased with annoyance, but he kept going.

"You shouldn't a turned the truck so hard with the kids in the back. They didn't have time to brace and now he's hurt. Pull over!" I checked the box of eggs on the floor. "And if you don't watch those potholes my eggs'll be mush and not worth a red cent." It was a good thing I'd wrapped them in rags.

Harlon glared at me, drumming his thick thumbs against the

steering wheel as he continued to drive.

"You really want to pull into town with a child covered in blood? You know how people talk." I knew that would get his attention. Unfortunately, his drunken behavior wasn't one of those things he cared to hide.

"Fine." He swerved the truck to the shoulder and came to a halt. There was a yell and a thump as something, or someone, careened against the cab.

I opened my door and jumped out.

Luddie was sprawled across a spare tire against the cab, and Helen crouched in the corner. Madder than a wet hornet at their father, I reached toward my son.

"Are you all right?" I touched the gash under his brow. The cut was oozing red, and he had smeared a fair amount into his hair. Pulling a hanky from the pocket of my dress I wet it with my tongue and dabbed at the cut.

"It's nothin'," Luddie pushed my hand away.

"Let me clean it up. Don't seem too bad." I continued to lick and dab.

Helen pushed from the tire and crawled across the truck bed. "I hit my head too." She pushed out her lower lip and rubbed at the side of her head.

"Did you now?"

"You did not, Henny," Luddie said.

"Well, not as bad as you." The little girl pulled herself up to eye level with me and in a voice just above a whisper said, "Daddy's a bad driver."

I stifled the urge to grin, stopped fussing over Luddie, and leaned toward her. "I s'pose we need to learn to hold on a bit tighter because it ain't never gonna change."

"Maybe I should sit up there and help him. I could tell him where the holes are."

I put my hand on her head. "You just sit back here and take care to hold on. Keep an eye on your brother for me."

Harlon came out of the cab. "You ain't bein' a crybaby now are you, boy?"

Luddie shook his head and crouched into the corner. I handed the blood-stained handkerchief to Luddie in case he still needed it.

"Let's go. I got things to do." Harlon jumped back in the cab.

Oh, how I wanted to give him 'what for.' I returned to the passenger side and as I gripped the open door and stepped onto the running board, Harlon gunned the motor. The truck lurched forward nearly tossing me to the ditch before I swung inside.

Within a mile, the outskirts of town came into view. The steeple of First Congregational Church rose through the leafy trees and a sign proclaimed, Peeksville, WI, population 2,632. We drove past the grand old houses on Kollmer Street where my best friend Ruby grew up. The houses gave way to Lincoln High School on the left, the train depot and onto Main Street where shops and restaurants lined the sidewalks. Oh, to come to town someday with time to stroll the streets, browse in the stores, stop for coffee and pie at the Robin's Nest, and have money to spend. That would be a fine afternoon.

The truck lurched to a stop in front of the brick and glass facade of Nelson's Hardware. A large wooden sign overhead in red with green letters proclaimed it so. Harlon ordered the children to wait on the bench out front. I helped Helen down over the wheel-well while gazing for anyone I knew among the few people milling about.

I saw to the children and gathered the eggs.

The bell over the door chimed a welcome as I entered the store, and I had to take in the scent of dusty wooden floor, musky leather, animal feed, and mineral oil. Einar and Cora Nelson gave me a job here after my mother pulled me out of school to help support the family after Pa ran off. As much as I hated leaving school, working for Nelson's gave me purpose, and there was a whole new world of learning within these brick walls. I soaked in all I could taking care of customers, stocking shelves, helping Mrs. Nelson with the books, inventing new displays. This place suited me just fine.

"Well, look who's here." Mr. Nelson's face split with a wide grin. "Esther, you're a welcome sight for these old eyes of mine."

He had his round, wire glasses set halfway down his nose as he did when going over receipts. The crinkly lines around his smile and his eyes seemed to deepen every time I saw him lately. He was getting on in years and it saddened me. Besides my grandpa, this was the kindest man I had ever known.

"Mornin', Mr. Nelson. How are you today?" I advanced up the aisle.

The store was quiet and not up to par. The shelves of household goods needed dusting, bags of oats needed to be stacked neatly, the hardwood floor needed sweeping, and someone had knocked over the display of saw blades. Without hesitation, I set the eggs on the floor and straightened the blades.

"Oh, I'm fine as fishing line. Thanks for doing that."

I hoped to find a female to visit with. Most days I ran into Doris Kronberger with the best gardening tips or Millie Jaros always ready with a recipe or two. Maggie Hartway had a good eye for color when it came to picking out bolts of material when I could afford some down at the Mercantile. Rita Thier knew the best gossip. Then there was Mary Cummings, ready with a smile, her four children in tow. Helen and Luddie would have enjoyed seeing them.

Mr. Nelson simply greeted Harlon with a nod of his head, then to me, "Good to see those eggs today, Esther."

"My hens seem to be taking a vacation this week." I placed the eggs on the counter. "Only six dozen today."

"I need to look at ax blades," Harlon said and walked to the back of the store.

"We'll put the eggs out right away and they'll be gone in no time. How are the children?" Mr. Nelson adjusted the glasses on his nose and began stacking the eggs in crates of his own after I took back my rags. "I've got some licorice for them when you leave."

"They will certainly love that, and oh, they're fine. Growin' like weeds." I always felt so comfortable with Mr. Nelson. I wished I could say the same for his wife, Cora. "How is Mrs. Nelson?"

"She's up at the church this afternoon setting up for the Sutton funeral. You know Cora. She's happiest when she's got the Women's Fellowship whipped into a frenzy." He grinned as he opened the cash register. "You hear from Teddy lately?"

"Haven't. I'm so worried about him." I thought of my brother. Such a goofball. I missed his practical jokes and wild stories of his Saturday night escapades.

"This darn old war, taking all these young boys," Mr. Nelson said rubbing a hand over his balding head. "You know that more than most, Esther, losing your oldest brother last year. He was a fine young man, that Jacob. Hard worker. Such a loss. And Teddy still over there. How's your Ma holding up?"

"She is so bitter and hard. I know she's scared for Teddy, she has to be, but she won't show it. I can't imagine losing another brother. I wish this war would end."

"Mr. Roosevelt is doing what he can. God willing, Teddy will be home before you know it." Mr. Nelson reached across the counter and patted my arm.

"I know." I nodded and pushed back the knot in my throat.

Mr. Nelson took the egg money from the cash register. He lowered his voice, leaned near and asked, "You ever think about a job, Esther? Cora'd like me to give up this foolishness already, but

I figure I got a few years left. Been talking about taking on some help though, just a few days a week. There's no one we'd rather have than you."

"I don't know..." Leaving the farm on a more frequent basis was appealing to say the least.

"It would give you some extra money. Help you to afford some of those finer things in life." His gaze cut to Harlon. "You know you've always had a special place in my heart, Esther, and I'd do whatever I could to help you out."

"That's very nice of you, but Harlon wouldn't approve. He says a man isn't providing for his family if the wife has to work. Guess it doesn't matter what the wife wants." I just shrugged as he counted out three dollars and eighty-four cents for the eggs.

"Thank you." I slipped the money into my pocket along with the two pieces of licorice for the children.

Mr. Nelson shot another glance Harlon's way. "Keep the offer in mind, won't you?" He hesitated a moment. "Just in case you decide whatever Harlon wants doesn't matter anymore." He winked.

"You know, Mr. Nelson, I just might take you up on that someday," I whispered back.

"Hey, there Nelson." Harlon came forward. "Goddamn tractor is actin' up. Needs some brushes for the generator again. Battery keeps goin' dead."

I turned away as I had no interest in tractor parts.

I checked on the children through the window and browsed the shelves of seed bags, feed for animals, and various household items. I could use some new canning jars as Harlon broke a few in one of his fits of rage. It was tempting to put them on the bill, but money was tight right now. Around the corner there was some of the bag balm Cora Nelson raved about using on her hands.

I held out my work-worn hands and grinned. To think women

30

would aspire to having hands as smooth as a cow's udder.

The bell over the door tinkled and I looked up hoping to see a friendly face, but that's not what happened. A tall man opened the door with morning sun blazing behind him, darkening his image. He wore a fedora on his head, which he removed as he stepped inside. I squinted to see him as he moved further into the store then, with a start, realized this was a face I'd seen before.

Staring back at me were the spectacled eyes of the stranger, the new neighbor, I had seen at the banks of the Redemption.

I couldn't breathe. The jar of bag balm tumbled from my hand with a thud and rolled across the aisle.

Harlon and Mr. Nelson turned their attention to the noise. I quickly bent to retrieve the jar, thankful for the moment to sink out of sight and praying the man would disappear or, better yet, the floor would open up and swallow me whole. The sound of his footsteps on the hardwood floor went right through me. I stayed crouched behind the shelf until I felt him peeking over at me.

Harlon's voice boomed, "What are you doing there, Esther? I can't afford to buy something just because you can't keep a hold of it." To Mr. Nelson he said, "Women."

Sure as I ever was, this stranger recognized me.

With a subtle shake of my head, I pleaded with my eyes, *'Please don't say you saw me.'* He gave me a brief nod and I knew he'd keep the secret. Slowly I rose and with a trembling hand, replaced the jar on the shelf.

"Can I help you there?" Mr. Nelson asked him.

The corners of the man's mouth curved upward, his face crinkling at the corners of his blue eyes.

"I've come in for some liniment for my horse. Old Zeke's taken lame and I'm hoping a good rubdown will help." His voice was pleasant and his smile sincere. He walked slowly to the counter, stopping a mere two feet from the husky bulk of a man that was

31

my husband.

Harlon rudely assessed the newcomer with bloodshot eyes and a glower.

"You new around here?" Mr. Nelson took a bottle of liniment off the shelf.

"Just bought the Kennedy farm out on Thornapple Road," he said, shoulders lifting with pride.

"Well then," a smile spread across Mr. Nelson's face, "you're standing next to your neighbor here." He gestured toward Harlon. "This is Harlon Foley. Harlon . . . ah, you have a name newcomer?"

"Robert Sommers." His name touched my ears like a song on a summer breeze. I silently mouthed the name, enjoying the way it played on my tongue.

Mr. Sommers drew a long-fingered hand from his pocket and extended it Harlon's way. Harlon stared at him and after a brief moment, he extended his own dirty hand with nails chewed to the quick. The two men shook. Robert Sommers then swung his hand toward the shopkeeper. "And you are?"

"Einar Nelson, young man. Welcome to Peeksville. My wife, Cora, is working at the church today, otherwise she'd be here as well." Their handshake amiable. Then Mr. Nelson asked, "Is there a Mrs. Sommers?"

Something unreadable passed over Mr. Sommers' face. "Ah, no, no there's not. It's just me."

Mr. Nelson gestured toward me and I held my breath.

"The young lady behind you there is Harlon's wife, Esther." Mr. Nelson eyed Harlon over the top of his glasses. "You don't mind my introducing your wife, do you Harlon?"

Robert Sommers turned, his eyes met mine, and mine met his.

"Mrs. Foley." Mr. Sommers came forward, his hand open and ready.

The Witness Tree

I took the hand he offered. "Mr. Sommers."

"Good to meet you." He had the kindest eyes. Blue as an autumn sky. A shock of auburn hair fell across his forehead.

As my hand found a home within his, a sensation shot through me—a kindred understanding of sorts. The definition of that understanding a mystery.

He released my hand, but the heat and tingle of the brief touch remained. I slipped the hand into a pocket as though attempting to preserve the feeling.

I brushed my other hand through my wind-blown hair that was surely a mess, feeling frumpy and foolish. I wished I'd thrown on another dress this morning and it had been a long time since I'd had a new pair of shoes.

"Nice to meet you Mr. Sommers," I said.

Harlon turned toward Mr. Sommers. "You say your horse is lame?"

"Favoring the right front. I'm not sure why. I'm rather new to farming." Mr. Sommers hung his head with a chuckle, and I noticed a slight dimple on the right. "Seems my idea to become a gentleman farmer may have been a bit lofty, but I'm enjoying the challenge."

"Gentleman farmer, huh? That's all we need, hey Einar. More city folk thinkin' they know a wit about the hard work a farmin'." Harlon returned his attention to the tractor parts catalog Mr. Nelson set in front of him. I seethed at his rudeness. Harlon was far from a model of the hard-working man.

"Now Harlon," Mr. Nelson offered Robert Sommers a sympathetic smile, "farming is a noble way to spend a life. Sometimes a body needs to try something new." To Mr. Sommers he asked, "What brought you here, if you don't mind my asking?"

"Like you said, time for a change. Come fall I'll be substitute teaching to pay the bills."

"Well, all the best to you, young man. I'm no farmer myself, but if you need advice, I'll do my best to hook you up with someone that can help."

"I appreciate that. Now, Mrs. Foley …"

I snapped to attention.

"Could you use a few ears of corn? My crop, rag-tag as it is, is nearly ready and I'd be happy to share."

I brought a hand up to my chest gripping the top button of the dress. My goodness, I was nervous as a mouse that just encountered a cat.

"I appreciate the offer," I said, "but no thank you. We got enough of our own."

He nodded and fingered the hat in his hands.

"Hey there, Sommers," Mr. Nelson held a bottle of liniment in his hand, "On second thought, I'm going to have you try this one. Just came in. Same price."

"Thank you." Mr. Sommers turned toward Einar Nelson and I breathed a sigh of relief.

"I ain't seein' what I want here." Harlon pushed the catalog across the counter and stomped down the aisle. "Let's go." He pushed past me and went out the door.

"Take care now," Mr. Nelson said to me.

"A pleasure to meet you, Mrs. Foley," Mr. Sommers nodded.

"As well." I turned and followed my husband.

CHAPTER 4

Helen

Since the discovery of the body that set Peeksville ablaze with gossip, I had to leave my phone off the hook, curtains drawn, and the doors locked. The first few calls were old neighbors from my days on the farm or at the hardware store. They offered care and concern, but all they really wanted was the scuttlebutt on the owner of the bones and the gruesome details. None of which I knew. Not really. Sherry Meyer came over with a plate of cookies, but that was just an excuse. I hadn't seen the girl in ages and suddenly, she bakes a plate of cookies to share? *Bullshit.* I didn't tell her a thing. After that, it was time to hole up in my house and keep the world at bay.

Problem was, as much as I savored my time alone, I grew tired and resentful of having to hide. None of this was of my doing. Not a bit. But the handle on my hoe finally split in two and the garden needed weeding something awful before the cold came on.

As I went through the glass doors of Convenience Hardware, I couldn't help but shake my head at the changes, but what in this life ever remained the same? When I owned it, keeping the name Nelson's Hardware, to honor Einar and Cora Nelson, the original owners who left it to Mama when they died, the place had a certain, cozy feeling. A place where townsfolk could find carpentry supplies, a few housewares, and what they needed to fix their broken plumbing and heating.

My store wasn't quite in such an orderly fashion, but I knew where every bolt and screw lay tucked amid the shelves, just like my mother had. Back then, the place smelled of the old, dusty oak flooring, linseed oil, and coffee from the pot I kept brewing on the counter for the customers. While I hadn't been much for small talk, then I enjoyed listening to the farmers and loggers, gardeners and shade-tree mechanics banter about life from my place behind the counter or as I stocked the shelves.

I was mighty proud of continuing on with the store in the same tradition as my mother when she inherited it from the Nelsons. Finer folks than the Nelsons could not be found, and they always said Mama was the best employee they'd ever had. Now, the new owners, a couple of newcomers from Madison-way, bought a franchise, changed the name, covered the old floor, put up new shelves and spiffed up the inventory.

I highly disapproved.

As I mulled over the selection of garden equipment, and not liking the prices one bit, out of the corner of my eye I noticed an old customer of mine, and he noticed me. I wasn't in the mood to visit and purposefully avoided Gus' gaze, knowing that he, too, had probably heard all the tawdry details of the discovery of the dirty bones. The whole thing was embarrassing.

"Why, if it ain't Helen Foley." Gus Jablonsky, the tall, tough old bird came around the row of shelves laden with fertilizers. Winter or summer, Gus wore a tattered hat on his cap of white hair, a red and black checkerboard shirt, and dirty wool pants held up with the nattiest pair of suspenders I'd seen. The pants were too short and showed the bottoms of his year-round long underwear over his work-worn leather boots. I gave him a solemn stare, but inside, I was grinning to beat the band.

Back in the day, Gus stopped into Nelson's Hardware at least twice a week, always to share a story of the old days in the lumber camps when he worked with Harlon, my father, and then later at the sawmill. Most of Gus' stories were funny, but some, regarding our father, not so much. Still, I couldn't help but like Gus. His kind were rare these days.

"Gus," I nodded.

"I come in for a repair link for the chainsaw, a bottle of mink oil, and a 'course I gotta have me a bag of peanut brittle." Gus stepped nearer at which I pulled in my chin and leaned back. "It ain't like the old days when you was here. These young kids here don't know where nothin' is."

"They'll learn in time." Well, just listen to me, I thought, being all positive.

"Anyway, I'm pretty dang good. How you doin' little lady?" The aroma of evergreen surrounded Gus and overpowered the industrial smell of the store. I liked that.

"I'm just fine." I knew what was coming. Just like everyone else, Gus loved a little gossip.

"Must a been a scare them findin' those bones on your land." Gus propped himself against the shelving unit with one of his big hands and leaned his long body forward.

"Wasn't me that found them."

The Witness Tree

"So, us old-timers think it's Harlon stuck in that tree. Ya think that might be true?" His beady eyes zeroed in on me under his bushy white brows.

A cold shiver ran through me and my throat felt dry. I hadn't expected this.

"Now why in blue blazes would you think such a thing?" I hugged my big old purse closer to my body. I'd bought it at the Hospital Auxiliary Thrift Store for three bucks. Despite being lime green, it had all the pockets I needed and a good, strong handle to grip. Anyone tried to accost me, one good whack with this purse would take 'em out. "You old poop, you're no better than the cackling hens in this town."

"Aw, you know how the rumor-mill works here. I ain't thought about your Pa in a long time. All this brings back memories. Hell, at ninety-four all I gots is memories."

"I know my father wasn't a saint, everybody knew that, but," and oh, how I hated to ask, "why would you think that?"

Gus straightened and rubbed the back of his neck, "Your Pa was a wildcat. Me and Harlon, we raised us some hell in our day. You know that. We sure did..." Gus grinned and rubbed his stubbly chin as his thoughts went back in time.

I silently chastised myself for asking.

"We liked to fight. Did I ever tell ya the time we was in Whitey's and Bruno Hill told Harlon he was nothin' but a lardass at the lumber camp? 'Not worth the weight of his snuss can,' Bruno said. Ol' Harlon didn't like that none. Wrestled 'im to the ground, then yelled for me. I held Bruno while Harlon sat on his face and said, 'How you like this lardass now?' Well, we all laughed at that like there was no tomorrow." Gus held up a finger. "That was until Bruno pulled hisself up from the floor. He grabbed Harlon, I grabbed Bruno, and soon the whole place went crazy. We had men beatin' the piss outta each other like you never seen before. Whitey's woman banned us all from comin' in for a month. 'Course old Clarice was a softy with us jacks. We was all back in there the next weekend." Gus's laugh boomed.

I checked to make sure no one else heard and leaned closer.

"You didn't answer my question, Gus. Why would you think it's my father in that tree?"

"Aw, Harlon, he made himself some enemies in his day."

"What kind of enemies? Who?" This certainly wasn't a conversation for the middle of a hardware store, but I couldn't help myself.

Gus hung his head for a moment. "Harlon had him some real trouble with that Pukall bunch. I wouldn't a messed with them. I think he bit off more'n he could chew." He pursed his lips and looked around the store.

"Go on," I challenged him.

"Nah, I ain't sayin' nothin' more. You're his little girl and all." Gus rubbed his gnarled hands.

"Nonsense. Tell me what you know, Gus. At this age, I'm old enough to know it all, don't you think?"

Gus shook his head and turned for the door. "Naw. I ain't doin' it. I'll come back for my stuff another day."

"Gus, you old fart, you can't leave me like this." But he did just that.

***

Damn Gus. I burned all the way back home. On the intersection of Cherry and Lyman I drove my old boat of a car right through the stop sign. I couldn't get home fast enough.

All I wanted was to hole up in the kitchen and cook until the demons of the past were stirred and whipped into a corner. Maybe a pot of chicken soup.

The Witness Tree

Reed wasn't going to let all this be. I was certain I'd be seeing him again. The rumors were circulating, and I was stuck in the middle of it all. The night after the good deputy was here, the story had been on the local news channel. The northern half of the state was going to be clambering for resolution.

The zinnias watering in an old enamel coffee pot on the kitchen table bowed their colorful heads. They understood as I chopped away, first celery, then onion, now carrots.

That old poop, Gus, had a secret and I didn't like it one bit. Chances are, it's something I'd heard before, but what if it wasn't? I wasn't immune to our father's reputation. Thankfully, most of the people that knew Harlon were long gone by now. I hadn't allowed thoughts of our father, or my first years on this earth, to crowd into my thoughts and now, some days I wasn't sure which of my scrambled memories were fact and which were unwanted fiction. And how cruel that I should have to recall any of it now that my life was nearly over.

I glanced out the window over the sink. The sunflowers nodded in agreement.

So, Gus thinks it's Harlon in that tree. The words played over and over like a train on a track of infinity. Of course, I couldn't be completely sure if it was Harlon or not. No one, not Mama or Luddie, Auntie Hat or Auntie Vee, our uncles Frankie and Eddie, no one ever mentioned him again. It was as though he vanished from the face of the earth, never to be seen or heard from again. And never to be discussed.

I angled the knife over a fat carrot and accidentally nipped the palm of my left hand, just under the thumb, making a neat slice. A quick line of red ran and dripped off my wrist.

"Look what you've made me do!" I exclaimed to no one.

I ran cold water over my hand watching the stream turn pink. Turning the water off, I held a dish cloth to the cut and leaned back against the cupboard. A picture of Ivy looked out at me from the door of the refrigerator. She must have been about twelve. Auburn braids and a dusting of freckles across her nose. Her brown eyes bright with promise, her smile toothy and wide and just a bit of mischief in her expression. Honestly, I liked that Ivy had some fire to her, but it made mothering her a trial.

Still, I looked upon the picture with warmth. Annabelle's daughter.

Annabelle. Just the sound of her name brought up a bucket of emotion I had no intention of deciphering. Remembering my sister was nothing more than a glance at her daughter, at Ivy. Both shared the auburn hair and fair skin. Annabelle wore her hair in soft curls that meandered down the middle of her back. She was slender and graceful and when she smiled, it seemed the sun smiled upon us all. I carried in my mind a picture of Annabelle about eight years old, skipping through the apple orchard, her hair highlighted with golden highlights amid the copper as it danced on her shoulders, apple blossoms wafting from the trees, and Annabelle laughing as I chased her between the trees in a game of hide-and-seek. When I finally tagged her, we both fell to the ground and lay there watching sparrows flit from tree to tree and puffy clouds entertain us with ever-changing profiles.

"Oh, Annabelle," slipped from my lips as I remembered. My heart ached with the beauty and the pain of the memory.

My sister and I, we were nothing alike. Annabelle wrote poetry. In fact, she'd won a competition in high school. She could paint beautiful landscapes and sing so pretty it would make the heart ache with the purity of her sweet soprano. Artsy-fartsy was what Luddie called her once, and he was right. Annabelle had many gifts, so many that I was jealous most of the time, yet Annabelle lacked the gift of a long life, and for that, I was supremely sad.

Annabelle wasn't much of a cook, and just pathetic when it

came to the barn chores. Luckily, I was able and willing to pick up the slack on that account. Someone had to. But everyone loved Annabelle. Especially our mother.

Mama doted on Annabelle something awful, but to the girl's credit, Annabelle was never spoilt because of it. All Annabelle had to do was enter a room and Mama lit up as though she'd won the lottery. The two were inseparable. For most of her childhood Annabelle slept with Mama, in the evenings she sat rapt as Annabelle sang songs from Sunday school or read her latest poem, the refrigerator was papered with her artwork. Annabelle was the most loving, generous person I had ever known.

When my sister met Samuel Burke at a church retreat, she was smitten. Mama was sad. She knew it was only a matter of time before Annabelle went off and made a life of her own. And secretly, I enjoyed having our mother to myself again, although it was never the same after Annabelle left.

Sam Burke was the golden child of his family as well. An only child to a Catholic physician and his socialite wife in Chicago, who expected their son to follow in his father's footsteps. The two maintained a long-distance courtship, marrying weeks after Annabelle graduated high school.

Mama had fretted so when they moved away. The two settled in Chicago while Sam changed his focus from medicine to engineering. This caused terrible friction between them all. His parents never approved of the match. It was nothing against Annabelle, but her background was not acceptable. Neither was her religion. But when Sam changed course, they blamed Annabelle. I always suspected Annabelle was simply part of Sam's rebellion, although he seemed to love her.

Annabelle was raised, with Mama's encouragement, within the Congregational Church in Peeksville. Every Sunday the two of them went to church and Annabelle stayed for Sunday School.

The Witness Tree

Apparently, all that hadn't been as necessary with Luddie and me.

When little Ivy came along so soon after the marriage, it did nothing to calm the waters between them all. Annabelle tried has hard as she could, but it was never enough, and Burke's took very little interest in their granddaughter.

And then tragedy struck and struck hard.

A drunk driver drove his loaded dump truck over the car carrying Sam and Annabelle as they were on their way to the hospital to deliver their second child, sparing little Ivy in the back seat. Sam, Annabelle and their unborn child lay dead in the aftermath. Devastated, Mama and I rushed to Illinois and the funeral, and returned home with a five-year-old girl to raise. After that, Mama's lung cancer took an aggressive turn, and it wasn't long, and she was gone as well. And I was a single parent.

I waved a hand in front of my face as though to wipe the memory away.

I checked the bleeding of my hand. It had stopped. I put the rag aside and reached for the basil. The soup was nearly done and so was I. I turned off the heat and while it cooled went to lay down awhile, but the memories of the past continued.

The black and white picture of Luddie and I on the bedside table seemed to call to me.

Mama had taken it of us in front of the chicken coop. We stood next to each other, Luddie a good foot and a half taller than I in his overalls, no shirt, bare feet and his left arm in a sling, a rag wrapped around two short boards protecting the arm. He'd fallen from a tree trying to build us a fort. I, with my blond hair in braids, looked up at my big brother as though he hung the stars, my legs and feet bare under the simple shift of a dress I wore. We must have been twelve and seven at the time. Just a year after...

As tragic as Annabelle's short life had been, Luddie was the most severe heartbreak of all.

The Witness Tree

I turned the picture face down.

CHAPTER 5

Esther

I tipped my face over the edge of the bucket to see what I had. I'd be lucky to get half a batch of jam with the berries picked so far. Raspberry was my favorite and it took a good amount of self-control not to stuff them into my mouth. Although, giving in just a bit wouldn't be so bad, would it? I took the largest berry from the bucket and popped it into my mouth and, oh my goodness, the sweetness rivaled the most decadent candy. It took me right back to the hard, butterscotch candies my grandpa always carried. I offered a berry to Petey, who lapped it up with his big, wet tongue.

With a hand on my back I stretched my muscles and savored the late morning sun when I heard the churn of an airplane overhead. I raised my face to the sky, shading my eyes with one

45

hand, as the plane came into view. It climbed high into the blue, looking like a silver dragonfly before it disappeared behind a cottony puff of white.

The brief interruption took me back to a time and place when I was young. When my name was Esther Peroutka. When life held the possibility of great adventure, roads to travel, oceans to view, cities to visit. That felt so damn long ago.

In particular, I was reminded of the day a flyboy came to our little town with his Curtiss Jenny biplane. The appearance caused quite a stir in Peeksville. The pilot, a nephew of Alfred Zingle who owned the creamery on River Road, offered rides out at Heier's field just outside of town. The only ticket required, a permission slip signed by a parent. I so begged my mother for that slip of paper, if for only a short time, I could break free from the daily drudge of life in this small town.

"I cannot afford funeral. So no," My mother, Rose, said in her clipped Bohemian accent.

Oh, I so wanted to soar high above Peeksville, to reach out, touch a cloud, fill my lungs with air so pure and sweet, and to dip and dance with the birds. And after all, it wasn't every day that adventure visited out tiny neck of the woods.

I begged. I pleaded. I even did more than my share of work in the barn to convince Ma, but the woman wouldn't budge.

Later that evening I secretly slipped a sheet of stationery from her bureau and penned a permission slip, signing Ma's name with flair. Pretending to go berry picking, I hid the pail in the brush and hitched a ride on Mr. Schmeedl's milk truck.

He dropped me off about a quarter mile from Heier's field and I nearly ran the whole way. When I saw that plane parked in the grass, I nearly split it two with excitement.

A young, curvaceous girl, her hair in a platinum bob, leaned against a wing of the plane flirting with the pilot, a tall, strapping young man in a leather jacket and leather hat from which a wisp or two of blond hair curled.

"Um, excuse me, I'm here for a ride." I interrupted, heart pounding so I could hardly breathe.

The pilot pulled his eyes from the tart in front of him and said, "Yeah, you got two bits? That's what it cost."

Well, my heart sank right to my knees. I didn't have a penny to my name, much less a quarter.

"I thought it was free." My dream of being the next Amelia Earhardt just crumbled.

The pilot threw his head back, laughed and the blond twittered along with him.

The girl, with her pink sweater dangerously tight across her young breasts, turned toward me.

"Oh, Esther!" Her blue eyes widened.

"Ruby Janisek? Is that you?" I asked. Didn't look nothing like the girl I remembered from school. This was perfect. Not only was I not going to get that ride, but I would be humiliated before one of the most popular girls in town.

Ruby brought red-nailed fingers to her new doo. "You like it? I wanted to look just like Jean Harlow. Did you see her in *Bombshell*?"

"Don't get to the movies much." I shifted my attention to the pilot. "I don't have a quarter. Is there something I can do to earn it?" Time was wasting, and I had to get home before Ma realized I was gone.

A mischievous grin curved one side of his pretty mouth. "That might be tempting if you had something to offer."

"Go jump in a lake." I crossed my arms over the flat of my chest.

"Just so happens," Ruby opened the pink sequined purse hanging from her elbow, "I've got an extra one." She held the coin between her forefinger and thumb.

That quarter glinted in the sun like a giant trophy.

"I…I can't take that." I wasn't ever one to take charity.

"Well, why not? It's just a quarter, silly." Ruby giggled.

"I…" I wanted that quarter more than anything in my short life. Besides, Ruby had lots of quarters. "Okay. I'll pay you back."

Ruby thrust the quarter at the pilot. "Here's for Essie and I'll get you one for me. You can take us both, together can't you?"

Sharing was not in my plans, but if it were not for Jean Harlow here, I would have no ride at all.

The pilot took the coins and promised us to double the airtime. Honestly, I think he was disappointed not to have Ruby all to himself.

"You want the permission slip?" I held the folded paper toward him.

"Naw, keep it."

Well, hell. All that for nothing.

"Ooo, this'll be fun." Ruby snapped her gum and smiled brightly.

As the pilot went around to the opposite side of the plane, Ruby leaned into me, took my hand, and whispered, "I saw him in town and he was so dreamy, but actually I'm afraid to go up in this thing. When you came, I was trying to find a graceful way to back out. It doesn't seem so scary to do it with a friend."

Ruby Janisek called me a friend. Well, glory be!

We squeezed into the seat and before we knew it, we were flying over farms, fields, forest and Peeksville itself, dipping over rooftops and steeples, buzzing cars on the highway and attempting to get the attention of the cows in Hilgart's pasture. Soon we were following the ribbon of Redemption River and I swear, I ain't never seen a prettier sight. It wasn't long into the flight that Ruby released her grip on my hand, and we cheered and waved to everyone we saw on the ground.

I had never felt so free, so alive. The wind whipped at my face and pulled at my hair, but I didn't care. I thrust out my skinny arms and tipped my face to the sun. I was Amelia Earhart with Jean Harlow in tow.

***

That summer me and Ruby began our friendship. It was a hot one and normally green grass, crunched underfoot, flowers ached for thirst, gardens refused to produce. The fields struggled and farmers worried something fierce. A few forest fires blazed to life. Nothing catastrophic, although the old farmers warned of a fire that could ruin everything. They said it could be another Peshtigo all over again.

On a Saturday in mid-July, I finished my chores early, washed at the sink, took the red kerchief from my head and pulled the curlers from my hair. I honestly didn't know why I bothered. In this humidity it wouldn't be long, and my light-brown curls would gain a mind of their own and hang on my shoulders like limp noodles. I put on my best baby-blue skirt and the whitest blouse I could find and went to the long mirror. I pulled the blouse tight over my chest and did an assessment. One would think, at seventeen, I would have more to show, but I didn't.

"Where ya goin'?"

Twelve-year-old sister Hattie had snuck into the room and lay back across my bed, her feet dangling over the hardwood floor, knees skun up and dirty, hands tucked beneath her brown braids as she looked up at me.

"I'm goin' for a ride with Ruby. That's all you need to know."

"Can I come?" Hattie's brows arched and she stuck her freckled nose in the air.

"No." I pulled a pink scarf from a dresser drawer and tied it around my neck.

49

"Why not? You up to no good like Ma says?" Half of Hattie's mouth turned up in a snide, little grin.

"Of course, not and you can tell that to Ma." At the mirror I fluffed my hair.

"Then why can't I come? Huh?" Hattie raised up on elbows.

"Because I said so. Now, get off my bed before you get it all dirty."

Ten-year-old Violet's dark little head peeked around the door jamb. "You look pretty."

"Thank you, sweetie." I kissed the top of her deep brown head.

The blat of a horn cut through the air outside the bedroom window. A shiny white Auburn 8 Cabriolet sat in the yard, the top down. Ruby waved from the driver's seat with the sun glinting on her platinum hair so, it was nearly blinding.

"Come on, Essie. Let's go," she called. I flew down the stairs and met with the hard glare of Ma.

"Where you off to?" She asked, her dark eyes glaring, gray hair in a lopsided bun at the top of her head, her round face red with anger.

"Ma, Ruby's waitin'. We're goin' to the pie social at the American Legion," I lied. Of course, we'd get there eventually. We were such snots at times.

"I don't like this." Ma stopped me with a tight grip of my arm. "You chum with this girl who has everything. We are hard-workin' people. We don't need the likes a her flauntin' her expensive cars and fancy clothes."

"Ma! Stop it. Ruby's not like that." I jerked my arm free. "She'll hear you."

"I don't care. You get these ideas in your head that you're better than this old farm. Well, Girlie, you're not." Ma poked a finger in my chest. She was always a hard woman, but when our father up and left us, she was worse, finding fault no matter what. I blamed her for his leaving and worried what the future held for Hattie and Violet, not to mention the boys.

"I worked hard today. The chores are done. There's nothin' wrong with havin' some fun." With that, I slammed through the screen door and ran toward my friend.

We were an unlikely pair, Ruby and me. In contrast to my plain wrapper, Ruby was all curvy girl and had the best of clothes with the moxie and beauty of a movie star. Ruby's parents owned the local sawmill and by Peeksville standards, the Janisek's were well to do. Our differences didn't really matter. We balanced each other nicely, I thought. I couldn't compete with Ruby and therefore, never tried. Maybe that was why jealousy never threatened us. And when Ruby's head was stuck in the clouds with talk of movie stars and Hollywood, I could always pull her back down. We were, as Ruby's mother said, as different as pearls and peacocks.

Ruby and I zoomed off in Mr. Janisek's car, the summer breeze threading our hair, leaving Ma on the porch alone with her disapproval.

"Anywhere special you want to go?" I gave Ruby a sideways glance and tightened the scarf around my neck. Ruby had obviously stuffed her bra. The mounds on her chest looked like little pillows.

Ruby grinned. "Whatcha got in mind?"

"Let's go out on Taggart Road." I tried a pretense of innocence and picked at a chipped nail.

"What's out there?" Ruby's dark eyes widened. "Oh, you want to see Harlon, don't you?"

"I just want to drive past is all."

"Sweetie, that guy's got a reputation." Ruby clucked and said, "You need to stay away from him."

"What's wrong with a little naughty? 'Sides, he's probably a sugarpuss underneath it all." Lordy, I was beginning to sound like

51

Ruby. I threw an arm over the seat and shifted sideways. "Hey, I heard his dad has a still out back and they make their own hooch. Sounds like a good time to me."

"Oh, Essie," Ruby giggled, "you be careful. Harlon's a big-time operator when it comes to the women. I tell ya, he's always on the make and I heard he can be a bit rough when he's drunk."

"How do you know that?"

"Mamie Mitford said he nearly had his way with her after the ball game a few weeks ago. If it wasn't for her brother looking for her, she would have been in big trouble. As it was, her brother pulled him off of her and Harlon gave him a black eye for it."

"Oh, look at the pitiful way Mamie flaunts herself." Then bit my lower lip hoping Ruby and her puffy boobs didn't take offense.

"That she does," Ruby agreed.

I reached over and flicked Ruby's arm. "I'm just havin' fun. What about the flyboy that gave us the ride? He nearly made quick work out of you. That was until you found his weddin' ring. He was a stinker if I ever knew one."

"We don't have to talk about that." Ruby grimaced. "Oh Lord and butter, he was a good kisser, though."

"Shove in the clutch and let's go. Whoohoo!" I threw my head back and laughed into the wind as Ruby put the car through its paces.

Within minutes Ruby turned onto Taggart Road and we whizzed past farm after farm.

"Okay, slow down." I squared my shoulders and smoothed my hair. "I want him to get a good look."

Ruby sighed. "I've created a monster."

The paved road curved to reveal the south field of the Foley farm. Old man Foley and his son Harlon were in the field raking hay into golden mounds. Harlon, tall and lean, his muscular arms moving back and forth to work the pitchfork, his black hair slick under the mid-day sun. He was as close to a perfect picture of masculinity as I'd seen.

Ruby tapped the horn as the we drove by, hands waving wildly. Mr. Foley simply glared, but Harlon bobbed his head and watched us go. As I looked back, his gaze was on me. Something passed 'tween us. I was certain of it.

Just south of the Foley farm, Ruby pulled the car to the edge of the road.

"He's so gorgeous," I gushed. "And did you see those muscles?"

"He's a hunk of heartbreak, that's what he is." Ruby reached across me to the glove box, a devilish grin on her face. "Okay, Essie, we're far enough out of town, I've got a surprise for you." I loved the way Ruby shortened my name.

"Whatcha got?"

Ruby pulled a brown satchel from the glove box. With a mischievous glint to her eye, she took out a small brown box.

"What is it?" I asked. "Let me see."

"Cigarettes." Ruby winked at me and held out a white stick. "Wanna try? Daddy rolls some every night and I helped myself to a couple. He'll never know."

"Ooo, you should have brought these out earlier so I could impress Harlon. We're gonna look so nifty. Light me up." I took one and brought it to my nose, smelling the tobacco. It reminded me of the pipe my grandfather had smoked.

"It takes some getting used to so don't inhale too deeply." Ruby lit the end.

"You've done this before?" I asked as she brought it to her red lips.

"Just last Sunday. Got sicker than a dog. But I sure felt important. Just like a movie star," Ruby said, grinning taking out another cigarette.

"Gee, if you had one of those fancy holders, you'd look just like Mae West in *I'm No Angel*. Without the boobs, of course," I said. Ruby had treated me to a picture show for my birthday in May. "Guess I'm more the Bette Davis type."

"Nothing wrong with that." Ruby hung a white stick from her lips and struck a match. I had an idea and stopped her with a hand on her wrist.

"Wait. Let's light these and drive past Harlon again. He'll think we're so sophisticated."

"Honestly, I'd stay away from him, sweetie. I've heard some things." Ruby's brows furrowed together. "Bad things."

"Okay, what have you heard?" I didn't appreciate her ruining my anticipation one bit.

"I didn't want to tell you this, but they say he's the one that beat the piss out of Jerry Newsome at Idlewild Landing last weekend. Poor Jerry doesn't have two brain cells to rub together and now he's laid up with a broken nose and a concussion. And, they say that Harlon's the reason Delcie Hoffman had to leave town last year. Her mother says Delcie went to take care of her aunt over in Crivitz, but we all know what that means."

"Delcie made it with half the junior class and I know all about the fight with Jerry. You know how people talk. Besides, Harlon was drunk, and Jerry probably had it coming." I wasn't about to admit the prickle of warning that shot through me every time I thought of Harlon, but I was hungry for adventure and Harlon was nothing like the other farm boys.

"Well, Harlon's not my type. Now Jim Cooley, that's another story. Cute as a button. 'Sides, he makes me laugh. Not like Harlon, he's too serious." Ruby set the rolled cigarette on the dash. "How did you get so hooked on this guy anyway?"

"The dance at Greenfield Hall. Remember? He was so darned handsome that night. I was goin' around the corner of the building

54

when I bumped right into him. Both of us nearly fell over and, I don't know what it was, but I haven't been able to get him out of my mind since. I heard him tell Barney Samson he's going to blow this old town and head for the city one of these days. Maybe Milwaukee. I could see him there. Just think of all the opportunities in the city. Why, a guy, or a girl, could do anything they want."

"True, but you better not run off with him and leave me here alone."

"Harlon's just…different. I think he's got a real future ahead of him. Take me past one more time. Please?" I brought my hands up as though I were begging. What a stupid girl I was.

"Fine, we'll do another drive-by so you'll leave me alone."

Ruby did a 'Y' in the road and we headed in the opposite direction. As we neared the Foley farm, Ruby pulled over and we lit our cigarettes, took the initial drags and coughed a few times. Harlon was still in the field but by himself this time. Ruby honked the horn.

I waved, took a drag from the cigarette, making sure to provide a good profile, and blew out a long puff of smoke. Harlon shook his head and watched us go. It was difficult to tell if he was impressed or not.

"Yuk." The smoke burned my lungs and caused me to cough again. "What do people see in these things?" I tossed the cigarette into the wind and as the little white stick left my fingers, creating a glowing arc, a jolt of energy pulsed through me—a feeling that time had slowed, that something exciting lay on the horizon. Couldn't quite put my finger on it.

By the banks of Redemption River, Ruby pulled the car to the side of the road. We sat on the rocks dangling our toes in the coolness of the gurgling water.

"You still thinkin' about college?" I asked as I sunk my feet further into the water. I hated the thought that Ruby might be leaving.

"Hmm, I don't think so." Ruby snapped off a weed and put it between her teeth. "Daddy is going to have a fit. He thinks it will make me a better wife, but I want to get out into life. Experience it. I don't need a college education to act. Can you just see it, Essie? Me in front of a grand audience with the lights lining the stage. Every seat in the place filled, and all the people hanging on every word while I make them laugh, cry, and sing along."

"You're right. Your dad is going to blow a gasket." I leaned back on elbows in the soft grass and looked through the leafy canopy overhead to the summer sky. "If I had a chance at a better education, I couldn't turn that down. I'm jealous you got to stay in school. I don't think I'll ever forgive Ma for makin' me drop out to work at Nelson's, even though I like workin' there."

"The shame of it is, between the two of us, you have the brains." Ruby twisted to look at me. "Say," she lay on her side facing me, "let's do it together. How about it?"

I laid back, hands under my head staring up at the clouds gliding through the blue. "Do what?"

"Run off and see if we can't get hired by a theater group." Ruby was pulsating with excitement.

"Are you off your rocker?"

Ruby pushed up from the grass. "Oh my God. Can you see it? I have one year left of school. We could squirrel away whatever money we could and take off the minute I graduate." She wiggled with excitement and grabbed me by the arm. "We could get on the bus to Chicago, get jobs and tryout for one of the theater groups. Some of the best performers in the world got their start in Chicago."

"I'm not much of an actress if you haven't noticed."

"Okay, but Essie, think of the team we would make. You could

56

work backstage and learn everything you could while I make my name out front." She was silent a moment, eyes wide, as though her brain couldn't contain all the ideas ricocheting through her head. "Down the road we could start our own theater company. You and me. You'd be so good at taking charge and making it all work, while I could find the best talent to make our shows a hit." She flopped back down onto the grass. "Oh, we'd be so famous. Everyone would want to be part of our productions. Think of the life we'd have. We'd travel the world."

"You might have somethin' there." A cloud overhead took on the shape of a bird. Another rippled into angel's wings. Although I wasn't religious, it had to be a sign. Wasn't it?

"We could travel the country. A band of vagabonds, living life to bring the classics to the masses," She giggled.

We were thoughtful a moment.

"You know, I think we should." I was suddenly filled with Ruby's excitement. "Life here has nothin' to offer me but work and more work, and down the road marryin' some dirty plowboy."

Ruby threw her head back and laughed, kicking her feet. She reached over, grabbed my arm, and shook me.

"That's it!" she yelled. "One year and we'll be off!" She waved her hands in the air like two poppies in the breeze.

"Old Rose is goin' to spin herself into the ground over this one." Pictures of our future flitted through my brain.

A truck came barreling past, then another. A look of intent on the driver's faces and neither bothering to wave.

"Somethin's wrong." I watched as they disappeared in a plume of dust.

"You and that intuition of yours. Sometimes I don't quite know what to make of it." Ruby reached into the water and sent a spray toward me. "Remember when you had a bad feeling when I told you Jane Wilson hadn't shown up for school one day last year?

She was supposed to help me that day with a presentation for geography. You said right away that something bad happened. Come to find out she died on the way to school and they didn't find her until that evening. Poor thing. Her heart stopped, just like that, and she was gone. Then there was the time you somehow knew my sister was going to be sick with measles, and she was. That's spooky."

"Don't know why those kinds of things hit me sometimes, but not always." I thought back to the night I dreamed I saw my grandfather in a bed, the whole family around him crying their eyes out because he'd died. The next day, dead of a stroke.

"See if you can tell if Jim Cooley will be at the social tonight."

I sat straighter on the grass. "No, somethin' isn't right." I searched the treetops and sniffed the air. "There … I can smell smoke. Don't you smell it?"

"No," Ruby sniffed the air as well. The forest was unusually still. "Wait, I do. There's a fire somewhere." Another pickup truck whizzed by.

"Let's go see. Lordy, I hope it's not our farm." I jumped up, grabbed my shoes, and ran for the car with Ruby right behind.

Over the top of the hill hazy smoke filled the air and people ran from all directions. Foley's field, the one Harlon and his father had been working in less than an hour before, was ablaze. Men were beating the flames with blankets, jackets, anything they could grab.

"We need to help." I yelled. Ruby parked along the road and we ran across the field. Mrs. Foley came running from the farmhouse with blankets. We each grabbed one, wet it in a water trough, and joined in beating the flames. After nearly two hours, and more neighbors lending a hand, the flames abated. The field smoldered and putrid smoke hung heavy in the air. Men and women gathered in the barnyard wiping their brows, drinking water and cursing the dry weather.

The Witness Tree

The cause of the fire, I knew, was the lit cigarette I'd flicked into the field. Feeling unbearable guilt, I slipped away to gather my courage before confessing to the Foley's. I walked past the pigpen and the chicken coop and rounded the weathered red barn.

As I stood there, arms wrapped around my middle, attempting to ease my fear, Harlon came around the opposite side of the barn. He didn't see me as he unzipped his pants and began urinating. Thankfully, he was turned enough so that I couldn't see anything I shouldn't. Just the same, I turned away, afraid to move for fear he see me.

Unfortunately, he turned in my direction just as I peeked over my shoulder.

I wished the ground would swallow me then and there. Harlon wasn't embarrassed whatsoever. He zipped his pants and came toward me, face blackened, hair in all directions.

"Sorry." I said quickly and bit my lower lip.

"You set our field on fire." He stood before me, so broad, filthy hands on hips.

"I know. Your Dad's goin' to kill me. I don't have any money, but I'll pay for anything that's damaged. Maybe I can work for your family. I'll do whatever I can." For all of my primping a few short hours ago, my clothes were a mess, and the new shoes I'd saved for so long, scuffed and scorched.

Harlon's eyes were hard.

"We'd have lost the whole farm if the wind had changed. I suppose a dame doesn't think of things like that. It was plain stupid what you did."

"I don't know what to say." I focused on the ground at my feet.

"Just what do you think you'll be able to do around here? A scrawny girl like you? You can't lift anything. You just proved you got the sense of a sheep. Your kinda help we can do without." He crossed his arms over his barrel chest.

59

"I've got to do somethin' to make up for this." I thought of all the times I'd wanted his attention. None of my fantasies had ever played out like this. But here I was, within five feet of him, and he was looking at me and no one else.

Suddenly his face softened, and he took a step closer.

"You got a boyfriend Esther?" A strange question.

"No."

"I didn't think so." He studied me. "I saw you lookin' at me out at Greenfield and thought about askin' you to dance, but you were busy with your girlfriends."

"You did?" I raised my face to meet his.

"I think you're different from those other girls, Esther." He moved closer. I could smell the sweat and soot that clung to him.

"You do?" I swallowed the lump in her throat.

He reached toward me, and I flinched. "Don't be a scardy-cat. You got black on your cheek."

I kept my eyes on his as he wiped my cheek with the back of a crooked finger. The simple touch caused a funny stirring in the pit of my stomach and a little below.

"You know, there's no need to piss off my old man. Not if I keep your secret." His mouth curved. "You ever been with a man, Esther?"

"That's for me to know."

I pressed my back against the cool stone of the barn wall. Harlon placed a hand next to my head and cantilevered his body over mine. He was so close I could barely breathe.

"You can make up for it. Let's go into the barn." He ran a finger down my forearm and, despite the heat of the day, sent a shiver into my bones.

All it had taken to get Harlon to look my way was to set his field on fire. It almost made me laugh, if I wasn't so nervous. For all my bravado in flirting with him, I was nothing but an inexperienced, uneducated farm girl.

"I…I think I should talk to your Pa right away. I don't want him to think I'm not takin' responsibility for this."

"Like I said, the old man don't need to know a thing about it." Harlon placed his blackened hand on my bare arm. "Let's go." He angled his head to the side with a wide grin showing his small teeth.

"I don't know..."

Harlon's face loomed over me. "I'll bet there's a fire blazin' under that skinny body you got there Esther. I bet it's just waitin' to show me."

"I … I can't breathe." I licked my lips and looked for an escape.

Harlon slipped his arm behind me and pulled me against him. My head was all the way back now as I looked up into his smoke-smudged face.

"There you are." Ruby came around the corner of the barn and relief flooded my body. Harlon released me. "Looks like I broke something up here. Hey, Harlon. Sorry about your field." Harlon glared. Then she said, "Guess I don't have to ask what you're doing back here."

"I had to get away to calm myself." I rubbed the gooseflesh from my arms.

"Esther and I have some business to discuss." Harlon glanced my way.

"We need to get out of here. I was supposed to have my Dad's car back by now," Ruby said.

Glancing up into Harlon's cold gaze, I said, "We have to go." I quickly followed Ruby but before rounding the corner, I glanced back to see Harlon lean against the stone wall of the barn, watching.

Part way through the barnyard, I stopped. "Ruby, I need to speak to Mr. Foley. He needs to know I started that fire." Mrs.

Foley was giving out glasses of water to the volunteers. Mr. Foley was railing to his neighbors about the damage done.

"You helped put it out. You've done all you can," Ruby said. "Being a martyr isn't going to help anyone."

"It just seems . . ."

Ruby grabbed my arm. "Let's go. I'm in trouble."

CHAPTER 6

Helen

I held the receiver and waited for the ringing to stop and someone to answer. And with each ring, I questioned my judgment in making the call in the first place.

"Helen?" It was Ivy.

"How'd you know it was me?"

"Caller ID."

Damn technology. At least it was a good sign the girl answered knowing it was me.

"Helen, what's up? Are you all right?" Cut right to the chase. That's the way the two of us had always been. I had been privy to conversations between families with all their small talk and words of endearment. That wasn't Ivy and I.

"I am just fine. Fit as ever."

"Good to know."

A palpable silence fell between us as I second guessed the call.

"There's some news you should know, and I suppose you should hear it from me, unless you've heard. Skeletal remains were found out back of the farm, back by the river."

"What! Where?"

"That hollowed-out tree I yelled at you to stay off of. Turned out it wasn't so hollow." I went on to explain the Jennings boy finding the bones that the authorities judge to be very old.

"Holy buckets, I didn't expect that. Do they know who it is? Any clues?"

"No, but I thought you should know."

"Huh. Well, yeah, that's big."

The moments ticked by.

"Have you been to the farm? Have you talked to the family?" Ivy asked.

"No. Not since I signed the papers. I don't know why I should have to talk to them. The place is theirs. It doesn't concern me anymore."

"The hell it doesn't, Helen. I know you were glad to leave it behind, but you can't tell me you aren't the least bit interested in who and how it got there. I find that to be very strange. Someone besides us knew that tree was hollow. This is freaky to say the least."

My face was warm, and I felt a bit dizzy.

"I will admit it's a mystery, but I don't need to concern myself with it. I won't."

"The police must be all over this. Have they contacted you?"

"That boy, your friend Reed, came over with all these questions, but I sent him on his way. How would I know anything that could help him? This probably happened before my parents bought the place."

"Reed? It's nice to know he's on the case. He'll do a good job. What did he want to know?"

64

I reiterated pieces of the conversation.

"Be nice, Helen. He's just trying to do his job."

"I know that!" My tone was too sharp. The last thing I needed was Ivy telling me how to behave or worse, suspecting I may know something by my being overly defensive.

"Next time you see him, say hello for me. Who am I kidding? I know you won't, but at least give him some of your time and if there is anything I can do, I will."

"I would help if I knew anything, you know that, but I don't."

"You know, Helen, you spent nearly your whole life on the farm and before that, your parents. How could something like this have gotten past you all?"

"I resent that! What are you suggesting? That I told someone they could hide a body on our property? And I'll tell you what I told the deputy, would I have taken you back there had I known? I don't think so, Missy. Be careful how you throw around your accusations."

"Calm down. I'm not accusing anyone."

I could hear her frustration with me. I was quite practiced at ignoring it.

"Let's change the subject for a bit. Would you like to know how *we* are?" I didn't like the condescending tone of her voice.

"Of course, I would."

"Maudie and Evan are good. Maudie's in sixth grade now and Evan in third. Maudie's quite the artist. In fact, she won first place in the city's poster contest for conservation. Evan is going to play in Little League next spring. He's not much for batting, but he's got a good arm on him and can run like the wind. With a little practice he might be pitching one of these days."

"Very good. Nice to hear." I missed those two kids. "I am knitting slippers for each of them for Christmas, orange for Evan and bright green for Maudie."

"Oh, uh, they'll like that. I need to tell you something. It's about Brad and me." Ivy's tone became icy. "Things aren't good. Not at all."

"How long has this been going on?" I could have forecasted this the day they married. *Don't gloat, Helen.*

"A month ago, he moved in with his girlfriend, but that only lasted a few days and she sent him packing. He moved back in while I was at work one day. It's just...not good. He won't leave and says it's all my fault. I didn't tell you because I didn't want to hear 'I told you so'."

"I wouldn't..."

"Oh yes, you would. You never liked Brad from the start. I get it, but..."

"No, I didn't like him, but I never wished for you to split after all this time. Those poor children of yours."

"What about me? I've been left holding the bag most of this marriage and I know, you warned me, but...I wanted someone to love me, Helen. I thought he did. I can't do it anymore."

"You haven't run around on him, have you?" As soon as the words left my mouth, I knew I shouldn't have said them. Maybe I was lashing out because she didn't listen to my warnings and she'd been so damned rebellious.

"How dare you! I'd like to think you know me better than that. Where the hell did that come from?"

"Oh, calm down. Marriage takes two."

"How would you know? And I will not calm down! How could you think that I would run around on him? Where the hell would I find time to do that between kids, a job and a house?" I could hear Ivy breathing heavily on the other end. "Of course, you would think it's my fault. Anything that's ever gone wrong has always had my blame written all over it in your eyes."

"Right there, Missy!" I pounded the table with my fist.

66

"Everything is always about you." I was losing my temper and it wasn't good. Never was.

"You can't even say my name! Do you hate me, Helen?"

"Now that's just foolish. You forget, *IVY*, that I put a roof over your head and kept you fed. I may not have been perfect, but I was there when you had no one else."

"Thank for the reminder. Do you know how pathetic that makes me feel? Why have you held yourself apart from me all these years?" Ivy threw the door open to territory I had never expected to breach. How could this call have gone so wrong?

"You know nothing of my life before you came into it." I looked out the window seeking strength from the sunflowers. They turned their heads away. I couldn't blame them.

"I can say the same," Ivy said.

She had me there. Had I ever taken Ivy's life before the accident into consideration? Was I so wrapped up in my own disillusionment with life?

"That's right, Helen. I had a mother who sang me songs, read me books, and held my hand wherever we went." Ivy's voice cracked. "I had a father who took me to the park and protected my every move. In the blink of an eye, I lost all of that. Forever!" She sniffled hard. "You know, you were thrust into my life just as I was thrust into yours. And rather than draw us together, you made sure we remained apart. I was only five! I needed a mother. What I got was an angry aunt who resented my interruption into her life. I was a little girl. I needed you."

"You ... you don't know everything," I said.   "Then by all means, enlighten me. All we had was each other, and we didn't even have that!"

"You've been so unappreciative!" Why did I continue to push? The undercurrent to it all was nearly swallowing me up and I had all I could do to keep my head above water. Everything was coming to a head all at once. Why? Did I deserve this?

Ivy voice quieted. "I have never been ungrateful for all that you've given me, but no one has ever asked me what I want. Not once."

"Stop it! Stop fighting!" I could hear Maudie in the background.

"Maudie, baby, I'm sorry," Ivy said. "I didn't know you'd come back in the house."

"I'm tired of you fighting with everyone. All you do is yell." The tone of Maudie's voice resembled a girl well beyond her ten years.

"Sweetie, I..." The slap of a screen door brought a momentary silence that hung heavy and incriminating between them.

"As you heard, Maudie blames me for everything wrong in the world, just like you. I guess that's my lot in life." Ivy's voice was wracked with exhaustion.

"I know how that feels." I felt no victory in those words. "I have one more thing to say. You lost your parents, not by choice, but by fate. Now, your children are being deprived of a home with both of theirs, and it's your choice. Think about that."

My answer was a resounding snap of disconnection. How did that conversation go so off-course? I was heartsick at the distress in Ivy's voice, yet I couldn't be supportive. Why? I took my empty coffee cup and threw it into the sink where it exploded in sharp, unforgiving shards.

***

I arrived at Gus's house with fire burning in my veins. I was still stinging from the phone call with Ivy and Gus's little tease in the store gnawed at me ever since, my brain spinning one possibility after another, and I knew eventually the good deputy would be back with more questions.

Gus lived in a tiny, gray house on Seventh Avenue with maroon trim and spindly trees growing close alongside as though they held the sorry structure from toppling over. Torn shades hung caddywampus in the dirty windows and the porch was leaning wearily to the south.

With my large purse dangling from a crooked arm, I pulled in my chin and resolved to step inside this ramshackle box he called home. Up the weathered, wooden steps I navigated and knocked on the rusty screen door once, twice, then again. Finally, Gus answered wiping his hands on a dirty, tattered kitchen towel.

"Well, lookey who's here." Gus grinned wide, his leathery face breaking into weathered wrinkles, rheumy eyes creased at the corners. He pushed the door open wide.

"You, Mister, are not leaving me hanging like this." I pointed a finger, then followed him inside.

"Shoulda figured you'd show up. You wanna beer? I could use one. 'Specially now."

"I do not. Gus, you can't tell me those things and not expect that I wouldn't want to know the rest of the story." I followed him in through the God-awful kitchen smelling of rotten food and mustiness, without an uncluttered space to be found. A metal table in the center of the room was piled with dirty dishes, some sort of car parts, fishing baits and the remnants of what looked like a baked chicken, the carcass dry and devoid of meat. I couldn't bear to look at the cupboards as I followed him into the dimly lit living room strewn with newspapers and clothes. In fact, it was hard to see had any furniture at all. And the carpet, a dirty brown path cut the room in half. *Oh, good heavens, how can people live this way?*

"My God, man, you need to clean this place up." I honestly couldn't hide my disgust.

"You offerin'?" His snowy eyebrows arched.

"You should be so lucky, old man. No."

Gus laughed at that, a full belly laugh that ended in a fit of coughing.

I pushed aside various papers and magazines and took a seat on the sagging red sofa. I was afraid to breathe too deeply in fear of what other odors lay in wait. I half expected to see a dead mouse or rat lying in a corner. So far, nothing. Gus plopped into the threadbare recliner.

A black cat jumped from a windowsill causing the shade to snap upward with a *'WHAP'*.

"What the hell?" I jumped as though someone had shot a gun.

"Go on now, Gopher." Gus shooed the cat. Light attempted to filter through the now exposed glass.

"Damn thing nearly gave me a stroke." I patted my face. "You have a cat named Gopher?"

Gus shrugged.

"I need you to tell me about my father, and don't pull any punches."

"Aw, I don't want to be the cause a you thinkin' different about your Pa." Gus rubbed his stubbly chin and angled into a rocking chair.

"There's a dead person on my old farm and I'm not completely sure who it is. I don't have time or patience for anything but the truth. Tell me about his troubles before he went missing."

"Oh, old Harlon, he was wild as a tiger. He, ah..." Gus rubbed his palms on his pants.

"The truth."

"Aw, geez. He was after one of them Pukall girls. Martha. She was a pretty little thing. Kinda rough around the edges. One night, after bar time, he took it too far and the girl accused him of rapin' her." Gus held up his hands. "Now, I don't know what was the honest-to-God truth. Harlon wouldn't say. Knowin' Harlon, I would say she weren't lyin'. Wasn't the first time he got in that kinda trouble. Martha had her some brothers and they threatened to

70

get even. Next thing you know, Harlon's truck is in the drink and no Harlon."

Conflicting images from decades ago fought for supremacy in my brain. I wasn't sure what was fact and what was fiction. The news of our father and Miss Pukall wasn't a total shock.

"Do you think they could be responsible? Maybe they did him in and tried to hide the evidence?"

"Wouldn't surprise me. Sheriff said he couldn't prove nothin'." Gus shrugged. "The girl turned up pregnant and said it was Harlon's. 'Course that was after he was already gone, so who knows."

The gossip regarding our father and Martha Pukall hadn't died with his disappearance, but it was years before I knew any of it. I was nearly twelve when I overheard Mama and her sisters talking about it in hushed tones, not realizing I was hiding at the top of the stairs. They'd whispered about a little girl across town. I asked Luddie about it, but he didn't know much, just that the Pukalls were plenty mad at the Foley's. At the time, I could tell he knew more than he was letting on, but I didn't press. My memories of our father were bad enough. I didn't care to add to it all. It wasn't until I was an adult that Auntie Vee told me the whole story. By then, Martha Pukall and her daughter were no longer in the area and honestly, I didn't think of it much after that.

"Poor Esther," Gus said, "here she was pregnant at the same time. No husband to support her and she had to know he had a seed growin' just across town." Gus shook his head and rubbed the back of his neck. "Esther was a good woman. I tried courtin' her after he was gone, but she wouldn't have none of it. Don't blame her after what he put her through."

I tried picturing Gus and our mother. *Hell no!* Gus took out a filthy handkerchief that was at one time white, and blew his nose, leaving a tiny bit hanging from his white nose hairs. I pointed and he wiped again before cramming it back into the pocket of his overalls.

"There had to be some in this town that questioned whether the Pukall boys might have had something to do with his disappearance. What other explanation could there be?" Maybe, just maybe, what I remembered from that night wasn't the whole story.

"I know those boys were hauled in for questioning, but there was also a hell of a storm came through that night and the law was stretched pretty thin as it was. Hell, there was trees down and roofs blown off and to top it off with a bad accident and then Harlon's truck in the drink. Those poor officers didn't know if they was comin' or goin'."

"One would think a disappearance would take precedence over storm damage."

"Harlon never made himself many friends which didn't help his case. Like I said, the sheriff's department had their hands full. You have to understand, there was no evidence, just some rumors."

I slapped my knees. "And now we have a body in a tree and no idea who or how it got there."

"That's the shit of it all. Don't make sense. Harlon's long gone, looked like he either drove himself into the river or someone put him in the river to hide a crime, or now, someone maybe put him in that tree. The truth is the sheriff wasn't gonna waste lots of time on someone like Harlon." Gus rubbed his chin again and looked away. "He weren't no upstanding citizen and it was perfectly acceptable that he ran off the road on his way home that night. I saw him earlier. He was drunk as a skunk. I didn't trust the Pukall boys or their Pa as far as I could throw 'em, but honestly, I think Harlon misjudged the road that night and ended up in the flowage."

"Who's to say the Pukalls are innocent."

"Yeah, I know."

"Still, the authorities are going to do their best to put a name to those bones. If it is my...father...well, I don't want the people I cared about dragged through the mud over it with all their unfounded gossip. I'm not about to accept that it's him. Damn their DNA."

"Their what?" Gus squished his features trying to decipher the meaning.

"Genetic testing, or something like that. Don't you watch the news?"

"Oh, well, nobody knowed that tree was hollow unless they been back there. And who else could a been back there? I'm sure you all didn't know that tree was hollow. And no way Esther coulda done him in and hid the body back there by herself."

"Exactly." I took a tissue from my purse and dabbed at my brow. It was suddenly very warm and the lines between what may have happened that night so long ago blurred, creating a chasm of doubt.

"Sides, Esther was a good person. She might have had reason to do him in, but I know she didn't. She was too concerned about you and your brother and the little one on the way."

"You're right there, Gus." I gave him a smile.

"Come to think of it," Gus leaned forward in his chair, "you want to know more, you want to talk to Clarice Luder. She might know more'n me. They owned Whiteys tavern where a lot of Harlon's shenanigans took place. She might remember more about the whole mess with Martha and the Pukalls. If somethin' was happenin' in town, Clarice heard all about it."

"She alive?"

"Last I heard, she was still this side of the sod. Livin' in Rose Manor."

CHAPTER 7

Esther

At the Greenfield Dance Hall, John Pesko and his band struck up *Happy Days Are Here Again*. Cigarette smoke hung like a blanket below the red, white, and blue banners strung from the rafters to celebrate the fourth of July. People of all ages sat on benches and chairs and told tales, while others danced like twirling tops. Young children snaked through the crowd, and raucous laughter burst above the music.

President Roosevelt had repealed Prohibition, and the dance halls were seeing new life. It was time to celebrate, shrug the oppressiveness of war, joblessness and bank failures, and live again.

Ruby and I sat on a bench along the wall, our feet tapping to the music, shoulders swaying from side to side, grape sodas in hand.

The side door burst open and a group of young punks spilled in, hooting and hollering, obviously drunk. Jim Cooley entered, and Ruby poked me in the arm. She was grinning from earring to earring. Harlon brought up the rear, cigarette dangling from his lips, beer bottle in one hand. He was so handsome in his white shirt tucked into brown trousers.

Most of the boys sloshed their way to the bar, while a few grabbed partners and joined in the swirl of dancers. Some of the adults wrinkled their noses and turned their heads from the ruffians.

From across the room, Harlon and I locked eyes. I could feel a blush burn quickly up my neck. I hadn't seen him since the burning of his field.

Harlon's gaze left mine and swept the room before he sauntered toward the bar with a defiant swagger that spoke of a self-assuredness that none of the other boys had.

Jim Cooley approached and offered Ruby a hand.

"I'll be back," she said to me and winked at Jim, "or maybe I won't." Jim hooked an arm around her waist and together they melded into the throng. I had to admit I was a bit jealous.

Virgil Baumgartner slid in beside me.

"Hey, Esther." His boyish face spread in a toothy grin. Virgil had been after me for the last few months, but I didn't give him the time of day. Virgil had no future other than fixing cars like his Pa. The boy bought more nuts and bolts than anyone in town. It got to the point Nelson's teased me every time he left through the door. It was pure pathetic how he couldn't take his eyes off me.

"Hey, Virgil," I said with a sigh.

"You wanna dance?" His droopy eyes reminded me of an old hound-dog. He pushed glasses up his nose with a finger.

"No."

"Why not?" Virgil slid in a bit nearer.

"Because, Virgil, I told you I'm not interested."

"We kissed and all," he whispered. Oh, for heaven's sake. He'd caught me one day in the alley behind the hardware store and said

75

he wouldn't let me by until he got a kiss. I had never kissed a boy and wanted to know what it was all about so, I let him. It was disgusting.

"We did not 'and all'. A kiss. That was it." I sure hoped Harlon didn't see Virgil drooling over me. "That doesn't mean we're a couple or anything. You forced me into it."

"Didn't you like it?" A blush crept into his cheeks.

"It was fine, but it really didn't mean anything."

"Fine." Virgil started to slide away.

"Wait." I started to reach for his arm but thought better of it. "I'm sorry Virgil. You're too good a friend. I don't want to ruin that."

"Lucky me." Within seconds he was out on the floor with Vivian Wendt, his knobby knees going this way and that.

Harlon was nowhere to be seen. More than likely he was outside where most of the rabble-rousers congregated. After the third song, much to my relief, Jim deposited Ruby on the bench.

He pulled a cigarette from his pocket, hung it on his lower lip, struck a match and as he lit it, winked at us girls. "I was just headin' outside. They got a game of poker goin' on in the parkin' lot. High stakes. You babes want to come? We got us some moonshine out there that'll knock your socks off. Old FDR, now there's a good old boy. He's my kinda President."

Ruby smoothed her bob. "What if I get cold? You gonna keep me warm?"

I rolled my eyes. "Don't be such a goo-ball."

"You bet I'll keep ya warm. Here's hopin' ol' man winter blows in." Jim pulled Ruby to her feet.

I could hardly contain my excitement as we followed Jim through the crowd. Harlon was sure to be out there somewhere. I was feeling a bit reckless for no reason other than the lively music and spirits were high.

The Witness Tree

Outside the cool night air caused gooseflesh on my arms. Young people gathered around cars or on the porch of the Greenfield, drinking, laughing, and smoking. Jim waved to several, as did Ruby. I was too busy scanning the dimly lit parking lot searching for Harlon.

And there he was. Illuminated by a lamp hanging from a wooden pole overhead, he and a few of his buddies were playing cards on the hood of an old Studebaker. A cigarette dangling from his lips, cards in one hand, a beer in the other. He seemed older than the others to me.

He looked up and saw me. It was if he could sense my presence. At least it was nice to think so.

He slapped his cards on the hood, took the cigarette from his mouth, held his beer bottle high and hooted into the night sky. Obviously, the cards had gone his way. The boys around him shouted in protest and threw their cards into the center in defeat.

Then his eyes settled on me and the heat of that gaze sent my gooseflesh running for the hills. He took a long drag on his cigarette, pulled it from his lips with two fingers, winked at me and sent the glowing stick sailing through the air. He was teasing me with what I'd done to his hay field.

I grinned at him and crossed arms over my chest.

"I'm out," Harlon said to the others and despite their objections, gathered his winnings. He shoved the money into the pockets of his pants, grabbed two bottles of beer from inside the car and came toward me.

His shirt was open just enough to show a dusting of dark hair, his stride purposeful and strong.

Harlon handed me a bottle, cold and wet. From his back pocket he pulled out a bottle opener, popped the top of his bottle and brought it to his mouth. His lips wrapped tightly to the top as he took a swig causing his Adams apple to bob. He savored the taste,

77

licking his lips, before taking the bottle from my hands, his warm fingers brushing over mine, and popped the top.

"Drink up," he said with a grin and clinked his bottle against mine.

I took a swig of the golden brew, tasting the bitterness.

"Come on." Harlon jerked his head to the side and began to walk between the vehicles.

I took another drink and with a quick glance at Ruby, who was fawning over Jim, I followed him. The anticipation of being a bit naughty had me quaking inside.

Harlon weaved in and out between cars and trucks, drinking as he went.

At the back of the parking lot, he indicated an old pickup truck. Moonlight lit the crooked grin on his face. "I want to show you my old Chevy. I've been fixin' on it."

I ran a hand along the edge of the box. "Nice." I didn't really know what else to say. One truck looked like another to me, although my brothers would berate me for that.

He ran his hand along the box as well until his fingers just barely touched mine. A queer twisting of my insides coursed through me. The shadows of the night played on his angular features making him seem a bit mysterious, a bit dangerous.

"You nervous to be out here with me, Esther?" He angled his head and studied me. His eyes were dark and penetrating.

My face burned under his gaze, but my lips were moist, just waiting to be kissed. A real kiss.

"No," I lied and tipped my nose into the night air trying to appear fearless. I couldn't help but notice how alone we were. "You don't scare me in the least, Harlon Foley."

He grinned and I noticed a slight dimple on the right. How I wanted to trace it with my finger.

I took another drink of courage.

The Witness Tree

He leaned an elbow on the truck, the bottle dangling from his hand, and with the other hand, reached out and stroked my arm. His calloused, work-worn hands were rough on my skin.

"You're shakin' like a leaf on one of them popple trees." His teeth were so white against the dark of night, his eyes held a mischievous glint.

"It's getting a little cool, that's all." No matter how hard I tried, I couldn't stem my nerves. I smiled up at him. Even though he didn't have a coat to throw across my shoulders, just maybe he'd put an arm around me.

He raised the bottle and took a good, hard pull, then threw it into the woods. "Better finish that while it's cold." He indicated mine with a pump of his head. "Warm beer ain't good for nothin'."

I took another drink, although my bottle was far from empty. "Guess I'm not that thirsty."

Harlon took the bottle from me and finished it, keeping his icy blue gaze on me all the while. He tossed the bottle aside and with a foot on the tire and a hand on the truck bed, he hopped over the side in one fluid motion.

"Good night to watch the stars." He thrust his hand in front of me. "Come on up."

I pictured my mother, face red as a Macintosh, warning me to behave like a lady. I would bet any money Rose Peroutka had never had an impulsive, carefree moment in her life.

I placed my foot on the tire and allowed him to pull me up and over the side. I anticipated the two of us sitting side by side watching the stars, his arm against mine, maybe an arm over my shoulder. Of course, he would kiss me. That was a forbidden fruit I couldn't wait to partake.

Harlon sat down in the box and ran his hand over the bottom. "It ain't dirty. I swept it out after the last load of firewood."

"I spent good money on this skirt."

"The stars look a lot better from here. Unless you're scared there, Esther." There was that dimple again. The moon dusted his features, highlighting his cheek bones.

"I'm not about to get my skirt dirty on account of your old truck." I swished the skirt before him.

"I said it's clean." He brushed his hand over the bottom again. "Come on."

It honestly didn't look too bad. I pulled my skirt around my legs and sat on the hard surface.

Harlon slid next to me and slipped an arm around my shoulders. "I've been waitin' for this."

"You have?" Excitement skittered up my spine as I settled in against him. Could it be that Harlon had been pining for me as well?

"You couldn't tell?" His voice was smooth as honey as he brushed his nose along my neck. I could feel the warmth of his breath on my cheek, smell the beer on his breath. His thumb brushed the side of my breast. My breath caught and I jerked.

"What's the matter, Esther?" His lips were against my ear.

"Nothin'." I looked to the black above. "Seems the clouds have covered up our stars."

"Then I guess we'll have to find something else to do."

"Like what?" I asked, then regretted sounding like the inexperienced girl I was.

"Like this." His thumb brushed my breast again and he groaned as he pressed against me. His hand came across my middle and toyed with a button on my blouse.

This was a bit more than I had bargained for. I brought my hand down on his.

"Harlon, I hardly know you." Where was that kiss I wanted? "Maybe we should go back inside. Ruby will be lookin' for me." I placed my other hand on his chest.

"Ruby's busy with Cooley. She ain't gonna care what you're doin'." The tone of his voice hardend.

"No, Harlon." I started to sit but Harlon roughly pulled me against him. My head snapped back against the cab.

"Ow." I reached up to rub it and Harlon put his whole hand on my breast.

"Harlon!" I tried to push up, but he had me firmly pinned against the corrugated bottom.

I put both hands on his chest and pushed as panic gripped me. "We shouldn't."

With his other hand he began pulling the skirt up my legs.

"You owe me for the trouble you caused." Gone was the dimple and the glint in his eyes was replaced with something treacherous.

"I'm not paying you back like this." I struggled to speak for the knot in my throat.

"Don't make this out to be anything more than it is."

"Harlon, don't." I brought a knee up and with my hands tried to force him off, but he was too big, too strong. His hand slipped inside my blouse and a button burst. His other hand was on my bare thigh and pushing higher. I was able to get an arm free and I pounded on his back.

"You're only makin' this harder, Esther."

"Noooo," but the sound and my innocence died in the night.

CHAPTER 8

Helen

The brick bulk of Rose Manor was a new addition to Peeksville. A stately looking building with white columns along the front entrance and some of the sorriest cedar bushes I'd ever seen surrounded by weed infested daylilies. If I ever get stuck here, I will need to take charge of the gardens.

Despite their sorry gardening skills, the interior was clean as a whistle, shiny tile floors, nice furniture in welcoming shades of blue and green. A doddering old man sat in a wheelchair, his body leaning to one side, although I could see he was strapped in. His trousers were way too short for him, his lunch was smeared down his shirt and white hair sticking straight up. A bit of drool ran down his chin. George Tesnoski. He was in my class in high school. I never thought he'd amount to much and this proved it. I sure as hell hope I don't end up like that, but who knows what's ahead. Guess I shouldn't be such a crabass.

The Witness Tree

At the front desk a young girl with a nametag that said Mercy asked if she could help me. I wanted to say '*keep me the hell out of here*', but I asked for Clarice Luder. The antiseptic smell of the place made me want to gag.

"Clarice? She doesn't get visitors," Mercy answered. The girl was clearly pregnant, about ready to pop, in one of those getups that medical workers wear in pink with little ducks all over it.

"She's got one now." I stared her down.

"You'll find her over by the window in the dining room just around the corner. She's the one by the windows." Mercy gestured to the right.

I walked a short way and sure enough, found Clarice sitting on a cushioned chair looking out to the gardens beyond the expanse of windows, gripping a large walking stick with one gnarled hand. Clarice pushed her fuzzy white head forward as she watched a flock of sparrow's peck under a bush. With her prominent nose, she reminded me of a hawk stalking its prey.

"Mrs. Luder? Clarice?" I pulled another cushioned chair up next to her and set my purse on the floor. The gardens outside the window were sad to say the least. No better than what was in front.

"Yeah." Clarice turned her head and narrowed her gaze as she considered me, then turned back to bird watching. "See them birds there?" she asked. "They's sparrows. Did you know they like to be in the tangles?" She angled her face toward the window. "The female, she's the one that builds the nest. The men, they just sit there and watch. Just like a man, ain't it?"

I leaned forward and watched as well. The tiny bird was busy indeed.

"Still and all," Clarice straightened her shoulders and brought the walking stick to rest between her legs, "I could use me a man." She banged the stick on the linoleum. "Been a while."

The old woman grinned showing off her crooked, yellow teeth.

"I'm guessing there's not many to choose from here," I said, instantly liking this old woman.

"You're damned straight there, young lady." Clarice smiled wide and it was then I noticed a tooth missing in the front. "You got yourself a man?"

"No." I cleared my throat. "No." This line of questioning was not what I'd prepared for.

"Didya at one time?"

"Maybe." There was Charlie but that was so long ago it really didn't count.

Clarice narrowed her eyes, bringing her brows together like two snowdrifts. "Either you did, or you didn't."

"I did for a short time. Didn't work. He moved away." The memory left a bitter taste.

"You didn't give up too soon, did you? You know, the beauty of it, 'tween men and women, is the back and forth and back and forth, but in the end, something beautiful comes. That's how it was with me and my Whitey. Sun's comin' out now." She waved her free hand toward the window. "Look at that maple tree out there, and the black-eyed-Susans, and the yarrow and the paintbrushes. Nature's artwork. Wish I could get out there and clean it up."

The old woman was speaking my language.

"So, who are you?" Clarice wrapped both hands around the walking stick, angled her head my way, studying me.

"My name is Helen Foley. I'm the daughter of Esther Foley. Do you remember Esther? She was married to Harlon Foley back in the forties. They had a farm out on Thornapple Road. I had the farm up until a few years ago."

Clarice scrunched her nose, thought for a moment before her eyes widened in recognition. "Harlon Foley? That old son-of-a-gun." She tsk, tsked and shook her head.

"Obviously, you remember him." Some might be honored to

have their family member well remembered within the community. Not me. Not where my father was concerned.

"My husband, Whitey and I owned a tavern back in the day. Whitey's. Best damn honky-tonk in the county. Harlon ripped it up many at time with his fightin'. My Whitey was right there with him, no good slug." Clarice grinned. "Yup, right up until the night old Harlon left and never came back. The night he ended up in the drink for good."

"The night he died." I gripped the arms of the chair. Now we were getting somewhere. "Can you tell me about it?"

"Never forget it. He was on a mean one. Rumor was he got hisself fired from the mill that day for stealin' from the company. Don't know if that's true or not. Harlon could be one ornery man if he was riled and that night, he was plenty riled. Said it had to do with the trumped-up charge by one of the Pukall boys he worked with." Clarice gave her a sideways glance before continuing. "He was after one of the Pukall girls. Can't remember the name."

"Martha."

"That's it. She accused him of rapin' her and if he hadn't disappeared, the wrath of her family woulda come down on 'im hard. He met his match with them. 'Course, maybe they did get their revenge. Who knows." Clarice pursed her shriveled lips and shook her head. "Hell, Harlon wanted his way with me too, but I could be just as mean. One night I broke a bottle over his head." Clarice cackled in delight then held up a finger, the veins on the back of her hand as blue as the Redemption. "I told 'im if he ever came at me again, it would be the end of 'im. Actually, I can't believe someone didn't do him in a long time before the river got 'im—if that's what got 'im."

"You're not sure?"

Clarice shifted her skinny butt in her chair and nodded. "People woulda lined up to give him what he had comin'. But kinda fishy, don't ya think? His truck is found in the Redemption and a body never shows up. You'd a thought there'd be some kind of sign."

I nodded. "Who were the other enemies he had?"

"Oh hell, coulda been anybody. He weren't a likable guy. Couldn't hold a job to save his soul. Drank up every penny he earned. Owed more people money than you could imagine. Hell, me and Whitey got stuck in the end as well."

"I'm sorry to hear that. Any names you can remember?"

Clarice blinked and looked up at the ceiling for a moment. "Naw. I got nothin' there."

"Human bones were found on the back forty of my old farm, Harlon and Esther's farm. Stuck inside a hollow tree. Some think it's Harlon, my father."

"I don't believe it. Bones?" Clarice shook her head. "If it's Harlon, after all this time, it don't really matter who done it, does it? I say water under the bridge. He never done nobody any good anyways."

I had a kindred spirit here and was mighty grateful.

"Coulda been the Pukalls, but they're all gone now 'cept for some grandkids still in the area."

"What happened to Martha and her baby?"

"Martha was a nice girl, but she drank herself to death, only lived into her forties, and the little girl died in her twenties. Some kinda cancer got 'er. I only remember that because I liked Martha. She bartended for us a couple times, but after the whole mess with Harlon she lost her way. Was a shame."

It was a strange basket of emotion I felt at having had a half-sister that I'd never known and never would. I'd lost one sister that I cherished, but this one...could we have been close? I didn't think so. And Martha. Harlon ruined her life.

"Do you remember the little girl's name?" I felt I should know.

"Oh, hell I don't know," Clarice said.

Seemed every life Harlon touched ended in tragedy. "Do you remember anything else?"

Clarice waved a hand in front of her face. "I'm nearly a hundred years old. Some days I can't remember squat."

The Pukalls seemed the most likely culprit, but it could have been someone he owed money, or revenge for something at work. The list was endless.

Clarice gave me a sly, bitter grin. "Harlon got me back for puttin' him off. He was good at revenge. I seen it many a time." Clarice hesitated a moment as though sorting through the memories. "The bastard stole my pearl ring. I know he did. One afternoon it was just him and me. I took the ring off to clean out the drain in the sink under the bar. Harlon sat there with his beer watchin' me. I went out back to grab a bucket. When I come back the ring and Harlon was gone. Whitey and I asked him about it, but he lied." She stuck a finger in the air. "But I knew. I could see it in his eyes."

"I'm sorry about that." I wanted to reach through the years and wring his neck. For so many things.

"I loved that ring." Clarice pursed her lips and stared off. Then, abruptly she banged the stick again. "Enough of feelin' sorry for myself. Don't get you nowheres."

"True." That had been my mantra of sorts. It got me through the toughest of times. Just another gift from my mother. She never wallowed in pity, after all she'd been through, kept moving forward, focusing on the next task at hand.

"Harlon had hisself a good woman there." Clarice sniffed and wiped her nose with the back of her hand. "Esther Foley was a hard workin' woman. Did what she could. Never understood why she stayed with that man. No body woulda faulted her for leavin'."

"Guess it was a different day back then." Auntie Vee told me that Mama had tried to leave him, but Harlon always got his way.

Why did he care to hold on?

"Not that different. Comes a point, a woman needs to take control. Be valued for her contribution." Clarice pushed up from her chair and grabbed her cane. I offered a hand and helped her straighten. "Now, I'm late to go bother the men in the lounge. Half a them don't know their backside from a hole in the ground. Walk with me."

Me and my big purse hanging from my elbow escorted the little lady down the hall, afraid that at any moment Clarice might topple over.

"You come see me again," Clarice said, her hand wrapped around my forearm. "I like you, even if you are related to that old river-rat."

I grinned as Clarice announced her arrival at the lounge with a bang, bang of her cane on the linoleum.

CHAPTER 9

Esther

By the time I hung the last of the clothes on the line to dry, my thin, pink cotton dress stuck to my body and pulled with every move. My hair was a fright in this humidity. I gathered what I could and secured it into a twist with a bobby pin from my pocket.

This daily drudgery was getting to me and I needed relief. Some time for me.

The river beckoned. It was the one guilty pleasure I was loath to deny myself, especially since I was home alone. It was rare that I sought the waters of the Redemption to soothe my soul, but today seemed perfect to indulge.

Fifteen minutes earlier Herman Gropp had pulled into the yard with his rattletrap truck and asked for the children to come help his wife, Magdalene, work in her large strawberry patch. The children agreed, knowing there really was no choice. Had they declined,

The Witness Tree

Herman would have gone right to Harlon to complain. At least Herman paid them for their time, albeit a pittance. They wouldn't be back for at least another hour.

I left the laundry basket on the porch and strolled across the hay field. Soon the golden aroma of newly cut hay gave way to the earthy pungency of forest. I stopped to pick raspberries as I went, enjoying the sweetness of Earth's bounty. A sparrow twittered from branch to branch as though keeping me company. A chipmunk darted across the path daring me to play along.

Soon I reached the stand of birch and my favorite pool of water lay just beyond. To the west, the rocky shore of Redemption River marked the edge of our property where a rotting basswood, jutting like a sundial from the ground, signaled the northern edge.

I pushed out of my shoes, pulled the stubborn dress over my head, then the slip, and stepped out of my bra and panties. Piece by piece I tossed them onto a boulder along the shore.

You know, if I'd been a religious person, this would be my church. This is where I was thankful for all that was around me and my two children.

I stepped into the current and my toes squished into the cool, muddy bottom. The chill wrapped around my legs, causing gooseflesh despite the warmth of the sun. As the water reached my middle, I shivered and bent into it. At the river's center, the mud gave way to a rocky bottom. In the pool at the base of the rapids I pushed off doing a breaststroke and flapped my feet against the current.

I couldn't help it, a twitter of a laugh escaped me and mingled with the birdsong.

A light breeze teased the leaves overhead as I floated on my back, my arms gracefully moving the water back and forth like an angel working her wings. A puffy cloud sailed overhead sending a fleeting shadow across the forest. I turned to see a young deer

90

come through the woods. It tipped its mouth to the pool for a drink, but upon seeing me, it stopped. The two of us stared at each other a moment before the deer took another quick sip and bounded off, it's white tail high in the air.

I rarely found contentment such as this. Just me and nature. Maybe I would bring Luddie and Helen back here after supper.

I remained as long as I dared. Supper needed starting, the children would be back soon, and Harlon would be home from the mill.

Reluctantly, my feet found the bottom and I pushed through the current to shore.

Chasing the water from my limbs, I dressed deciding to stay barefoot. Finding two more bobby pins in the pocket, I clipped more of the unruly strands that had come loose.

Despite all that waited at home, I walked along the shore heading north into Mr. Sommer's property. It was a pretty walk, and I simply felt too good to head back into the heat of the field. This way I could circle around, following more of the forest. Shoes dangling from my hand, I followed the river. The only sounds were the rustle of the breeze and the song of the gurgling water.

Completely lost in thought, I jumped at the snap of a branch. "Hello."

I gasped, tripped on a branch and fell to the ground. The new neighbor was standing over me. His tall form blocking the sun through the lace of leaves overhead.

"I startled you. I apologize." He pushed his glasses up his nose, leaned over and extended a hand.

At first, I simply sat there staring at him trying to gather my wits.

"Come on, let me help you." He pushed the hand closer. His dog came around his legs.

"Winifred, get back." He used his other hand to push the dog away. "Sorry about that. She thinks everyone is her friend. It's going to get her into trouble one of these days."

His long fingers curled around mine. There was strength in his grip, and tenderness too. And a feeling of...what? Recognition? The awareness of meeting a kindred soul? That sounded silly.

Mr. Sommers pulled me to my feet. "Are you all right?"

I steadied, withdrew my hand and took a step back. "I'm fine. Seems I'm a bit of a klutz around you, Mr. Sommers." My dress was a wrinkled mess and I tried to smooth it out.

"Again, I'm so sorry to have startled you like that. You were lost in thought. I should have made some sort of movement earlier to let you know I was there."

"I...I didn't see you. I was...where were you?" Oh, Lordy, had he seen me naked?

"Propped in the crook of this tree here." He gestured to a willow along the river with one thick limb curling out over the water. "I'm scaring the fish away." His face lit in a smile.

A kiss of breeze moved a shock of his hair onto his forehead.

His fishing pole was propped against the trunk. Looking back, there was no way he could have seen me.

"I went for a dip in the pool back there to escape this heat."

"I'll bet the water felt good on a day like today."

"It did. Thank you for the hand up. And now, I'm trespassin' again."

"It's a nice path along the Redemption here, isn't it?"

"It is at that. I was caught up in an old memory. Didn't see you there." I pushed a twig from the path with my foot, then smiled up at him.

"Must have been a wonderful daydream." He angled his head and studied me.

"Just a slip into my youth. You know, there's really no fish in this river other than blue gills that aren't worth spit."

"Bob at the filling station told me there are some excellent trout here."

I had to chuckle at that. "He's just trying to keep you out of his fishin' hole. When he's not pumpin' gas, he's in the narrows on Butternut Lake. He does that to all the newcomers."

"You don't say. Won't he be surprised when I show up?" He grinned, his eyes crinkling at the sides, he had a bit of a sunburn on his nose. "Please don't feel that you have to run off on account of me."

"Oh, there's always lots to be done on the farm." Although I really had no urgency to leave.

An amiable silence settled between us. Mr. Sommers crossed his arms over his chest and breathed in the clean air, face tipped toward the canopy of trees and the celestial rays dotting his face.

I took a seat on a boulder and slipped on my shoes.

He went back to his perch on the tree limb, his bare feet dangling over the water.

"Nice and cool here, isn't it?" he asked.

"Hmm." I patted my twist of hair and wound a strand around my finger.

"Your children, I saw them outside the store that day. Is your son all right? I noticed he had a good size gash over one eye."

Would have been nice if Luddie's own father had been as concerned as this stranger. "He's fine. He bumped himself on the bed of the truck on our way into town. You almost can't tell anymore."

"Good to hear. What are their names?"

"Luddie and Helen. He's named for my grandfather, Ludlow, the kindest man I've ever known. And Helen…I always loved history and so, well, she's named after Helen of Troy. You know, so beautiful she could bring a nation to war. I was always a bit of a romantic back in my younger, more foolish days. But Helen is a

93

name of strength to me. I wanted my girl to be strong and that she is."

"There's nothing foolish about a romantic. It gets you through the rough parts of life." He hung his head, cleared his throat and a slight pall smoothed the features on his face. "Well, most of them."

Does it? I wondered. Something in the subtle change in his voice that told me something darkened his door at one time, still did.

"Do you read poetry?" He angled his head to the side as he waited for my response. A gentle smile graced his face, and his cap of auburn hair caught the sun.

"No, although I used to. Back in school, I loved Emily Dickinson."

"I do as well. In fact, I was just running a poem through my head when I saw you come through the trees today. To me this place inspires words to flow."

"Are you a writer?" I could easily see him pecking away for hours on end at a typewriter.

"No, no." He chuckled. A very pleasant sound. "I simply enjoy poetry of any kind. It seems to soothe the spirits."

"That day I saw you at the river," I was compelled to ask, "you were reciting something then. What was it?"

"The poem was 'Annabel Lee' by Edgar Allan Poe. It's a haunting tale of lost love." His eyes held a far-off glaze. "I run it through my brain every once in a while. Probably shouldn't."

"Hmm, 'Annabel Lee'." I pondered the beautiful name and the mystery in his final words. I wanted to ask for an explanation, but thought better of it. "I think I read that in school."

"You know, Mrs. Foley, you look very different with your hair swept up that way." Some of the heat I sought to escape at the river was beginning to return in a very different way. "Forgive me if that was too forward." Although, he didn't look the least embarrassed.

94

I raised a hand to the still-wet hair plastered to back of my neck. "My hair is a fright in this humidity. And please, my name is Esther."

"With your hair up like that makes you look, oh, I don't know, queenly somehow. Like Helen of Troy." His lopsided grin was so engaging, I couldn't help but smile back. "Esther is a lovely name."

"Oh, I think it's too stodgy. My best friend always called me Essie and I liked that, but my grandfather called me Bess. I loved that."

"Bess?" He swung his bare feet back and forth over the water.

"My middle name is Elizabeth." I hadn't thought of my middle name in so long.

"Ah, now there's a queenly name." He brought a finger to his lips then pointed it at me. "Good Queen Bess."

I had to chuckle at that. "Mister Sommers, feel free to call me Bess anytime."

"Bess it is. And please, my name is Robert. There's no need to be so formal between friends, and I do hope we'll be friends." Dappled sunlight glinted off his glasses.

"Robert." I liked the feel of his name on my tongue. I also like the easy way he was looking at me. I should have probably looked away, but I didn't want to.

A welcome breeze stirred the canopy overhead and bent the grass at our feet.

"Einar Nelson is a fine man, isn't he?" Robert reached for his pole and jiggled the line.

"Yes, he is. He's been runnin' that store since I can remember." I lowered my voice as though sharing a secret, "Although, be mindful of his wife. She can be a battle-ax if you owe money."

Robert chuckled. "I'll take that into consideration." He sighed and said, "The sun's starting to swing to the west and I've got cows waiting to be milked. I suppose I should mosey on back."

"Oh, my goodness, I've completely forgotten the time." I pushed off from the boulder and started back along the path. "Goodbye, Robert."

"Bess," he called with a hand in the air. I turned, enjoying my new name and the sound of it coming from his mouth, "thank you for taking the time to visit with me."

I waved a hand over my head and continued on. I hadn't felt that good, that appreciated, in forever.

CHAPTER 10

Helen

I opened the front door to Deputy Reed Bolton. He took off his hat and bobbed his head.

"Well?" I stared him down. I knew he'd be back, but this time I was ready for him.

"Thought I'd see if you remembered anything more. Could we sit down and have a conversation?" He gestured toward the interior with his hat. "I won't take too much of your time, Helen."

"Oh, come in. I'll find a can of soda for you." I led him inside, through my cozy living room with overstuffed furniture in floral patterns, afghans strewn here and there, a few end tables with antique lamps I'd brought from the farm and a bookshelf overloaded with my mother's favorite books. I directed him to a seat at the dining room table before going into the kitchen and returning with a can of orange soda.

"That'll have to do. It's all I've got." I took a seat opposite and spread my hands on the hard surface of the old, oak table marked with the history of family dinners, teaching Ivy to cut her meat, Luddie drumming to the music on the radio, Annabelle painting her pictures, my mother playing solitaire.

"This is just fine, Helen. I haven't had orange soda in years." Reed cracked the can and took a swig. He leaned his elbows on the table and he looked me straight in the eye. "How are you doing?"

"How do you think? I'm old. Each day is an adventure in sore knees, an aching back and arthritic hands." I leaned forward, focusing on his face, remembering the little shit he'd been as a kid. He must have been about six years old when he broke a light fixture in the hardware store. I made his father pay for it, I did. Ivy complained once of his picking on her in school, although later on it was clear he had a crush. Well, enough of that. "I don't like all this talk going around about my family and my farm. Someone at that sheriff's office has loose lips. This should have remained a quiet affair, but now the whole town is talking about it. I was accosted three times in the grocery store with nosy townsfolk wanting to know the scoop. And all I was there for was a lousy box of beef broth."

"Helen, it's news. You must have seen the article in the newspaper. People have the right to be informed of a crime committed in their community. This kind of thing doesn't happen very often in a small town. You have to expect people are going to talk. It will die down in time."

"I let my newspaper subscription go last year." What use was it when I no longer recognized the names? I watched him take another pull on the soda then wipe the corner of his mouth with a finger.

"So, what can you tell me about your father's death? Anything new?"

"Not much," I said. "I was a little girl then. My mother did what she could to shield me and my brother when our father disappeared. It was never discussed. She kept us close to the farm for quite some time after. At that time, most people were polite enough to respect our privacy. Not like these days. Of course, there were those that brought out food and offered to help with the farm."

"I've been going over county records. Everyone in your family and the surrounding neighbors are accounted for. Everyone except him." He took another drink and stared at me.

"That's because he's somewhere at the bottom of the flowage." I brushed a crumb from the table.

"Are you sure about that?"

"That's what the consensus was at the time. Why would I question it? The man was drunk and couldn't swim a lick. As many times as he drove over that bridge when he was soused, I'm surprised it didn't happen sooner." I leaned toward him in challenge. "You know something I don't?"

"I've read the report of the investigation. I have to say, they did a half-assed job." He tapped his fingers on the can.

I simply glared at him, the only sound was his tap, tap, tap on the can with a fingernail. How it grated on my nerves.

"If Harlon was in the flowage, you'd think he would have shown up after the spring thaw. Something would show up, a piece of clothing, his wallet, a boot. I'm inclined to think he was never there."

"You've been to the flowage. There are millions of places a body could get caught, islands and logs and driftwood. Lots of hungry fish too." I sat back in my chair determined to let him know he was not getting to me. He was interrogating me as though I was a common criminal. Oh, how I wanted this to go away.

"You know, it's interesting, that you can talk about your father that way." Reed sat back as well. "With all due respect, it's kind of cold, don't you think?"

"He wasn't much of a father." I refused to flinch at his assessment of my lack of emotion. "If you're expecting me to be all mushy over it, it's not happening. I hate to think where we'd have been without my mother. The woman was a saint. And don't you forget it." I pointed at him to highlight the point.

"I'm guessing Harlon wasn't much of a husband either." Reed angled his head. "Someone with his reputation isn't generally any different at home."

"No. He was not."

"Tell me more about that."

"I am sure you can guess what he was like, so let's end it right there."

"Was he physically abusive to you all?"

"Quit pushing," I said through gritted teeth.

The deputy only paused a moment before continuing.

"I looked back through court records. He had quite a sheet. Even got into trouble a couple of times for bothering the ladies, if you know what I mean. One in particular. Martha Pukall. Seems old Harlon was quite smitten with her. Wouldn't leave her alone."

My spine grew steely under my cotton blouse.

My mother's clock chimed in the living room ting, ting, ting. The sound echoed through the stillness. I worried he could hear the beat of my heart.

"I'll bet your mother was none too pleased with her husband's behavior. Martha's family either. She had five brothers. Seems to me there's other scenarios back then that should have been explored and weren't."

"I remember the Pukall's. Wouldn't surprise me in the least if one of them put a bullet in him." I leaned forward, elbows on the table. "But then, he owed money to half the county and caused his share of problems at the mill before they fired him. If I was you,

100

I'd put my attention on the Pukalls." I paused a moment. "If you're insinuating my mother had anything to do with this, she had every right to do him in, but she didn't. I bet my life on that one."

"Women have disposed of husbands for less," he said. "The Pukalls were questioned when Harlon went missing, but there was no evidence to prove anything. From what I can see that lead wasn't explored nearly enough. Do you remember any gossip, any rumors?"

"I was too young, but you might want to talk to Gus Jablonsky. He knows all about the Pukall incident." I wasn't about to set him on the trail of Clarice. The woman didn't need the nuisance.

"Will do. Did Harlon have other enemies that you know of?"

"From what I heard, around every corner. No one missed him when he was gone. Trust me."

"You really hated your father." He tapped on the damn can again. I was sorry I'd offered it to him.

"I don't remember him much, but what I do wasn't pleasant. Sure, there were times I missed having a father around to help out, take us fishing or swimming, be a guiding force, but that wasn't him."

"Do you think it could it be that someone staged it to look like something it wasn't?" he asked.

"I do. The question is, who?"

"The fact that the truck was found in the river and no body to go with it seems very fishy to me. Too easy considering his reputation."

"You're the cop here. I think you just answered your own question and shouldn't be sitting here with me. Get out there and see what you find."

"Sorry, Helen. Just trying to do my job."

"I suppose someone could have tried to hide a crime, but if you're right, that person is long gone now. That's why I don't understand all this fuss trying to figure it out. If I don't care, why should anyone else?"

"Seems odd to me that you don't want to know the truth." He leaned forward on his elbows again. "He was your family after all, and your father disappearing must have made your lives quite difficult after he was gone. If someone is responsible for that, wouldn't you want them to pay?"

He had no idea how difficult our lives had been. "My mother worked her fingers to the bone at the hardware store on top of the house and the farm. Why she kept the farm, I can't fathom. Her life would have been much easier if she had sold it, but while Luddie and I were there, we took on a lion's share of the work so Mama could work in town. Luddie offered to leave school, but she wouldn't hear of it. She valued education."

A new thought occurred and ripped me to the core. Was our mother protecting a secret by keeping the farm? It made sense. By holding onto the farm, she was ensuring that no one else would go back there and discover the remains. I folded my hands together to keep them still.

"I do find it interesting that she held on to it" Reed said. "After all, it wasn't handed down from any other relatives for sentimenal reasons. Other than your home at the time, it should have meant nothing to her but bad memories of her marriage to a difficult man."

"She was a proud woman. Would it change anything now? No. The end result is the same. If you find that's my father in the tree, you'd best leave it as a mystery and stop wasting taxpayer dollars to solve a crime no one cares about." *There, take that.*

"Helen...," Reed sat back in his chair, a queer smile on his face. "There's something I didn't mention during my last visit. When I pulled into the yard after the initial call to our office from Joe Jennings, I saw a woman in the window upstairs. She was looking out toward the crime scene. Hair up at the back of her head, a dress and apron on. When I interviewed the family, I asked about her. They said there was no one else in the house." Reed looked away briefly. "I know what I saw. Carrie said they have a ghost but had never seen her."

"Oh pooh! There's no ghost there." The thought was ridiculous. Reed simply shrugged.

I slapped the table between us and pushed out my chair. "And now, on that note, Mr. Deputy, we're done. I've given as much of my time to this as I care."

"I'd like you to give a DNA sample. You don't have to, but it would certainly help."

"Absolutely not. I will not help this circus one bit." I knew this question was coming. I was the only tie to Harlon Foley now and they would have to hog-tie me to get a sample on the off-chance Gus was right about his suspicions.

"Makes me wonder why, Helen. The sooner we can wrap this up, the sooner you won't have to think about it anymore. And I'll stop pestering you."

"We're done." I could feel my face redden and was gritting my teeth so hard I was afraid they'd break.

Reed drained the last of his soda and stood. "Thank you, Helen. If you think of anything else, you'll call, won't you?"

I nodded knowing that neither of us believed I would.

CHAPTER 11

Esther

I pushed the venison around the skillet on the cook stove and silently berated myself for allowing the meat to cook too long. The leathery strips were much too dark, and I knew they would be tough. Turning my attention to the carrots, there was no water left and some of them stuck to the bottom. I quickly stirred to pull them away from the scorched pan before taking the boiling potatoes to the sink in a cloud of steam. I drained the water and began mashing. Some of the potatoes had not finished cooking and fought the masher. *What was the matter with me?*

Perspiration tricked down the back of my neck. Closing my eyes, I sought the calm I had found at the Redemption that afternoon when I'd come upon Robert as he fished.

No matter how hard I tried, I couldn't stop thinking of him. His face was before me, his kind and gentle voice sang in my ears. I'd felt alive for the first time in so long.

Beyond the kitchen window Harlon's truck pulled into the yard in a swirl of dust.

"Pa's home," Helen said from her chair at the table where she was drawing pictures of flowers.

"Better get the table set." I stopped mashing. "Come on, Helen, help Mama, please."

Helen gathered her pencil and papers and scissors, set them on the sideboard, and began setting the table.

I watched as Harlon approached the house. It was like a dark cloud rolling in from the west bringing a nasty storm.

"Where's Luddie?" I asked.

"He's outside." Helen continued setting the plates around.

Luddie was in the yard petting one of the few barn cats. Harlon stopped and spoke to him. Luddie left the cat and followed his father to the house.

As soon as Harlon entered, the smoky tang of the tavern filled the room. Surprisingly, he must have only stopped for a few for he was early.

"Come and eat." I spooned the potatoes into a dish.

The children were already seated after Harlon washed his hands. He cuffed the back of Luddie's head on his way to his place at the head of the table. The boy's head jerked forward, but he steadied himself. Helen glared at her father as he plopped into his chair, then reached over and tweaked one of her braids.

My fingers tightened on the steaming bowl of carrots. How I wanted to hurl it at him, watch it smash against his skull.

We ate in relative silence. I missed dinners in the Peroutka house, the constant flow of laughter, stories of the day, jostling to get the last chicken leg, Ma bustling about trying to keep us all fed, barking orders as she did so.

"Did you have a good day?" I tried to make pleasant conversation as I took a bite of tough venison.

"I spent it at the sawmill on a day that was so hot you couldn't breathe. Yeah, Esther, I had a great day." He took a drink of milk. To Luddie he said, "You didn't clean out the trough like I asked, did you?"

The boy dropped his fork, brought his shoulders up, and braced. "No, I…"

"Herman came for the children to work in the strawberries with Magdalene. We hadn't expected him. It disrupted our day a bit." I flashed a reassuring smile toward Luddie.

"I can do it after supper." Luddie swallowed hard and waited, expecting the worst.

"Damn right, you will." Harlon shoveled in a forkful of potatoes. "I ask you to do a job, I expect it done. Old Gropp better have paid you both."

"He gave us each a dime." Helen produced the shiny coin from her pocket. "When can we go to town? I want to go to Zillinger's and get licorice and a root beer and some bubble gum and maybe new ribbons for my braids." She pulled out a braid and flapped the end.

Harlon chuckled. "A whole dime he give ya? Gropp is a cheap SOB. I'm surprised you got that much."

"Luddie, how are you going to spend yours?" I asked the boy.

He began to answer, but Harlon cut him off.

"Henny, you get yourself them ribbons, you'll be the prettiest girl in town." Harlon said.

I leaned toward Luddie. "How will you spend your money?"

Luddie raised his soft, brown eyes to me. Oh, how I wanted to wrap him in my arms and hold him forever. "I want to save for a bike."

"That's a wonderful idea." I looked across the table to where Harlon was having a hard time cutting his piece of meat. Dark clouds rolled across his face and I knew any bit of normalcy of a family meal had just ended.

"This meal ain't fit for a hog." Harlon's voice boomed through the house. The windows shivered with it.

"I suppose I spent too much time in the garden and rushed the meal to get it done on time. Let me get you another piece." I began to stand.

"Luddie said you'd been down at the river when they got home. You lyin' to me?" He stared me down like a cat eyeing a mouse for dinner.

I offered a quick smile to Luddie and sat back down. "That's right, I worked so long in the garden that I felt woozy. That sun just wouldn't stop today. I took a quick walk and cooled off in the water." Luddie glanced at me and quickly averted his eyes. "Maybe you can take the children to the river after supper. I could do the evening chores for you." I calmly placed a forkful of scorched carrots into my mouth and chewed.

Helen piped up. "Wish I could have gone swimming rather than pick dumb berries for Mrs. Gropp. She's crabby. I snuck a few though. They were so good."

That was all the fuel Harlon needed. He slammed his fork down with a crack. "Wish I could have gone swimmin' too. I had to work in a sawmill with one-hundred-degree heat. Someone's got to pay the bills around here while you're out swimmin'. You think I wouldn't like to just drop everything and run off to play in the water?"

I pushed the food down my throat. "Harlon, I was feelin' ill, that's why I went to the river. It wasn't to escape the work around here. I needed to cool off, that's all, and now I'm offerin' to do your work for you tonight so you can go."

"This meal is nothin' but pig slop."

"I think it's good." Helen took a bite of her meat and chewed defiantly.

107

Harlon stood, his legs pushing his chair into the wall behind him. The children jumped in their seats but kept their heads low.

"Harlon, I can make you somethin' else if you like. It'd be no trouble at all."

"And let you ruin more of the food I have to work to put on the table?" The wild look in his eye frightened me.

He took the plate of venison, then came around the table, grabbed me by the arm and pulled me to into the kitchen.

"Harlon let go. This isn't going to fix anythin'. Just let me make you somethin' differ'nt. It'll be fine." He shoved me against the sink, his mouth in an evil snarl, the plate of meat still in his hand.

"I hate beer and I hate taverns." Helen yelled from behind us.

Harlon's released his grip slightly as he turned to face our daughter. I peered over his shoulder at Helen who stood under the arch between the kitchen and dining room, scissors in one hand, a braid in the other.

"I hate beer and I hate taverns." She repeated.

"What's this?" Harlon set the plate down. I held my breath. Luddie gripped his chair, his face ashen.

"I don't like it when you get drunk." Helen said. "You're not very nice."

"What do you plan to do with those?" Harlon waved a finger toward the scissors.

Helen pulled the braid straight out. "Next time you get drunk, I'm cutting off my braids."

"You wouldn't cut off them pretty braids. The kids in school would laugh 'atcha."

"I would cut 'em off if you don't be nice to our Mama." She continued to hold the braid hostage.

"I don't want no short-haired little girl." He glared. Helen stood her ground. Neither relenting.

"Harlon, let me fry up some of the sausage Frankie brought us."

Esther said.

"Fine," Harlon said.

Helen dropped the braid, set the scissors on the credenza and with a rigid set to her spine, returned to her seat at the table.

Harlon watched her for a moment. "Quite the little general, ain't she?" Pride evident on his face.

I nodded, then turned to take the sausage from the icebox while Harlon returned to the dinner table.

I sliced that sausage with angry, deliberate cuts. The knife felt mighty good in my hand.

CHAPTER 12

Helen

Autumn leaves choked the walk to my front stoop, and I swept the broom from one side to the other to push them away. I liked a clean sidewalk, not that I wanted anyone to use it. All part of staying busy, pushing away all thoughts of investigations and skeletons in trees. This little house provided lots to do, especially this time of the year. I still needed to wash the windows and take the screens down, after all the first snow could be here in mid-October already. The spent flower beds needed to be cut back and the bistro set in the back yard put away for the season.

Out of the corner of my eye I spied the new neighbor a few houses down across the street. An elderly gentleman. I noticed his moving in a few days ago. He now stood at the corner of his house—hands on hips, wearing a red tee shirt tucked into blue jeans, a pudgy middle and balding head—watching me. Didn't he have enough of his own work to do?

The Witness Tree

No doubt he'd heard the gossip from the neighbors regarding the body found on the farm. I was beginning to feel like a curiosity on show for everyone's entertainment. And I didn't like it one bit.

I gave him my back and, taking the broom, went to clean the glut of leaves from the flower box below the living room window. A few days ago I had dug out the geraniums and put the root balls in the basement for next year.

The maple at the corner of my house rustled its leaves. *Be calm, be calm,* they said as if I needed some sort of warning of coming events.

"Helen?"

My shoulders slumped with the knowledge that I was being interrupted.

"Helen? Is that you?" With a heavy sigh I turned his way.

The new neighbor crossed the street with a purposeful stride. There was something familiar about him. I couldn't put my finger on it. Nor did I want to. Couldn't he tell I was busy?

"I thought so," he said with a broad grin spread across a face for which smiling was no effort whatsoever. "My, it's been a long, long time." He stopped just short of the curb, hands in his pants pockets. What was it about him that had me searching the past?

"Do I know..." The air rushed from my lungs. No, not Charlie. It couldn't be. Not now.

He broached the curb and took a few steps into my yard. He didn't have the height I remembered, but the eyes knew me, and I knew them.

"It's me, Charlie. Charlie Soderberg."

The broom fell from my hand. I grabbed for it but missed and it bounced on the grass. I felt dizzy and one knee buckled slightly.

Charlie rushed forward and took my elbow as I regained my footing and my dignity.

Never again had I expected to lay eyes on Charlie Soderberg.

He had been the only one for me all through high school and then some. I'd noticed him the moment he and his parents moved to town in our freshman year, but he waited until our junior year to ask me to a movie. From then, our relationship grew slowly as I had many responsibilities in those days, but once we graduated, I thought we were bound to make a future. Charlie had other plans. Now, his face was a mere foot in front of my own. His hand on my arm.

"Are you all right? I didn't mean to startle you." His voice wasn't as deep as I remembered.

I shook him off as the steely walls of my heart came around me.

"I'm fine. You didn't startle me." I lied. "I saw you move in. You and your helpers were loud enough." I bent for the broom as my heart banged in my chest. "Those Stanley kids couldn't wait to push their father into the nursing home and sell his house. He was a good man. They should have shown him more gratitude than to stick him in the home. Not everyone has a father the likes of him."

"Helen, he had Alzheimer's. His kids work. The nursing home was their best option. I went to visit him yesterday. He's doing quite well. Enjoying himself actually." His eyes crinkled at the corners in a pleasing way.

I adjusted my light blue jacket. "I hope you're better at mowing the yard. The man skirted the corners just awful. And when it was time to rake the leaves, he left it all go. Looked just pathetic." I gripped the broom all the harder to stem the trembling in my hands.

Charlie laughed.

"There's nothing funny about a shoddy yard," I stubbornly held onto my crabbiness. It was my only defense. One I'd honed for a good many a year.

"Since when have you gotten so nit-picky?" His old gray eyes glinted in the sunlight.

The Witness Tree

"Since life became so damn fun." The words came out a bit more acerbic than I intended. I hadn't wanted to touch on those old wounds, but they settled in closer to the surface than I'd realized. Now it hung between us, heavy and uncomfortable.

He studied his loafers, rocking back and forth on his heels.

"You left me, Charlie." I couldn't stop the words from leaving my mouth and it was embarrassing. The walls of my heart crumbled as I pried open the door to our past.

"You wouldn't leave Peeksville." He his gaze met mine. "I begged, but you said no. Remember?"

"I trusted you and you left me just like everyone else." What caused me to say these things? The last thing I wanted was his pity or have such a private conversation in the middle of my front yard.

"Helen, I…" The once pleasant eyes were now glassy. Was he going to cry, for heaven's sake?

"We are not having this conversation. You left me here. Plain and simple. Please leave." I turned from him and from over my shoulder said, "I don't want you in my yard. Not on my street. Not in Peeksville."

"Helen, that's ancient history. Can't we move on? Please?"

"It's not ancient history to me. I waited but you were off making your name as a war hero. When you were done, Peeksville wasn't good enough for you. I wasn't…you left and never looked back."

"If you remember right, I pleaded with you. I even went to your mother about it, but you were adamant. You made your choice."

"You know so little about the choices I made." The bitterness in me rose up like a thundercloud chewing up the sky. I knew he'd gone to my mother and I didn't appreciate it one bit. Mama tried to convince me to follow my heart, to follow Charlie, but Luddie had already left for Tennessee to try his luck with his music. There was still the store, a sister to watch over, and the farm. I was needed

113

and good thing I didn't go, for even though Charlie continued to write letters, Annabelle soon left us and Ivy needed raising.

"We had such dreams, Helen. You can't blame me for the sense of responsibility you felt toward your family. I had already created a career in the service. I couldn't give that up. When your sister died, I asked you to come anyway, bring Ivy with you, but you said no."

"But I do blame you. My mother was sick by then. What kind of daughter would I have been to leave then? If you really loved me, you would have come back." The blame I hung on him was so deeply rooted, a gushing undercurrent to all the life that came after him. And all the life that didn't.

"Why didn't you continue to answer my letters?" he asked.

The wind chimes hanging from the corner of her house sang, *be strong, be strong.*

"It was pointless. Anyway, we're too old to relive this now." I started sweeping again thinking of the letters from him I burned. One after another. His letters were full of descriptions of brave adventures and exciting places. Would he have wanted to hear about the drudgery of working at the hardware store, slopping pigs and milking cows, watching my mother deteriorate, and having to look into the eyes of a child devastated by death?

"I thought you were my future and I yours." He kicked at the leaves with his foot. "In the end we simply wanted different lives. There's really no one to blame."

How could he be so blind? Did he really think the life I got was the life I wanted? As the bristles of my broom moved over the sidewalk they whispered, *'truth, truth, truth, truth.'*

"Different lives? Yes, Charlie. We wanted very different lives. It's all over and done now." I swallowed the prickly ball of hurt. "It was for the best."

"I'm sorry, Helen."

The Witness Tree

"Why did you come back here, Charlie? And why, for heaven's sake, did you have to buy a house on my street?" I stopped the broom and looked him in the eye.

"I assumed you were still out at the farm. My wife died," his face clouded, "and I've always longed for Peeksville since I retired. Beth and I moved our family around so much that no place else ever felt like home. Not like this. Besides, my son lives in Duluth and a daughter in Madison, and my youngest daughter in Minneapolis. This is perfect. Between all three. I count myself very lucky that they all settled in the Midwest."

"I can't see how this little village can compare to the streets of all those fancy places you lived." I felt so small in the face of his big life.

Charlie raised his bushy eyebrows and grinned, "You've kept up on me."

"Hard not to when your Aunt Elodie kept putting articles in the paper about your exploits. I'd have been embarrassed if I was you." Charlie's aunt wrote for the Peeksville newspaper and it was a stab to my heart every time Elodie mentioned him in her column.

"She was proud of me. With no children of her own, she doted on me. I miss her."

"She was a nice lady," I conceded, remembering the little white-haired lady, always a twinkle in her blue eyes.

"I came for her funeral. I looked for you, but you weren't there," he said.

"I had responsibilities. Business to run, child to raise." How could I tell him how hard it was to stay away knowing he'd be there? He and his wife and three children. Good God, I even knew the names of his children. Lisa, Charlie Jr. and Amy.

"Too bad. Would have been nice to catch up."

"You know, this isn't the same town it used to be," I said. "I hardly know a soul in the grocery store these days."

"Of course, it is. The people may have different names and faces, but Peeksville is still breathing life into its place on this Earth. Small towns are important. So many flock to the cities in search of all they have to offer, but the best childhoods are here in small towns. The best retirements too. I'm banking on that."

"Well, aren't you the philosopher." I suddenly felt very tired. "Go back to your life across the street, Charlie." How in the world was I going to go about my days with him nearby? I looked to the yellow house I'd come to love so much. Yes, this was a mistake.

"I came here hoping to find peace, Helen. I hope I haven't stolen yours." He had such a doleful look on his face.

A baseball rolled out of the leaves on the heels of my broom.

"Aha!" I stooped to pick it up. Holding it between my thumb and forefinger I shook it toward the house next door. "I knew I'd find that little brat's ball." I turned toward Charlie and thrust the ball at him. "Do you know how many times I get stuck picking up the toys that end up over here? I have told those kids hundreds of times to stay out of my yard. Do they listen? Not once! This ball hit my window yesterday. I knew it was still out here. The little snot tried sneaking into my yard to get it, but I saw him. He knew he better skedaddle."

I laid the broom on the sidewalk and went to the front door. I reached inside, grabbed a bucket and held it out for him to see. "Look at this."

Charlie peered over the side at my collection of baseballs, tennis balls, golf balls, small cars and trucks and one naked Barbie doll. "My, do all those belong to the neighbor children?"

"Yep," I said, gloating. "They never learn."

Charlie grinned at me, eyes twinkling. "Dear Helen, I promise to never leave anything in your yard, ever." He turned, shaking his head, and left.

All I could see was that young man walking away to take the

train to parts unknown, shattering my dreams of a future.

I wanted to scream, 'You have left something in my yard, Charlie Soderberg. You've left my heart lying amid this mess of leaves. And I will never find forgive you for it.'

CHAPTER 13

Esther

The funeral crowd faded from view and tears filled my eyes as they had so many times since the telegram came. Holding a handkerchief to my mouth to stem a sob, I closed my eyes tight and let the tears seep down my cheeks and onto my neck wetting the collar of my dress.

The weather was as cold and gray and as dismal as my heart. Pastor Bales was speaking to the grave diggers. The short service had ended, and the crowd dispersed slowly.

Sister Hattie stood at my side, tall, straight, and angry. At only twenty-three, she was as resolute and stoic as our mother. Hattie refused to accept any words of comfort offered. Her hard, brown eyes glared at the casket under a sweep of deep chestnut hair.

"First our older brother and now our youngest," I wiped my

face with a hanky. "How can this happen, Hattie? I just want to see his face one last time, count his freckles and wipe that mop of blond hair from his forehead."

"That's a fine sentiment," Hattie said, "but the undertaker said there wasn't enough of him left. We sent the government a healthy, eager young man and what they sent us back doesn't amount to squat."

"Don't say such a thing." I whispered as many of the mourners glanced their way.

"Two brothers gone," Hattie said, her voice rising, "all because of this damn war."

Brothers Eddie and Frankie looked to me to calm her down, but I didn't have it in me.

"I can't stand this," said Violet as she turned from the grave, tears streaming. The girl was shaking life a leaf and the ashen tone of her face made me worry she'd be sick.

"Vee," I grabbed for her arm, but she shook me off and ran through the crowd, her dark curls bouncing on her shoulders.

"I'll go after her," Eddie said and followed. Eddie, as tall and strapping as he was, had a heart as deep as the Redemption and then some.

"I worry how this will affect her," I said to Hattie. "They were so close."

The days of the seven Peroutka children laughing, splashing in the river, playing in the barn, seemed so long ago. I was desperately sad.

Ma glared at the coffin, a vengeful snarl upon her round, red face. She abruptly turned from the grave and stomped down the hill of the cemetery toward the luncheon hall, her silver bun and the black hat tottering from side to side. Ladies from the Homemakers Club followed offering comfort that was promptly refused with a swipe of her meaty arm.

119

Some of the black-clad mourners filed past the grave and followed to the luncheon.

Brother Frankie left the gravesite with his young wife and two children. Luddie was already at the luncheon with Harlon's mother. Helen was at Schoenfelds for the day. This was too sad for a little girl.

I couldn't bear the thought of attending the luncheon just yet. I needed some time to gather my emotions before playing the gracious host. At the town hall they would pass the plates of sandwiches and desserts and share stories of Teddy's silly exploits. They would laugh and slap shoulders. Then, they would remember the tragedy of Jacob that lay in the grave next to him. The people of Peeksville would come out in droves to make certain the Peroutka family was well looked after. Women would bring food, men would offer help with the farm. At least for a while.

Hattie continued to glare at the open grave and I noted a slight tremor in her chin.

"We have to be watchful of Ma, Hattie," I said. "She's always had to be so strong, but this might be too much."

"I know." Hattie took a breath and squared her shoulders. "I know." She glanced at me then followed the others.

I looked down at my feet, willing my knees to keep me upright. From the corner of my eye, I noticed Harlon standing just down the hill.

Our eyes met and held. He took a long drag from the cigarette dangling between his thumb and forefinger, then blew a plume of smoke into the air that curled about him in a ghostly veil. It was a battlefield on which we stood, and the ravages of war lay between us.

He licked his lips, flicked the cigarette, and came toward me.

"Come have some lunch," he said and uncharacteristically touched my arm as he passed. I nodded. Harlon had liked Teddy, said he made him laugh.

The gloomy sky overhead mirrored the darkness in my soul. An oppressive, gray mist unfurled across the cemetery as I stood there with nothing but a box holding my dear brother amid a sea of weathered stones. The smell of freshly moved earth mingled with the moisture in the dank air. Soon, men would come and lower Teddy in, cover him up and that would be that. Ma would never mention him again just as she would never talk about Jacob.

I broke off a lily from the spray on Teddy's coffin and lay it across Jacob's grave. I kissed my fingers and touched the cold stone.

Suddenly, I knew I was not alone.

"Essie?"

I turned.

"Ruby?" I blinked. It couldn't be, yet it was. My old friend stepped through the blanket of fog. Ruby was home from Seattle.

"Oh honey, I'm so sorry." Ruby rushed forward and grabbed me in an embrace so tight it chased the breath from my lungs. "Teddy was a good egg. He'll be missed."

"I know." I cried into the soft brunette curls as she held me.

After a few moments, I cleared my throat, brushed the tears from my face, and stepped back.

"What are you doin' here?" My eyes swept over Ruby, who still looked so young and pretty, although very different from the Ruby of our youth. This Ruby was a mother and a wife.

"Don't know if you've heard, but my mother had a slight stroke. She's doing better, but this was as soon as I could get here. We arrived this morning and I heard the news about Teddy. I would have come in time for the funeral if I had known." Ruby pulled her coat tighter around her to cover the sweater and modest dress she wore.

"You're here now and I'm so grateful." A strand of hair had

loosed from the twist at the back of my head. I tucked it behind my ear. "Tell your mother I'm thinkin' of her."

Ruby gestured to a concrete bench, "Let's have a seat."

We sat side by side as a biting breeze nipped our ankles.

"Funny, isn't it," I gazed toward the grave, "the sum of our lives amounts to our name and some dates on a rock."

"No," Ruby patted my knee, "no, it doesn't. The sum of our lives is kept for keeps in the hearts of those that love us."

"I know you're right. It's just that all the wonderful things about Teddy are in that box waitin' to be lowered into the ground. I can't hardly bare it." I wiped at my nose. "Losin' Jacob was hard enough."

"You know, I had such a crush on Jacob in school. He was dating Katie Doering at the time, so I kept my distance. Gosh, he was handsome."

"You never told me. How did I not see that?"

"The way he looked at Katie, I knew he'd never see me."

"She waited for him to come back. When he didn't, she left town. Went to live with an aunt in Iowa."

"I can't imagine her sadness." Ruby shook her head. "I met Harlon as I came up." Ruby glanced over her shoulder. "How are things?"

"Same as ever. Harlon will never change."

"Mom has heard some unflattering things about him. Moreso than normal."

"Whatever it is, it's keepin' him away from home and that's fine with me." I admired Ruby's new hair color. "Remember your Jean Harlow phase?" I sniffed and attempted a smile.

Ruby brought a hand up to her dark curls. "Jean's long gone. Can you believe I have four children now? Whatever happened to those girls we used to be?"

"Wish I knew." I raised my face to the wooly sky. "In my heart,

I'm still Amelia Earhart in that plane. Remember that? When I look in the mirror, well, I try not to look too long."

"Be careful, Amelia Earhart is either dead or living on a deserted island." Ruby nudged me and smiled. "I've enjoyed your letters. Sorry it takes me so long to answer. Seems I'm always being pulled between this child and that one." Ruby picked at a fingernail. "Look at these hands. They haven't seen nail polish in I don't know how long."

"Are you happy?" I was desperate to know someone somewhere was happy with life.

Ruby shrugged. "I am. I love being a mom and Eldon is on the fast track to working his way up at the bank. He's never home. Even so, we have a nice life."

"I'm glad for you." I twisted the white, damp handkerchief in my hands.

Ruby slipped an arm across my shoulders. "Come to Seattle, Essie. Just bundle up the children and come by me. You can stay with us. It'll be a new beginning. You and I could start that theater group we talked about so long ago."

"I have to say, I think about that every now and then."

Ruby took my work-worn hands into her own smooth ones. "You deserve better than Harlon Foley. Eldon and I have a spare bedroom you could use. Luddie and Helen can bunk with the children. I'm sure Eldon could get you a job at the bank. He'd be happy to help."

"Honestly, I can't leave Ma and the others after this. Not yet. Besides," I sniffed and wiped at my nose again, "Harlon says if I leave, he'll track us down and take the children. I can't chance that."

Ruby's brows knit together. "Honestly, you think he would bother? He doesn't give two shits about those beautiful children of yours. As far as your mother goes, she's a strong woman and you have brothers and sisters that will keep an eye on things."

"I don't know." Suddenly I felt the need to save some dignity. "It hasn't always been bad, you know. Havin' Helen melted his heart a tad and things were good for a while, but it didn't last."

"Oh, honey, I'm leaving on Wednesday. Think about coming with me. If not now, in the future. I'm only a train ticket away."

I thought how to answer. "I can handle it for now."

Ruby wrapped her arms around me. "When you're ready, you just say the word."

"Where is that girl I used to be, Ruby? Why did she go so far away?" I turned my gaze to the grave again and felt my heart harden. "Harlon should be in that box."

CHAPTER 14

Helen

I sat alone in the dining room with my chicken soup and liver sausage sandwich. I reached for the remote and clicked off the television, having seen enough of the foolishness and heartbreak there. So much of my world spun in turmoil, I didn't need to see more. I had been safe here in this little house. But now my home was violated. Violated by my past with Charlie and an investigation I wanted no part of.

I pushed aside my dinner. My appetite wasn't what it had been a week ago. All this fuss with the remains and then Charlie, was simply too much.

I placed my wrinkled hands on the table, a map of a hard life upon them. and pushed up from my chair. With leaden bones warning of a change in weather, I shuffled to the bedroom. There I opened the closet door, reached into the far corner of the top shelf where my hand found the wooden box amid old purses and clothes no longer worn. Carefully I pulled it down.

The Witness Tree

At one time, the box held my mother's jewelry, what little she had, until she removed the inner compartments to create another use. A hiding place. After she passed, I found it carefully covered in a corner of the attic. She had to know I'd find it one day and have a bucket full of questions she could no longer answer.

I ran my hand over the dark wooden top embossed with decorative gold swirls and tiny pink roses barely visible now. A brass latch hung off the front over an open lock. The key disappeared years ago but then I was able to jimmy it open with a butter knife, careful not to lock it again.

Gingerly, I held it to my chest with closed eyes as though embracing a most precious gift, and at the same time, holding tight to a cursed secret.

After a moment, I sat on the edge of the bed and lift the top. A copy of *How Green was my Valley* by Richard Llewellyn lay inside, a bit tattered and worn with age. Once, when asked, our mother named it as her favorite book of all time. Back then, I had no idea why, no idea what the book represented to her.

With a shaking finger I eased the book from its casket. Heavy in my hand, the book was weighted with secrets that had, at one time, shocked and saddened me. A sense of longing swept through me for the conversations this box would have spurred. Conversations I wished we'd had, Mama and I. My heart ached with it.

Amid the yellowed pages of the novel, our mother had tucked letters, aged and yellowed. I couldn't bring herself to read the letters again. Couldn't do it. Couldn't experience the tragedy of it all again. How I wished I didn't have them. Maybe it was time to take them into the yard and start a fire or give them to Ivy. In my heart, I knew their next home needed to be with Ivy, to read the truth of her family. The entire truth. Would she hate me when that day came?

I set the book aside and eased the piece of green felt loose that

126

covered the bottom exposing the browned, brittle newspaper article. *Elgin Couple Killed in Auto Accident* it said. There was no picture of the mangled vehicle, but a description of the horrific collision that left a young married couple, Samuel and Annabelle Burke, dead as they were on their way to a concert in the park. Their little girl in the back seat was spared any injury.

Refolding the article, I tucked it between the last page of the back cover of the book. I had wanted to protect Ivy from the details, but she was an adult now and this was part of her history. And if I've suddenly learned anything, I now knew that failing to talk about the past served no one.

Carefully, I returned the article and book to the box with its cache of secrets and closed the lid.

Weariness assailed my heart. I wished I'd never had to deal with the box and what it held. Perhaps, there was a lesson in it all. If so, I was damned if I could tell what it was. So much sadness in this family of mine. Some days it was nearly too much to bear. I didn't know why, but with all these reminders of growing up on the farm, of my mother and Luddie, of Annabelle, of my own losses and yes, that of Ivy. I needed, perhaps, to punish this broken spirit of mine by revisiting the box now and then. But not today. I should have left it in the closet.

I put the box back on its shelf. The house was so still and quiet except for the spirits of those long gone and the memories that prodded and poked at me.

As if I indeed had a need for punishment, I went to the attic.

The paneled wooden door opened with a groan and I stepped into the heavy, musty air. I reached for the string hanging from the light and illuminated the space with a ghostly glow. As a rule, I only went up to the attic twice a year—to take out the tiny ceramic Christmas tree lit from the inside with a bulb and to put it away at the end of the season. It was my only concession to a holiday and that was because it reminded me so of Mama's delight at Christmas time. She always displayed this very tree in the living room the months of December and January. It had been a gift long ago from Nelson's for her help at the store. Although back then it was lit from the inside by a candle. Ivy had been so fascinated by it, I feared the girl would knock it over and burn the whole place down which prompted me to update it to electric. While it was a safer alternative to the candle, it didn't carry the same glow.

With hands on my hips, I studied the smattering of boxes spread out before me filled with outgrown toys and clothes, dishes and books. Why I'd brought all of this from the farm was beyond me. I should have taken it all to the Hospital Auxiliary Thrift Shop, but I didn't. They didn't need to know my business, and now, because of my need for privacy, I will have to deal with all of this again one day. Or Ivy will, and probably curse me the whole time.

There was an antique radio that made me think of Luddie. He'd bought it for our mother before heading off to Tennessee. I couldn't very well get rid of that. In fact, I should move it downstairs. There was a dressing table that had been in Annabelle's room. I smiled as I remembered the hours Annabelle sat at that table drawing her pictures, writing her poems, primping for a party. Now it was piled with old curtains collecting dust. Against the lathe and plaster walls a few old prints leaned, one of them, a girl dancing among the daisies in watercolor, was done by Annabelle. I set it by the stairs. Ivy should have it. Had the girl helped with the move to town, she would have it by now, but her husband said they had other plans that week. I left it at that and hired movers. There were pieces of a rocking chair that Ivy found at a garage sale and planned to restore one day. How I ended up with it was a mystery. A simple headboard was against the northern wall, its veneer chipped and curled. This had been from my bed at the farm. I should have hauled it to the burn pile long before this. And over by the window, in the peak, stood an antique Victrola cabinet. Mama and Luddie spent hours sitting alongside the thing playing old records. Somehow, after our father was gone, Mama managed to buy it from the estate sale held at the Sommers farm up the hill from ours. I cherished that Victrola.

I ran my hands over the top. Lifting the heavy lid, the inside was now devoid of the mechanisms needed to play albums. All that remained was the blue felt lining the inside. I opened the bottom doors and found old albums, heavy and scratched. Jimmie Rodgers and Rudy Vallee, Stuart Hamblin and Clyde McCoy, Irving Kaufman and Will Osbourne with his Orchestra, and so many others.

I was reminded of the time, looking into the living room window of the farmhouse, I heard a mournful tune playing from the Victrola and my mother sat alongside, head in hands, bent at the waist, weeping. Too young to understand, I was panicked at the sight, but never intruded. It was a scene I remembered many times over the years.

At first, Mama didn't use the Victrola much, but in time, music filled the house on a regular basis again. And it was those times when she seemed the most joyous. It was as though she was able to shed all her worries and, although her countenance seemed wistful at times, she was happy as she went about her daily chores. Those were good times.

I wished I hadn't stuck it up here to be forgotten, but there simply wasn't room in my small house.

That's when I noticed the trunk. It sat squat along the wall, tucked under the eaves, all alone. The rounded top caked with dust, the leather straps cracked and dry. A relic that certainly could tell many a story if it could talk.

I pushed a few of the boxes against the wall creating a trail through to the trunk. I knelt before it, my knees as creaky as the

129

rusty hinges that squealed as I pushed open the top. Inside lay a clear plastic bag covering quilted pieces of fabric. I carefully removed the contents to find a quilt cover in shades of blue and white in a starburst pattern. I touched the delicate stitches and tiny seams. My mother had never been able to finish it before the cancer made her life a living hell. I wasn't much of a seamstress, but what was there would make for beautiful pillows. I set it aside to bring downstairs as well.

Stacks of embroidered items, table runners, pillowcases, dish cloths, and aprons lay folded underneath.

There were a few items of clothing. A blue-flowered dress, a pair of suspenders, a tablecloth. Random items. Then a few old photos in a brown bag, mostly sepia-toned portraits of people long gone. Some were black and whites of a rag-tag group of children, Mama's brothers and sisters, taken by the by the Redemption on a summer's day. Auntie Hat, her skinny body clad in dungarees and a blouse, Auntie Vee in a swimsuit, her dark hair curled about her shoulders, the shirtless boys in crude cut-offs. Mama must have been the photographer.

Then, a picture of my big brother and I crouched together under an apple tree heavy with blossoms. I found the guarded innocence in Luddie's eyes haunting. I quickly placed it back in the bag with the rest of the pictures.

Sunlight streamed in through the one window illuminating the dance of dust mites. In a corner of the trunk, sat a Mason jar with a metal top. It was empty but for one object at the bottom.

I held the jar up to the light. I was certain this was the jar our mother used to save her egg money so many years ago. As a girl, I questioned our mother about the money in the jar when I'd been snooping in her bedroom. With a glint in her eye, she said it was her egg money She was saving for us to have an adventure.

"What adventure?" I had asked. She said we just might go see the Pacific Ocean someday. Of course, we didn't.

Now the jar was once again in my hand and holding it up to the light from the window, something glinted at the bottom.

It was a woman's ring, thin gold band with a pearl in the middle. I unscrewed the cap and the ring easily slid into my palm.

I'd never seen Mama wear it. I slipped it on my ring finger, but my arthritic knuckles wouldn't allow it. Then a thought struck me.

Could this be Clarice's ring? It certainly fit the description. How in the world would it have ended up in Mama's jar? It didn't make sense. Clarice said Harlon stole it, but did he give it to our mother? Did Mama know the rightful owner?

CHAPTER 15

Esther

I turned the ordinary letter over in my hands. It had been mixed in with our mail. The postmark read Fall Creek, Wisconsin. No return address. It was a letter for Pastor Robert Sommers.

Pastor Sommers? Our new neighbor was a minister? That took some pondering, but of course, I could see it. He never struck me as a man that was much for physical labor. His owning a farm didn't quite fit him. But he'd said he was a teacher. If, in fact, he was a man of the pulpit, why would he not openly share that?

I rolled the question over in my mind. This new information, if true, caused a bit of a conundrum. A church was not a place I frequented, nor did I feel the need. Yet, somehow, he was affiliated with a church. Would my lack of religion bother him? Would he think less of me?

I shouldn't a been having such thoughts.

At any length, the letter needed to be properly directed. I could put it back in our mailbox with a note to Don Schmeedle, the mailman, or...

I was not sure if I should curse Mr. Schmeedle, or thank him. The neighborly thing to do would be to take it upon myself to make sure Mister, or Pastor Sommers received his mail. I smiled and slapped it against my palm a few times as I contemplated my next move.

Petey waited up the drive. The old dog never made it all the way to the mailbox with me anymore. He watched me with doleful eyes as the breeze blew his shaggy red fur.

"Petey, go home." I shooed the dog. Petey dipped his head and limped away.

I stuffed the rest of the mail back into the box for now and walked up the hill toward Robert's farm. A slight breeze floated in, causing the yarrow to dance and the leaves of the maple to lightly applaud my good fortune. My heart rate skipped a notch as I approached the curved, gravel drive that led to the white farmhouse with the windowed porch on the south side. A lilac bush, flowers long spent, graced the eastern corner.

The house appeared neat and tidy, much like I imagined its owner. A weathered barn flanked the south side of the yard with an empty garage off to the west. It appeared Pastor Sommers was not at home.

I was disappointed at that. It was tempting to take the letter home and return later on when he returned. But that would be silly. Still, I thirsted for adult conversation. Robert Sommers intrigued me, and after all, returning his letter was the right thing to do.

Yes, it was.

Feeling quite brave and somewhat adventurous, I peeked in through the windows. The porch was a pleasant enough place to spend a rainy afternoon. A sofa strewn with newspapers and a multicolored afghan adorned one side while a table and two chairs filled the other. On the table a tray held small pots with sprouting seedlings. What was he trying to grow at this time of the year? The growing season was nearing it's end.

My curiosity got the best of me and I rounded the southeast corner of the house and went to the large picture window. Carefully, I peered in at a comfortable living room. Overstuffed chairs and a burgundy sofa, a bureau with a radio atop against one wall and books. Books were stacked everywhere—on an end table, at a corner of the sofa, under a chair, and in shelves stretching along one whole wall. Why, the man had a library all to himself. How exciting! I imagined books of wonderfully interesting people and far-off places. All to himself!

I pressed my face closer to the glass and tried to read some of the titles. How I missed afternoons lost in a good book before I married, hiding away from Ma. Now if I found the time to read a book, I'd have to hide from Harlon or be accused of laziness.

Something cold touched my leg and I let loose with a mighty shriek. Pastor Sommers' dog Winifred looked up at me, tongue dripping, dark eyes wide with excitement.

"Bess?" Robert Sommers came around the corner of the house clad in denim shirt and brown slacks.

"Oh,my." Embarrassed at my nosiness, I dropped the letter and quickly bent to pick it up. The dog sniffed my legs.

"Winifred, mind your manners." Robert waved the dog away who willingly obeyed her master. "I was washing my old jalopy by the spigot out back. I was just going to the garage for a sponge when I saw you go around the corner. You just missed Principal MacDonald. Seems his history teacher will be out on medical leave later this year. I'll be gladly filling in." He smiled.

"I…I…well, you caught me." A blush crept up my neck. "I was admiring your books. I love to read but haven't in quite some time.

You've got quite a collection there."

"I'm an avid reader, as you can tell." He rubbed his palms together. "It engages my brain and makes the time go quickly."

"The last book I read was *Gone with the Wind* by Margaret Mitchell. My sister Vee lent me her copy. I so wanted to see the movie, but…" I turned my palms to the sky and shrugged.

"Oh, that was a wonderful book. We'll have to find a book for you to borrow. In fact, we'll find more than one." Then his gaze held mine and for a moment we were silent. "You know, you're looking lovely today. That shade of pink is very becoming on you. And you've got your hair up."

"Oh, ah, thank you." I touched a hand to the twist at the back of my head. Since he'd complimented me at the river, I was wearing it that way more often.

"What have you got there?"

I'd completely forgotten the letter. "Oh, yes." I waved the letter between us.

"We received a piece of your mail today. I thought I'd bring it over."

He took the envelope from me as his brows knit together. The muscles of his jaw tightened, and his mouth was a thin, pulled line. His chest expanded with a deep breath as he considered the letter.

"I didn't realize you were a preacher."

His head snapped up. "I'm not a preacher. Not anymore. That life is over. I wish these letters would stop." He held the envelope as though uncertain what to do with it. Then he simply folded it in half and stuffed it into his shirt pocket.

"I'm sorry. Maybe I shouldn't have…"

"An old parishioner of mine won't let it drop. She will in time." He smiled, yet his eyes held a far-off detachment.

"I should be going."

"I hope it wasn't a bother bringing it up here."

"None at all." I was lost in the warmth of those brown eyes of his.

"Bess?" His hand lightly touched my upper arm.

"Yes?"

His hand fell away from my arm and his eyes settled on the perfect outline of fingers in purple and yellow that stained my skin.

I covered the bruise with a hand. "I ran smack into the door of the truck a few days ago. I'm such a klutz." How embarrassing.

"Looks painful," he said, concern etched in the lines of his face. He wasn't buying my story.

"It's not. In fact, I had forgotten it was there." I didn't like the pity in his eyes one bit.

An awkward silence fell between us. I knew I should leave, but I didn't want to and I didn't think he wanted me to.

"Do you like music?" he asked.

What? Had I heard that right?

"Music. Do you like it?" A corner of his mouth lifted, and his eyes shone bright.

"Yes, I do," I said. "Very much."

"I'm yearning for a cool lemonade and a good tune or two. Care to join me? Old Winifred doesn't appreciate my music, do you girl?" He nuzzled the top of the dog's head.

The children were gone with Harlon to Ashland to buy a part for the pickup and wouldn't be back for at least a couple hours. If I was careful, I wouldn't be caught. And how I wanted to hear his music!

"That would be lovely." A sensation of recklessness bubbled within me.

His kitchen was a wash of yellow cabinets, yellow curtains on the window over the sink, and yellow and green linoleum. He reached into the icebox and brought out a glass pitcher, filled two glasses and handed me one. The cool felt good against my hand.

I took a sip. "That's nice."

With a pump of his head, I followed him to the parlor.

"You have to pardon my mess." He moved a stack of books and newspapers from the sofa and gestured for me to have a seat.

"This isn't a mess at all. To me, it's wonderful. When I think of all the hours of entertainment you have here."

"Just a moment," and with enthusiasm he went through a stack of books on the credenza. "Here it is. I bet you'd enjoy this one."

I set the glass on the end table and took the book from his hands. It was a copy of *How Green was my Valley*. I savored the feel of the smooth cover in my hands and the smell of paper and ink.

"Have you read it?" he asked.

"No, I haven't." I turned the book over in my hands. "I heard good things about it in a letter from my friend Ruby."

"I saw a bit of myself in the young man that tells the story. Would you like to borrow it?" His eyes were wide with invitation as he waited for an answer.

"Yes, I would." I held the book close to my bosom as though he had just given me a treasured gift. And honestly, he had.

A photograph on the sideboard caught my eye. It was a young woman kneeling on the grass, a towhead little girl on her lap. Robert followed the direction of my gaze.

"That's my wife and daughter." Robert's face paled as he went to the sideboard and took the picture into his hands.

"You're married?" I hoped I hadn't sounded as stunned as I was. Mr. Nelson had asked Robert that very question, and the answer had been 'no.'

"I was. They were killed in an auto accident." His voice took on a stony edge, the soft planes of his face tightened.

"I'm so sorry." Tears gathered at the corners of my eyes. His wife had been a beauty and the girl so full of innocence and happiness in the picture.

"It was a long time ago. Polly, my wife, was driving to visit a parishioner. Little Emily was with her in the front seat." He swallowed hard. "Polly didn't want to go, but I pleaded with her. Mrs. Warburton was a thorn in my side. She had gone to the trustees to whip them into a frenzy that I was spending inappropriately. But she was ailing and needed a visit. The Women's Circle quilted a lap-blanket for her and asked me to deliver it. I suspect none of them wanted to visit with her either." He chuckled, but his eyes remained sad. "It was my responsibility to visit the sick, not Polly's. I had been invited to fly fish with Axel McCutcheon and couldn't see spending time with Mrs. Warburton. So, I asked Polly. I reasoned that Emily would brighten the old woman's day. It should have been me in that car." His voice dropped to a whisper. "It should have been me under that train."

"How terrible for you." I set aside the glass of lemonade and the book and went to him, laying a hand on his arm.

His hands shook as he clumsily set the picture back on the sideboard.

With a faint smile he said, "Emily would be eleven this year. Your daughter reminds me of her. I don't know if it is something in her eyes or the color of her braids."

I had an overwhelming desire to embrace my children good and hard when I got home.

"That is why I am here. I sunk to the lowest depths a soul can go for several years, but I am trying to make a new beginning. Unfortunately, I'm not much of a farmer, but I need to fill my life with a challenge. Something productive. I must say I am looking forward to the start of school. This old farm needs a break from me now and again." He rubbed his hands together. "Don't feel sorry for me, Bess. That's a part of my life I've had to set aside. I've had years to practice how to put the pain away and continue breathing.

138

It's time to live again."

He strode to the corner of the room where a Victrola waited in a slender cabinet.

"I promised you music and music you shall have." His smile was genuine now.

Robert pulled the record album from its cover and placed it on the hard disk. The sound was scratchy at first but the strains of *I'll Be Seeing You* filled the room. I sipped my lemonade, holding the book again, and began to sway to the rhythm while Robert took a seat in a large Queen Ann chair.

"I loved to dance when I was younger. My friend, Ruby, and I would go to Greenfield Dancehall on Saturday nights. I had forgotten how I missed that."

"When is the last time you danced?" He sat straighter in his chair, hands on knees.

"Oh goodness, it's been forever. I don't know." I chuckled. "Yes, I do. The last time was when my Uncle Alfred pulled me onto the dance floor at cousin Bertha's wedding in '42. It was a disaster. Uncle Alfred's a mess on the dancefloor. As his partner one needs to protect her feet at all times, and I suspect he's put many a back out from his treacherous twirls."

We laughed at that.

"Come on, Bess, we're dancing." Robert stood and held out a hand to me. "Neither of us has danced in far too long."

"I suppose one wouldn't hurt, now would it?" I set the book and the lemonade on the table next to the sofa.

"Wonderful." He took my hand in his. I felt the smoothness of his palm against my own. His fingers gently entwined with mine. He touched my waist with his other hand. I put my hand on his shoulder, touching the fabric of his shirt, feeling the warmth of his skin just beneath the cotton weave.

He smiled down at me as his body began to sway to the music,

139

ever so slightly at first.

A trickle of perspiration moved down my back. I felt his every muscle as he moved. He smelled of leather and fresh air and the soap he'd been using on his car. This wasn't at all proper, but I didn't care. My body, my soul, was thirsty for the gentle touch between a man and a woman.

His hands remained as tender as a new leaf. How could he know the touch of a man in this way was as foreign to me as the far-off places I dreamed of visiting?

Closing my eyes, I let the music fill me, lift me away like sparrows rising into the bluest summer sky. A sigh slipped from my lips. I hoped he hadn't heard. Looking up, his eyes were closed.

Being so close, I studied the planes of his face, the thin lips, prominent cheek bones, the brown lashes resting on his skin. Then, he opened his eyes and caught me looking at him.

I smiled and looked away.

Much too soon, the song ended, although the glow it produced did not. Reluctantly, I stepped back.

Robert released my hand and went to the Victrola. As if he'd read my thoughts, he asked, "More?"

Sentimental Journey began playing, and Robert claimed my hand once again. We were so close I could see the tiny hairs on his neck. The rise and fall of his chest made me want to push my chest against his, feel his body working to breathe. Match my breath to his. And have the world fade away.

Soon, he bent his head and placed his cheek against mine. Then, with a start said, "I'm sorry."

We were two adults, one of which was married, alone in his home, and sharing a slow, soul-lulling dance in the middle of the afternoon. It wasn't proper and if anyone found out, we'd be the talk of Peeksville.

140

Not to mention having to deal with the reaction of Harlon. "It's fine."

One song blended into the next and by the end of the fifth, Robert's body was full against mine. I allowed my face to touch his shoulder. His clean, masculine scent filled me until I was dizzy.

Suddenly, a bark from Winifred outside the house jolted us to our senses, interrupting the reverie.

I quickly stepped away and smoothed my wrinkled dress. Robert went to the window. "Winnie's got a chipmunk up a tree."

"I need to go. Har . . ." I meant to say Harlon and the children would be home soon, but I couldn't bring myself to ruin this moment by saying his name.

"You didn't finish your lemonade." Robert hesitated. "I understand."

"It was wonderful, really. I have to get going." I moved toward the door.

"Wait." Robert quickly bent for the book and handed it to me, his hand lingering a moment on mine. "Don't forget your book, and take your time reading it. As you can see, I have plenty to keep me occupied."

"Thank you, Robert." Our gaze held. We were different now.

I left him standing at the door of the porch. Winifred followed me down the drive.

"Go on, girl, go back."

From the house I heard Robert call the dog. I turned and waved. He waved back. Once I was safely out of sight, I stopped, amazed at what transpired from the simple act of returning a letter.

The rest of the day I was a bumbling idiot. Harlon and the children returned shortly after. *How Green was my Valley* lay safely hidden amid the linens in the closet.

Harlon left later in the afternoon and failed to show for dinner, which was just as well. The beef was over salted as was the corn.

What was wrong with me? I couldn't concentrate. The children laughed when I completely missed Luddie's glass with the milk.

With the meal finished, the children went to the barn for their evening chores while I stood at the window over the sink, reliving the feel of Robert's arms around me, his whispered breath upon my neck, and the sweet sounds of his Victrola.

That evening I read the book he'd given me until my eyes would no longer open. Then, carefully, I tucked the book under the bed.

It was nearly two o'clock in the morning when I woke. The bed beside me was empty. Harlon was on another bender.

I checked on the children. They were sound asleep. Angels in slumber. I touched each of their heads and kissed their foreheads. I went to a silver-glazed window. The moon was full and bright and spilled milky upon the barnyard.

Suddenly headlights swung into the drive as Harlon's pickup came to a stop by the barn.

He stumbled from the truck slamming the door and nearly toppled over as he came toward the house. I left the children's room, shut the door, and stole back into bed as I heard him enter the kitchen.

I pulled the sheet up to my neck and held it there hoping he would fall asleep in the parlor chair as he sometimes did. Soon I heard the clop, clop, clop of his boots on the stairs. He came into the room, bumped the wooden chair against the wall and cursed.

The room immediately smelled of beer and cigarettes. I wanted to gag with it. Despite the stench, I took in a breath and let it out slowly to steady my nerves. I knew I wouldn't sleep this night.

Harlon laid upon the mattress and spooned against me, reaching around to pull at my nightgown.

"No, Harlon, you're drunk." I pushed his arm off.

"Come on, Esther." He nipped at my ear with his teeth.

I tried to stem the churn of my stomach and pushed my shoulder into his bulk.

"I said no."

"Don't tell me no. It's been too long." He roughly grabbed my breast and held it. I pulled at his arm without success. He was trying to force his other hand between my body and the mattress.

"You'll wake the children. I'm not feeling well."

"You don't feel sick to me." He chuckled, hooked his leg over mine and turned me over.

I grabbed the edge of the mattress and attempted to pull away. He put his hands inside the opening of my nightgown and pulled. The material gave way, buttons flew.

"Stop it," I said. He placed his hands around my neck and squeezed as he lowered his face to hover above mine.

"Show your husband how you missed him, Esther."

I opened my mouth, but no sound came. He pushed me harder against the bed and my lungs stung from lack of air. He forced his knee between my legs.

A voice sounded beyond him. It was Helen.

"Mommy, I'm sick."

Harlon ground out a curse, let go of my neck and rolled off. I bolted from the bed gasping for air. I pulled the torn nightgown around me and quickly ushered Helen from the room and down the stairs.

"Do you feel warm, honey?" I placed a hand on my daughter's forehead. "How about a drink of water?"

Helen looked up at me and said, "No Mama, I feel better now."

CHAPTER 16

Helen

I stood in line at the post office waiting my turn for a book of stamps, putting a good distance between myself and the tall, black-haired woman in front of me trying to decide what design of stamps she like best. For crying out loud, they all share the same purpose. I had to button my lip not to say something.

This was one of my favorite buildings in Peeksville. The three-story brick structure with marble floors was built in the thirties and a talented painter adorned the walls with a mural of a log drive, the loggers navigating the slippery logs as they made their way down the Redemption toward the mill in Park Falls. It was a beautiful depiction in muted colors that I appreciated for the heritage of our small town.

The woman in front of me finally chose the flowery stamps and as she turned to leave, said, "Why, Miss Foley. Hello."

I gave her a blank stare.

"It's me, Justine. Ivy's friend." She had a pleasant smile, her hair now a short pixie from the long, sleek mop she'd had when younger. I remembered the times Ivy brought Justine to the farm. The two girls were fast friends, yet when they entered high school, they took part in their share of shenanigans of which I didn't approve. Being called to the principal's office was humiliating enough but having to pick them up from the police station in their junior year for drinking was the last straw. I did my best to keep them apart after that, but in their senior year Ivy met Brad and then Justine was the least of my worries.

"Good to see you again." I turned away, stepped up to the counter and Justine left.

As soon as I had my own book of stamps, with no care for the pretty design, I exited to find Justine waiting for me.

"Miss Foley, do you have a moment?"

I sighed heavily, letting her know this was an interruption. I still had to make it to the pharmacy before they close. "I suppose you want to know about the bones as well."

"No. I read the article in the newspaper and there's nothing more I need to know. That's your business."

How refreshing. "Then what can I do for you?"

"I'd like to talk to you about Ivy. She told me about your last conversation." Justine gestured toward a concrete bench under a white birch. "Let's sit."

I could only imagine this wasn't good. Was she going to chastise me for my accusing Ivy of having an affair of her own? I hadn't heard from Ivy since our nasty conversation regarding the state of her marriage.

Justine and I sat side by side. A pleasing breeze caused the leaves to twitter.

"I'm worried about Ivy," Justine said. "I have begged her to leave Brad for so long. Once she was face to face with his affairs, I thought that would be the end of it. He's mentally abusive, Helen. I've seen the effect of it, his put downs, name calling, telling her she's not worth the dirt on his shoes. She pretends it doesn't hurt, but of course it does. And he does it in front of the kids. We've been talking a lot lately and she's starting to realize she deserves better, but she needs support."

"Our last phone call wasn't pleasant."

"I've asked her to call you, Helen, but she won't. And she'll probably be upset with me for letting you know all of this. I've offered her a place to stay, but I live in a one-bedroom apartment. She has no money because Brad spent it as fast as she can earn it. He's drinking on top of it all and Ivy is so unhappy. The kids are seeing all of this and they shouldn't have to live this way."

I closed my eyes to steady my nerves. This story was all too familiar. "I said things I shouldn't have." I cleared my throat. "I saw things in him when the two of them started up with each other, but she was so besotted with him. I gave up. I'm not very good with...feelings and such. She and I, we butt heads like a couple of ornery goats."

"I wish I would have said something to her about him back then, but I didn't. Maybe she would have listened to me."

"She was so headstrong back then. When she got pregnant, I felt as though I had let it go too far. I told her they didn't have to get married but marrying him seemed a better solution to her than living with me. History simply repeated itself in a way."

Justine angled her head. "How's that?"

"Oh, nothing." I couldn't help but see the parallels between my mother's and Ivy's similar situation. It was maddening. And frightening. Guilt flooded through me. "I suppose I shouldn't have allowed her and I to grow apart the way we have. Marriage with Brad...I was angry with her for the choices she made." I put a hand on my forehead feeling the pulse of blood pounding through my brain. The whole situation made my stomach tight.

Didn't I have enough at the moment? Fate was not being kind in the least. In fact, fate could kiss my flabby ass.

"Well," Justine held up her palms, "I'm afraid for her. I think things are worse than she's letting on."

"I don't know what I can do. She's made her bed and now..." Why did those words spill from my mouth? I don't think I meant to say them aloud, but they did.

"And now, Helen, I'm really sorry I bothered you." Justine stormed away leaving me with my new book of stamps and a knot in my heart that grew with each breath.

Esther

I took a seat on the back porch in the black of night. The children were tucked in their beds and because Harlon hadn't come home again, we'd had a pleasant supper. Afterward, we listened to the Abbot and Costello show and later, Gene Autry's Melody Ranch. Luddie sang along to *Back in the Saddle Again* while Helen and I joined hands and danced in circles. How I lived for evenings like these.

A cool breeze came through the trees and with it the sweet scent of evergreen and wood. I kicked off my shoes and relaxed into the rocking chair I kept out there. A cowbell clanged from somewhere in the pasture. A bull frog called from the ditch along the road and an occasional firefly danced against the black of the night.

It wouldn't be long now, and I would have enough in my freedom fund. Trying to help, Hattie and Vee had lately sold some of the hats and mittens I'd knitted, and the jar was filling up. I could hardly wait and refused to think of the trouble I may have with Harlon. Instead, I preferred to think he'd be happy to be free, despite all his warnings of the past.

The Witness Tree

Mr. Nelson said the job was still mine if I wanted it. I had my eye on an apartment above the barber shop and dreamed of the patterns of curtains and tablecloths I'd sew for our new home. Finally, both children would have their own bedrooms. I'd find pretty wallpaper for Helen's room and maybe afford to buy Luddie a guitar at some point. I wouldn't have a car, but living in town, I wouldn't need one. And if Peeksville didn't work out, and Harlon gave me too much trouble, there was always Ruby's offer of a life in Seattle.

Lights came up the drive and swung against the house interrupting my thoughts. It was a police car that parked close to the hosue.

Sheriff Bergey stepped out.

"Sheriff." I met him at the corner of the porch, arms crossed over my chest, waiting for the bad news he was sure to bring. "What can I do for you?"

"Mrs. Foley, wish I was here with better news." He pushed his glasses up his nose and put his hands on his hips. Short and stocky, with a pudgy middle, he stood with legs wide, appearing to weigh his words before beginning.

I braced. Maybe Harlon was dead. A feeling of hope skittered up my spine.

"Thought you'd be wondering the whereabouts of your husband. Appears he drank his supper tonight." Sheriff Bergey scratched his jaw.

"That's nothin' new."

"This ain't pleasant, but you need to know what's goin' on. I hauled him into the joint about an hour ago." Sheriff Bergey spit a stream of chew and wiped the corner of his mouth with his hand.

"What'd he do this time?"

"He, ah, well, we got a woman sayin' he raped her in a ditch over by Patterson Road tonight." The Sheriff gave a jerk of his

148

head toward the north.

I bit my lower lip and nodded. "Who is she?"

"A gal by the name of Martha Pukall, a barmaid at Whitey's and a few other taverns."

I thought a moment, and then replied, "I know the family. Martha's quite young, isn't she?"

"Seventeen or eighteen. I guess old Harlon's been chasing after her for quite some time. She said he won't leave her alone."

"Hmph." I rubbed my forehead. If only Harlon would find someone else and leave. I should be so lucky.

"You ain't defendin' your husband?" Sheriff Bergey looked at me over his glasses.

"Should I?" I had no energy or inclination to defend him.

"Well, if it's worth anything Mrs. Foley, I know you ain't had it easy with him. Harlon says Martha led him on from the beginnin'. From what I saw, somethin' definitely happened between 'em. She was in quite a state and he was awful drunk. Whether she was askin' for it or not, I can't say. I agreed to keep him overnight to cool off. You can expect him in the mornin'."

"*If* she was asking for it? I doubt a woman would ask to be raped."

"She's a bit wild and workin' in a tavern is gonna expose her to that kinda behavior. Anyway, that's where we're at."

"I appreciate that, I mean, I appreciate your telling me. This way I won't stay up half the night worrying." Did he catch my sarcasm?

The sheriff nodded.

"Is she all right? Martha?" I was not Harlon's only victim. In a way, that brought a measure of comfort that someone else understood, but it also brought a bucket of anger. Was there anyone out there that could stop him?

"I think so. Her daddy took her home." He looked down for a

moment as though he were weighing his next comment. "You know, Martha's got some brothers. They're pretty hot about this. I tried calmin' them down, but if I was you, I'd be on the lookout. Rafe, the oldest, vows he's gonna make Harlon pay. I think he's just blowin' hot air but be careful for a few days till he cools off."

"Thank you for the warnin.'"

"That husband of yours just isn't the same when he's drinkin'. He's always been a bit rough around the edges, but when he's hittin' the hootch, well, I'm sure you've got your hands full."

"Yes, Harlon's a...a hand full."

The sheriff turned to leave, then stopped. "I almost forgot." He dug in his pocket and pulled out a ring. A pearl set in a gold band.

"Martha gave this to me. Harlon tried to give it to her as a present. She told him she didn't want it. Said he got awful mad at that. It was the beginnin' of their altercation tonight. After that, one thing led to another." He held the ring out to her. The light of the moon illuminated the gold band and created a milky sheen to the pearl.

I took it in the palm of my hand. My husband gave this gift, one he couldn't afford, to a girl he tried to seduce when there was never a mention of a wedding ring for me. A bitter taste filled my mouth and the cool of the evening filled my bones with a cold that turned my heart to stone.

"I don't want it either." I held it out to him.

Sheriff Bergey held up his hands. "Might be worth somethin'. Maybe you could sell it."

I thought of my freedom fund. He had a point. I slipped the ring into the pocket of my dress. Later on, I'd put it in the jar in the attic.

"'Night, Mrs. Foley. You take care now."

I nodded in response and as I returned to the house, looked up to see Luddie in the window above me. His face pressed to the glass. I spent the rest of the night trying to sleep, a shotgun tucked under the bed.

CHAPTER 17

Helen

If I had been prone to physical abuse, the tiller in front of me would be a pile of parts by now. It was arguing with me over breaking ground for a small bed of spring bulbs along the walk to my front door. I envisioned a pretty flounce of yellow and white bloom along the walk, maybe a few tulips as well. Wasn't sure what I'd do once they stopped blooming in the spring, but I'd cross that issue next summer.

But at present, I was determined to win the war of the tiller, but the thick mat of grass simply would not budge. The blasted piece of metal became bulkier to handle every year. And damn how I hated to admit that.

It was more than the tiller today, I knew. It was the visit from the deputy and the talk with Justine. And the letters. I hadn't read them in many years and for some reason, they seemed to be calling to me again. Even though, I knew the confused emotions they would fuel in my heart.

"Let me give you a hand."

I snapped to attention. Charlie Soderberg stood at the end of my walk. While it would be a relief to have help, the last thing I needed was a man. This man.

"Go back to whatever you were doing. I can handle this." I shooed at him. But he didn't leave. Instead, he stood next to me and nearly pushed me out of the way as he gripped the rubber-clad handles.

"Excuse me, but from what I see, the tiller is handling you," he said. He was wearing a Green Bay Packer jersey and blue jeans. Was he trying to look like a teenager?

I tried to barge in front of him, but he wouldn't move. "I didn't ask for help." I pushed my shoulder into him with no luck.

"Nonsense. I'm here. Now, what are you trying to accomplish?" He firmly stood his ground. The few straggly white hairs on the top of his head lifted in the breeze.

"Oh, you are a stubborn cuss. I want a bed of daffodils along the walk for the spring."

"I'm stubborn? That's fresh. Now, how long and how wide?" His face wore a determined set. "I can be just as stubborn as you, Helen."

I gave him my best glare. It was tough to concede I did, indeed, need the help. But I was angry and hard work was the fix. He broke my stride. Worse yet, he made me feel weak.

"Come on," Charlie waved a hand toward the grass, "show me."

I put a hand alongside his on the handle and nudged him one more time.

"I said go. The last thing I need is help from you. You've done quite enough," I said.

Charlie refused to let go. "Helen, I've watched you struggle with this thing for nearly ten minutes. I knew you'd be angry, but what kind of neighbor would I be if I simply let you fight with this machine on your own?"

"You wouldn't be any different than the other ninnies on this street. You don't see them rushing to help me. Besides, you shouldn't be a neighbor of mine in the first place." I could feel the blood pumping through my heart at a dangerous clip. It would serve him right to be the cause of my having the big one right there in the front yard.

"My God, Helen. Can't we move on?"

Why did Charlie feel the need to torment me this way? My life was coming apart at the seams no matter which way I looked. Fighting with the tiller gave me an outlet to vent. Now he'd spoiled that as well. How much more was I going to have to endure?

"I'll ask again. How big do you want it?" We were nearly nose-to-nose. "I'm not leaving."

I huffed and relinquished my hold. "Five feet long and the width of the tiller."

"That wasn't so hard now was it?" Charlie chuckled. It only took a moment before the tiller scooped up the grass and churned it back into the soil. It was embarrassing to stand here and watch while someone else did my work.

"Well, that didn't take long at all," he said when he finished. "Now if you'll direct me where to put this thing, I will put it away."

"I can do that."

"Again, where can I put this for you?"

"Oh, you old goat! Follow me."

I took him around the back of the house to the little red gardening shed in the corner of my yard. He parked the tiller inside and closed the double doors.

"Is that a Mock Orange bush?" He pointed to the nearly fifteen-foot bush in the corner of the yard that gifted me with thousands of white blooms in mid-summer with a heavenly scent.

"Yes, it is, and you can't have it." I turned and began walking toward the back door.

At that Charlie broke into laughter. "I don't make a habit of stealing shrubbery."

The Mock Orange tittered in the breeze like a child's giggle.

I turned back, realizing how ridiculous my accusation, and smiled. In the short space of time that I watched him work the tiller, my heart melted a tad. Just a tad.

"Helen, you crack me up." He had the nicest twinkle in his eyes. "I want you to come with me. Come to my house."

"I'm not going anywhere with you." The smile slid from my face. Damn, now I'd opened a can of worms simply by letting him help. Would I ever learn?

"I need your advice on a Spirea bush on the west side of my house. It looks mighty sickly. I'd like to save it if I could, but I don't know what to do. Would you look at it?"

I hesitated. Having him in my yard was one thing. Following him to his was quite another. But, I couldn't deny, I was curious. Besides, I'd noticed the sorry shrub before he'd moved in.

"Fine, but I don't have a lot of time." I kept the tone of my voice even.

"Have a busy schedule, do you?" The corners of his mouth lifted in that enticing way I remembered from so long ago.

"Don't mess with me, Charlie." The sound of his name felt good on my lips. He chuckled again.

I followed him across the street and into his yard. I had always admired the Craftsman style home of Charlie's with its broad front porch, triangular roof lines and half-paned windows.

Charlie went straight to the corner of the house where the spindly bush struggled.

"Here it is. A sorry specimen, don't you think?"

155

"Hmph." I studied the poor thing. "It doesn't look like anything is eating it." I knelt on the grass. "The base seems healthy enough. I would cut it back to about six inches high. It'll come back in the spring. I suspect it simply needs to rejuvenate." It was then I realized I was going to need help to regain my footing. Damn knees. I attempted to push up when Charlie stuck a hand in front of my face.

"I'm fine." Although my old joints screamed otherwise.

"You keep saying that, but a little help now and then does a body good." He pushed his hand closer.

I reluctantly placed my hand in his. All those years ago, placing my hand in his was as easy as breathing. Hands that were once smooth and strong were now gnarly and dotted with age spots. Even so, he had a good, strong grip as he pulled me to my feet.

I reclaimed my hand with a jerk.

"How about sitting on the porch and having a cup of coffee with me," he asked.

"Oh no." I blurted a bit too forcefully. "That's not going to happen." I started across the lawn.

"Helen, I could really use the company right now. Today is the third anniversary of Beth's death. I would appreciate it if you could stay." His eyes pleaded with me and the joviality in his face disappeared. "I'm feeling a bit lonely today."

"You expect me to comfort you on the death of your wife?" The nerve! His insensitivity was mind-boggling.

"I don't need comforting. I just need a friend. I'm sorry for the past, but we're not those young sweethearts anymore, Helen. If we can put the hurt aside, we have a strong basis for friendship. I'd like you to be my friend."

"I don't have friends." I hated those words as they left my mouth before I could stop them. They sounded so hard and pathetic.

"You would do me a big favor if you could spare a little of your time." His eyes teared just a bit. "More than you know."

"Oh, I suppose." Only a complete shrew would refuse.

"Wonderful. I baked a batch of Snickerdoodles. They're good dunkers if I do say so myself."

"You bake?" I didn't know of any other man that baked. I wasn't quite sure what to make of that.

Charlie winked at me. "You'd be surprised what I can do." His melancholy dissipated awfully quick.

For reasons I could not comprehend, I followed him into the house. The kitchen was a pleasing shade of green, neat and organized. The only items on the counter were a cookie jar and a standup mixer. He had a violet thriving in the window over the sink and a bowl of apples, newly washed, waiting alongside. The braided rug in the middle made it all look so comfy. I wondered what he would think of mine with stacks of cookbooks and scads of canning equipment and vases for my flowers. My kitchen was not a showplace and that suited me just fine.

Charlie handed me a cup of steaming brew, then took his cup, a plate of cookies and led me through his comfortable living room, passed a brown sofa draped with a lacy afghan and a bouquet of fall flowers on the coffee table, and into the porch.

"I'd rather not sit out front." I stopped just short of entering the sunny porch filled with wicker furniture and house plants.

Charlie turned, brows arched.

I remained firmly in place. "I don't need the whole neighborhood talking more than they already are. As it is, my family is providing great fodder for the gossips in this town."

"It's just coffee, Helen, and some wicked good cookies. My teenage granddaughter says everything is 'wicked' these days." He chuckled at that. "I may be old, but I think if I wanted the neighbors to talk, I could do better than this." He continued out to the porch and set the cookies on a table to match the rest of the furniture. "Come sit." He motioned toward a pillowed chair. "It's a beautiful day, isn't it?"

"Fine." I lowered into the chair opposite him. "Are you always so happy?" It struck me how we resided in opposing corners.

"Are you always so glum?" His squinted his eyes. He was making fun of me and I couldn't hardly blame him.

"Drink your coffee before it chills." I tipped the cup to my lips and tried to hide the smile that wanted to spread across my face.

Charlie proceeded to talk non-stop. Normally that would have annoyed me to no end, but his life was interesting. College was a grand time for him, then he joined the service where he met Beth and they had the three children in rapid succession. They traipsed all over the country for the service. He retired from the Air Force and became an airline pilot traveling to every corner of the globe. After their children were off on their own and he retired for good, they settled in Chicago. The children scattered across the Midwest and twelve years later, Beth's heart attack left him alone. The city bored him, and he longed to return to the simplicity of Peeksville, if only for a while.

As he spoke of flying and the places he'd been, his face lit with a light from within. It was a wonderful thing to see. I wanted to be jealous, but the emotion eluded me.

Then, he asked about my life.

"Nothing to tell." I downed the last of my coffee. This conversation had just gotten too close.

"Would you like another cup?"

"No." I shook my head. "That's my limit for the day." I picked up my purse, preparing to leave. I had repaid his good deed.

Charlie settled back into his chair. "It's only fair you tell me about your life. All the years we missed. You and I."

"You say that like you missed me. I don't think that would be true. You have had an awfully full life, Charlie. I can't imagine you had time to think about me. I should go."

"Don't. Please. A part of me always missed you, Helen. You were a fireball." He laughed. "That's what my father called you."

"I always liked that man." I thought back to Mr. Soderberg and his kindly face. Charlie looked at lot like the old history teacher now.

"He got a kick out of you. There was never any guessing what you were thinking. He liked that. You made him laugh." Charlie's eyes became wistful at the mention of his father.

"I was never one to mince words, I suppose. No time for it." I cleared my throat. "You were lucky to have him."

"Now, what's Helen Foley's story? How did you fill those years?" He waited as though I had some grand story of my own to tell.

"Running a store, raising Annabelle's child, and working the farm. That's it in a nutshell."

"Such a shame about Annabelle and her husband. What's become of their daughter?"

"Ivy and her family live in Amery. They have two children. Girl and a boy. I don't hear from them much. Ivy and I don't get along well. She thinks I was too hard on her. Anyway, she and her husband are having some problems right now."

"I think most kids think their parents were too hard on them. Parenting is a slippery slope. I hope they work out whatever problems they're having."

"I do as well. I suppose I wasn't much of a parent. Hadn't been in my plan any longer."

A heavy moment hovered between us. When Charlie left, my hope of marriage and parenthood left as well.

"Look, Helen," he leaned forward, elbows on knees, "I won't pretend I didn't see the story in the paper about the remains found on the farm. Do you want to talk about it?"

"Not particularly."

"I only know what I read. They said they're looking into your father's death. Do you think that's a possibility?"

"Absolutely not!" Anger boiled within me now. "Is that why I'm here? So you can get the scoop firsthand?"

"Of course not, Helen." He reached to put his hand on mine, but I pulled away. "You know, I met your father once. Did I ever tell you that?"

"No, you didn't." I braced.

"I was about eight years old. I was walking along Main one day when a man in the upper window of the jailhouse yelled down, 'hey kid'."

A bitter taste filled my mouth. Did he honestly feel I needed to know this?

"He tossed a quarter down to me and said, 'get me a can of snuff and a paper.' I did as I was told. When I got back with it, he told me to bring it around to the front door. 'Tell 'em it's for Harlon Foley' he said." Charlie chuckled. "What was he in for, anyway? Do you remember?"

"Probably a bar fight." Our nice visit had just hit a wall.

"Maybe I shouldn't have told you. I didn't mean to open an old wound." He sat up straight. "If you want to talk about it, I'm here for you. If you don't, that's fine too. I just want you to know that if you need someone, I'm all ears."

I set the cup on the table between us and stood.

"I've got bulbs to plant." I pushed my chin defiantly in the air.

"I can see I've upset you. I'm sorry." He stood as well. "I hope we can do this again sometime."

I crossed the street to the black-eyed Susans calling *come home, come home.* I felt his eyes upon me as I went. Daring to look back, he was watching from the porch, lifted a hand and waved. I bobbed

160

my head in response.

Oh hell, the bulbs could wait. I went in through the front door and pulled the shades.

CHAPTER 18

Esther

As I strolled along Thornapple Road, the setting sun dusted the fields with gold and shafts of pink. I picked a few daisies and brushed the soft petals under my chin as I went. It was my favorite time for a walk. For at this time of day, the scent of wildflowers was more pungent against the earthiness of the forest, and as the world slipped toward dusk, I found comfort in the stillness, broken only by birdsong and the slight kiss of a breeze.

As I reached the rise of the hill before Gropp's farm my steps slowed as my heart rate kicked up. Intuition pulled at me. Something was wrong. I felt it in my bones.

The rumble of a truck came from behind. I felt it as much as I heard it and moved closer to the edge of the road. I turned to see a pickup truck barreling up the ribbon of black top. As the truck passed, I and the driver, Rafe Pukall made eye contact. My breath caught. The passenger was his brother Louie. Their tires ground to a halt on the shoulder and dust rose in angry, tornadic swirls.

I braced. Sheriff Bergey's warning about the Pukalls exacting revenge alarmed every nerve ending in my body.

The doors of the truck swung open and the brothers jumped out.

"Don't do this, Rafe," Louie said to his older brother as they rounded the back of the truck.

"Shut up," Rafe said without taking his hawkish eyes off me. "It's time for ol' Harlon to pay up for messing with Marty."

My heart boomed like a fist beating against the door of a house on fire. Terror choked any attempt at pleading for mercy. I pointed a shaking finger.

"Stay away from me, Rafe. I didn't do anything to your sister. That's Harlon's doin'."

"I don't give a shit," Rafe said. "Might as well have us some fun, too. What ya think, Louie?" Rafe spat into the ditch.

I threw the daisies onto the road and in a single leap, crossed the ditch and ran into the forest.

Daring a look over my shoulder, Rafe was closing fast, hooting and hollering like a deranged escapee from an asylum. Louie wasn't far behind. Instantly, I knew I shouldn't have run. Perhaps, if I'd remained on the road, I could have reasoned with them but now, because I ran, panic rose with every step I took. Had I stayed on the road, someone might have come by that I could have flagged down. But it was too late now.

Branches scratched my bare legs and arms, pulled my hair, and clawed my dress as I pushed through the undergrowth, dodging trees, stumbling over fallen logs, nearly falling into a fox hole. Where I was going, I didn't know. Would I come out on another farm, find a hunter or a logger to save me, another road? All that mattered, was that I stay ahead of them.

"We'll getcha," Rafe yelled with glee as though chasing a stray animal or a deer for slaughter.

"Stop it, Rafe!" Louie called from behind.

I stopped abruptly and nearly careened into a deep gully. Desperately I grabbed a sturdy tree trunk and swung my body down into the deep cut into the earth thinking I could hide. It was then, I realized my mistake. I was a caged bird. The banks were too steep for a quick, easy escape. *What a stupid mistake!*

My heart pounded with frightening force and my breath came in quick heaves of exhaustion. A large stick lay at my feet. I tightened my grip around it, waiting.

Looking up, I saw Rafe staring down. He had me, and he knew it. A satisfied grin thinned his lips.

Taking control was my only hope. With a deep breath, I drew on every ounce of courage I'd ever possessed.

Rafe angled his body along the lip of the gully, then sat and dangled his legs over the side leaning forward with elbows on knees.

"Looks like your goose is cooked Mrs. Foley."

Louie caught up and nearly fell over the edge. He grabbed on to the same tree trunk and tried to catch his breath. He and I locked eyes. I knew I had an ally in Louie, but how far would he go to rail against his brother?

"Stop it! Stop right now!" I held up the stick and thrust it forward like a steel beam.

The lecherous look in Rafe's eyes was terrifying. He rubbed his dirty hands together as though he were salivating over a plate of fried chicken.

"Don't do this! You're good boys. I know you, Rafe, you're a hard worker at the mill. They say you're the one that saved Roy Hanson from goin' through the chipper last month. Louie, you're on the fire crew. You saved the Johnson kids last year. They say if you hadn't found the youngest under that bed, she'd never made it out. You're good boys. Don't stoop to Harlon's level. You're better'n him."

"We are better'n Harlon," Louie said.

"He ruined our sister's life. That ain't somethin' we can overlook." Rafe turned to Louie. "Don't be no pansy-ass when it comes to Foley. Where's your loyalty to the family, to Marty? She ain't never done nothin' to nobody and Foley comes along and…and has his way with 'er. I ain't standin' for it and you shouldn't neither."

"Harlon does need to pay. Marty's never gonna be the same," Louie said to Rafe. "But this ain't the way. His wife ain't done nothin'."

I took my chance. "You think hurtin' me will make it all better? Well, it won't. Harlon won't give a care. What your sister went through is only a fraction a what I go through. You don't think I don't know what he can be like? Don't allow him to ruin your lives as well. If you do, then he wins."

"Rafe, you gotta think about that," Louie said.

Rafe cuffed his brother's arm. "Don't go soft on her. That son-of-a-bitch didn't go soft on Marty."

"I'm sorry for Martha," I said. "Truly I am. But Harlon won't give a fig if you hurt me."

"She's right. We want to make Harlon pay. We need to deal with him directly." Louie looked to me with pity in his eyes.

Rafe slid down the hill to stand before me. I struggled to stop shaking and hold the stick still.

He came forward and leaned into me. "Does he care about his kids?"

"No! Please!" I threw the stick and placed my hands on his chest, my fingers curled into the fabric of his shirt.

"Rafe! No!" Louie slid down the side of the gully.

"Please don't hurt my children. They're innocent in all this." Tears ran down my face. "Would you want Harlon as a father?

Would you?" I released his shirt with a little shove to his chest.

Louie grabbed Rafe by the arm. "For Chrissake, Rafe, I ain't hurtin' kids. Neither are you."

Rafe backed off, his mouth twisted in a hateful line.

"We won't hurt your kids," Louie said to me, "and we ain't hurtin' you. I mean it, Rafe. We ain't doin' this."

I nodded, grateful. My body shook as I wiped the tears from my face.

Rafe pointed a finger at me. "We'll get him. One of these days he'll pay. You tell him."

"I will. I hope your sister will be all right."

"C'mon, Rafe." Louie touched his brother's shoulder. "Let's get out a here. The old man will have our hide if we don't get home soon."

Rafe ran a hand though his hair. "I ain't gonna stand for Harlon's shit. He keeps it up he's gonna find hisself six feet under."

"Rafe, let's go." To me, Louie said, "Sorry."

The boys crawled up the side of the gully and disappeared over the edge. My body shook like a leaf holding on against a torrential storm. I wrapped my arms around my middle and sunk to the forest floor. There, I bent, covering my face with my hands and sobbed as though every hurt in my world were coming out at the same time.

CHAPTER 19

Helen

I answered the ring of the phone. It was the damn deputy again.
"Helen, how are you?" Reed asked.

"Fine. Just like I tell you every time we talk." I took a deep breath to stem the anger at the interruption of my afternoon game of solitaire. "You have an idea who is in that tree?" Might as well cut to the chase.

"Wish I did. The Crime Lab is going to take their time with this one." Oh, he sounded so important on the other end. I wanted to reach through the phone and cuff him one.

"Why do you say that?" I moved the queen of spades to cover the king.

"For one, it's a painstakingly complex piece of work to separate the skeleton from the trunk of the tree. They're taking the trunk apart bit by bit, bone by bone. Any growth of the trunk may have absorbed oils from the body and bits of clothing as it decomposed.

We're also checking with the register of deeds to get a picture of the families that came and went over the years."

"I'm happy for you." My sarcasm certainly wasn't lost on him.

"Have you remembered anything, Helen?"

"No. Not a thing."

"Have you heard from Ivy?"

"Why do you ask?"

"Purely personal. I haven't seen her in a while and well, we were friends in the past. Just wondering how she's doing. I, ah," he chuckled, "I thought of her the other night when I drove under the overpass on County H and saw what remains of her artwork. That really was a work of art, you know. Too bad the county tried covering it up."

I was mortified every time I had to take that road. The outline of the little girl's hand letting go of the heart shaped balloon and the giant eye with the tear was still slightly visible. It was a cry for attention, plain and simple, and a stab at my parenting skills. How the hell was I every supposed to make up for a little girl losing her parents?

Still, the girl did inherit her mother's gift with a brush and paint. Too bad she didn't do something with it as an adult. The detail in the painting on the overpass was impressive, but the message was embarrassing. Even though it was no longer completely visible, I still couldn't look up as I passed underneath.

The school counselor had called me in and suggested counseling for the girl, but I didn't believe in all that hooey. Still, I agreed for Ivy to go. After all, what would people think if they knew I didn't comply. Ivy went, but I later learned she'd skipped out and that was the end of that.

"You might as well know, she and her husband are having problems." I moved the ace of hearts to the side.

"Yes, you mentioned that last time. That's too bad."

Ha! I almost laughed at that. He's not disappointed in the least.
"Tell her that I wish her all the best."

"Ivy and I aren't on the best of terms, as I've said."

"That's sad, Helen. A person needs family around. Especially at
a time like this. Any time for that matter. Families go through ebbs
and flows of their relationships just like marriages. You and Ivy
need each other. You are all the other has. It'd be a shame not to
embrace it. I'm sure Ivy's mother, your sister, wouldn't approve.
Had fate not been so cruel, you wouldn't have any family near
you."

Who the hell did he think he was, preaching to me like that?
Didn't matter that he was right.

"Hmph. I suppose."

"Guess it's really not my place to stick my nose in, but I am
blessed with a big, wonderful family and I wish everyone could
have that in their life. Anyway, back to the investigation..."

"This has nothing to do with me or Ivy. I simply owned that
land at one time and that's all. I have no knowledge of a dead body
in a tree."

"I'm just concerned..."

I hung up. The cards were no longer cooperating. The game was
over and so was my patience with this investigation.

Just then, a knock at the back door. Now, who in the world
would use that door and not the front?

Fueled by my annoyance with the nosy deputy, I stomped
through the kitchen and grabbed the doorknob, only to see Ivy
staring back at me through the window.

"What are you doing here?" I asked as I opened the door.
"Where are the children?"

"They're spending the weekend with Brad's parents. Helen, we
need to talk. Justine told me she filled you in on what's been going
on. She shouldn't have done that."

169

Dressed in a flowered blouse and jeans, with her long auburn hair in a braid over her shoulder, she looked so much like her mother with her brown eyes and dusting of freckles that my heart ached with longing for my little sister.

"Oh, come on in." I ushered Ivy into the dining room where we took seats across from one another. I pushed the playing cards off to the side.

"You know, I'd like to see Maudie and Evan once in a while myself. They must be growing like weeds. Anyway, I could make us a pot of coffee," I offered and began to stand.

"No, I'm good." Ivy crossed her arms in front of her. "I needed to get away, to clear my head. I'm staying with Justine, for the weekend."

"I have a perfectly good spare room here." I took umbrage with that as I sat back down.

"After our last conversation, I didn't think I'd be welcome."

"Well, of course you would be." I smoothed the lacy tablecloth in front of me. "What are you planning to do about your marriage?" Reed's words swam about in my head. I am a cantankerous, crusty old fool at times.

"It's over, although Brad doesn't agree. I just need some space to plan. I don't think I want to stay in Amery, but I'm not sure."

"Where would you go? If you leave, what will you do about work? Who will help you with the kids?" Panic made my heart pump harder. What if she took the kids and moved farther away? I had always known they were within a few hours ride, and if needed, I could get to them, or they could get to me, quite easily. If they were farther away, I would truly be alone. The thought was gut-wrenching.

"Helen, I'm working on all of those things. I may go back to school. I'm not sure." Ivy's shoulders slumped and she looked exhausted and, honestly, I felt for her.

I knew this was my chance to step up, be the parent Ivy needed, the parent Annabelle would have relied on me to be. Reed's words still hung before me and I knew I was being granted another chance.

"You know," I tapped a long fingernail on the table as thoughts formed. "you might want to think about pursuing your art. There must be something you could do with that. It's a talent you inherited from...from your mother."

Ivy simply stared at me, picking at a fingernail as she always did when nervous.

"I should have encouraged that a long time ago I suppose, but I was never one for the arts." A few beats of silence ensued. I slapped the table and said, "I would pay for your schooling if you decide to do that. There's that college not more than an hour's drive from here. If you go there, I could help with the kids. You could live here if you need to."

Ivy's jaw dropped. She looked as though I could knock her out of her chair with the touch of my finger. My heart was beating like a bass drum. I think I surprised myself as much as Ivy.

"I've got money socked away and I'd like to do that for you. The sale of the store and the farm has left me comfortable and it's time to spend some of it. Not as though I can take it with me when I bite the dust." Surprisingly, it seemed a giant weight had lifted from my shoulders by offering this gift.

"Ah, okay. Where is my Aunt Helen and will you be bringing her back?" Ivy looked at me as though I'd grown three noses. I couldn't help but smile. "I can't believe you would do that. That's very generous of you. I'll think on it, Helen."

"Do that." I wanted to chuckle at the stunned look on her face. What a tremendous day this turned into.

"I have a lot of planning to do and dealing with Brad is going to be a challenge."

"He hasn't laid his hands on you lately, has he?"

"Laid his hands on me?"

"Abused you physically?"

Ivy shook her head and pressed her lips together in a way I feared she was lying.

"If he is, don't take it, Ivy. No man should get away with that."

"No, I... I don't want to talk about Brad anymore. I realize you are dealing with a lot right now. I'm concerned at how this discovery at the farm is affecting you. Please be honest with me."

"What are you getting at?"

Ivy leaned forward, "The remains, Helen. This must be upsetting for you on some level. It is for me. I was raised there and so were you. I know you like to think you're tougher than most, but this can't be easy. Someone came onto your land and deposited a body. That's horrifying."

"I'm handling it. There's nothing anyone can do. They say they can solve it and that will be that."

"I was thinking of going to see Reed and see what he can tell me."

"I just spoke to him, in fact. He was on his way out of town for the weekend." It bothered me to lie, but I wasn't ready for Ivy to stick her nose into all of this. There were things that affected her as well and I simply wasn't ready. "I'm right here. You want to know something, you talk to me."

"I'm sorry to have missed Reed. As an old friend, I think he will be helpful to have on the case."

"He's a pain in the patoot, is what he is."

"There's the old Helen. Welcome back." Ivy grinned. "He's just doing his job. You know, it wouldn't be so bad for you to accept help once in a while. I mean to be better at that in the future for myself." A sly grin softened her features. "I had a bit of a crush on Reed at one time. Gosh, that was so long ago. I was a different person back then." She got up and went to the window. "Your gardens look as though they've done well this year."

"They have."

"You know, I don't know if I've ever seen you have a bouquet of cut flowers from your gardens in the house. Why is that?"

"Then they'd die before their time. I've seen enough of that in my life."

Ivy nodded and turned from the window. "Helen, would you like to have dinner with me tonight? We could go to that little diner you like. The Five Sister's Cafe."

"That's the only place in town a body can get a decent bowl of soup."

"Is that a yes?"

"You know, I've got soup in the freezer. Made up a pot last week."

"I don't want you to fuss, so I'm taking you out. We're going to have a nice dinner and go for a drive around town. I want to see if anything has changed."

"I suppose we could, but the last time I had their soup it was too salty. They have a new waitress there, not sure of the name, but she's about as worthless as they come. Still and all, it's better than the rest. I guess I could get a sandwich. And a drive? What for? It's not the nice town it once was. Did I tell you they tore down the old Kollmer Hotel and replaced it with a pawn shop? Place looks trashy to me. You'll see."

"Yep, the old Helen is back." Ivy reached over and patted me on the arm. "But a better version I think."

The Witness Tree

CHAPTER 20

Esther

"Hurry it up, Hattie. I don't have all day," I said as my sisters and I bounced along in our mother's old rust-bucket of a pickup. Hattie insisted on driving. Vee sat between us, legs up against mine to avoid the stick shift.

Hattie shifted into gear and said, "You know the old lady's going to have a coronary if she finds out I drove you all the way to Judge Shadduck's." Her curly brown hair was pulled tight into a ponytail and her freckles darkened a bit with exposure from the sun after working in the hay field. Hattie wanted nothing more out of life than the farm. And while our mother's constant nagging pushed the others out, Hattie didn't take it one bit. That's probably why the two lived together without a hitch.

"You aren't kidding," Vee said putting one hand on the dash as Hattie pressed the gas. Vee looked pretty with her dark curls

174

bouncing on her shoulders. With her wide doe-like eyes and creamy skin, she was so pretty. I often though she should be a singer with her talent for music. But Violet was hopelessly in love with Bucky Clemson, a schoolteacher and football coach, and they were to be married next fall. All Vee wanted a houseful of babies she could sing to.

"Ma knows I want a divorce, but she's not about to help, so it only fits that I use her truck to do it." I craned my head out the window feeling the wind thread through my hair.

"What kind of trouble do you think you'll have with Harlon if this goes your way?" Vee asked.

"He's going to have a shit-fit." Hattie said, glancing at me. "If the judge gives you what you want, where you gonna go?"

Vee stared at me with wide, fearful eyes.

"I been cleanin' out Harlon's pockets every time he's come home drunk in the last year. His spare change and the money from my egg sales are addin' up. Plus, I sold a quilt Harlon doesn't know about. Mr. Nelson offered me a job in the past. I'm hopin' the offer's still good. Even so, I could always waitress. Maybe do laundry or housecleanin' on the side. I can make it." I nodded as though trying to convince myself this might work. After the run-in with the Pukall boys, I was more determined than ever.

"I will watch Luddie and Helen for you whenever I can," Vee said.

"That SOB Harlon won't help you." Hattie rolled down the window. "You know he's going to make your life a living hell." Warm summer air flooded the cab.

"He already has."

Vee reached over and patted my knee.

"No one can breathe a word of this to Harlon, or anyone for that matter, or I'm dead for sure."

The color drained from Vee's face. "Oh my God, do you really think so? Don't do this, Esther. We'll think of something else."

"Vee, it's time Esther stood her ground." Hattie glanced at Vee. "A woman shouldn't have to stick with a man who treats her like the shit under his boots."

"Like you would know. When's the last time you let a guy near you?" Vee shot back and Hattie glared.

Vee made a face at her and turned to me. "Okay, why don't you get yourselves on the train and keep going. Try for a job somewhere with room and board. I'll get a second job and send you what I can."

"Ruby offered to have us come out to Seattle, but Eldon's had a stroke, and she's got her hands full. Peeksville has been home my whole life. I don't want to leave all of you. If it gets bad enough, I may have to, but until then…"

"I hope you know what you're doing." Vee's eyes got watery.

"Oh, hush now, Esther knows what she's doing. If he doesn't back down, we'll shoot him. Put him in the meat grinder and feed him to the pigs where he belongs."

"Hattie!" Vee jumped in her seat while I broke into giggles.

"My pigs have better taste than that." I was grateful for the chance to laugh.

"What if Luddie and Helen say something about today?" Vee asked.

"We've been over this. I came over to visit with the children and you asked me to run in to Nelson's with you and Hattie. That's it. The children are having too much fun in the barn with Eddie to think about what we're doing. And Ma thinks we're looking at the new bolts of material Nelson's just got in."

"What would we have done if Ma had asked to come with?" Vee wrung her hands.

"We'd be looking at material right now," I said.

"Trust me, we aren't going to spill the beans to anyone, not even Ma. We'll stop at Nelson's on the way back just for show," Hattie said.

We parked in front of a brick house surrounded by a white picket fence. Hollyhocks danced along the gate with daisies and black-eyed Susans. My heart pounded in my chest something awful.

"Good luck," Vee said with brows and shoulders raised.

"Go get your life back." Hattie shooed me toward the house.

I ventured through the gate and down the brick walk.

A thin, petite woman with a pinched nose and a cap of gray hair answered the door. "May I help you?" The judge's wife was known as a dour old woman with no sympathy or compassion for anyone.

"Yes ma'am, my name is Esther Foley. Would the Judge be at home?"

"Is this business or personal?" The woman's expression narrowed making her look like a baby hawk stretching its neck for a worm.

"It's personal business, ma'am."

"This is Saturday. Have you thought of making an appointment at the courthouse? He is a busy man after all. Call him there Monday morning." She began to close the door, but I couldn't let that happen.

I put a hand on the door. "Please, Mrs. Shadduck. I cannot be seen at his office. I need only a moment of his time."

The door swung back, and the judge stood there looking me up and down.

"I'll see her." Judge Shadduck stepped into the doorway. His wife stepped back. The judge was a portly gentleman with a generous white mustache and round glasses.

"What can I do for you?" He studied me with small eyes behind thick black frames.

"I want to divorce my husband, sir." I folded my hands and

177

squared my shoulders. "How can I go about that, please?"

The judge narrowed his eyes and puffed out his cheeks. "Aren't you Harlon Foley's wife?"

"Yes, I am." I was buoyed by the fact that the judge knew Harlon. Certainly, he would understand my desperate situation.

The Judge looked beyond me to the truck parked along the fence.

"Well, come in then." He stepped back inside and, as I followed, a flock of sparrows lifted from the rooftop, their song dusting the breeze.

CHAPTER 21

Helen

I parked my old station wagon in the barnyard. Today, I had an overwhelming need to return to the farm, a nudge at every turn. Why? I couldn't say. Ivy and I had driven past before the girl went back to Amery and maybe that stirred some longing to step back in time. Maybe it was sheer nosiness regarding the finding of the bones, a macabre need to revisit the scene of the crime. Besides, I had canned goods and frozen soup to give away and it seemed the perfect excuse to make a trip out.

Chillier than expected, the afternoon air was sweet and woody, redolent with the scent of a Wisconsin autumn. A mist hung heavy over the land enveloping the old white house like a shroud. So many memories inside that house.

I stood, with a brown bag full of goodies and my purse, staring up at it from the yard. It had been too long since I'd seen it, but yet, I suddenly didn't feel the need to go inside. Leave the memories as they were. Maybe I was being a coward.

I walked over to inspect the fenced-in garden plot. Tomato vines held onto a few green, unripened orbs. Pumpkins lay plump and orange. Golden cornstalks waited to be cut. In the corner grew clumps of black-eyed Susans that still thrived, but the daylilies were lifeless and the dahlias a shriveled-up mess, the bulbs needing to be dug up before the cold weather arrived.

Beyond, the apple orchard looked sad compared to what it once was. Shortly before I moved, a storm took out some of the best trees. The ones that remained now held strong under their sweet bounty and the grape vines, already done for the season, lay with arms stretched in repose.

Overhead fuzzy clouds churned and warned of rain.

Chickens clucked intensely from the hen house and cattle chewed from a bale of hay out in the field, while a pony in a corner of the corral ignored them all. Ivy had begged for a pony. I said no.

Looking out over the field, stubbly after the hay harvest, I noted the yellow crime tape stopping anyone from entering the tree-lined path created by the cattle looking to escape the summer sun. I knew it so well. The hoof-worn path pitched and leveled with the landscape, broken here and there with root and rock, bending around stumps and fallen logs until it dipped toward the river. And the place where a tree once stood.

As a child, I ran that path on my way to the river, a gangly, barefoot girl with yellow curls flying, freckled nose turned toward the sun, and knobby knees stained with grass and soil. Back then, then animals were my only friends and the land my escape from all that haunted me.

And suddenly, I felt foolish. I shouldn't have come. What had driven me here? Was there anything I thought I'd accomplish? No. It was time to leave and hope no one saw me.

"Miss Foley? Helen?" Joe Jennings called from the side yard

where he leaned on a shovel.

"Oh," I nearly tripped at the start, "I hadn't seen you there." Damn. I crossed the lawn carrying the grocery bag of food, taking care to avoid looking in the direction of the woods behind the farm. I didn't need to be reminded of the mystery the Crime Lab was now scurrying to solve. Too bad about this thing called DNA.

"'Hello, there." Joe placed one booted foot on the shovel and one long arm draped over the top of the handle. He was a handsome man of medium height, an engaging smile and brown hair pulled back into what the kids called a man-bun. I had to catch myself from rolling my eyes at the sight. He had a leather string tied around his neck with some sort of pewter doohickey hanging from it.

"Is it all right that I'm here?" I asked. The bag in my arms was getting heavy.

"Of course. I'm trying to shore up this clothesline. Damn pole has been threatening to fall over for about a year now." He pressed his hand against the pole to test it.

I simply nodded.

"Carrie should be home shortly. Said she was leaving the flower shop a little early today. The kids are still in school." He wiped his brow with the sleeve of his denim shirt.

I looked to the sky, ignoring the memories that circled like ghosts hanging in the breeze. "They say we'll be getting a bit of summer back before the cold begins." I shifted the bag onto my hip. "I don't think they know what the hell they're talking about."

"I don't put much store in weather forecasts, myself." Joe grinned. "What's in the bag?"

"I made a kettle of squash bisque a few days ago. Thought you all could use some." I stopped just short of him. "I've got a few jars of pickled beets in here, applesauce and stewed tomatoes, too. I didn't really think anyone would be home. I just planned to leave it on the stoop."

"How generous. Let me take that." He laid the shovel down, came forward and took the bag from me. I rolled my shoulders in relief.

A flash of something caught the corner of my eye. I turned abruptly but saw nothing. A prickle of recognition warmed my skin.

"Are you all right?" Joe was studying me.

"Right as rain. I see you haven't fixed the tractor yet. It's still in the same place as it was shortly after you moved yourselves in." I suspected Joe was a touch lazy. This sealed it.

"Yeah, I never quite got that far. Always something needing fixing around here." He bounced the bag on his hip.

"How was the garden this year?"

"Carrie's been so busy so I'm trying to pitch in. We're learning as we go."

"Looks like you've sold off most of the livestock. Why did you buy a farm in the first place? You're not much for gardening, no animals, and field is looking shabby. You better not let that grow up. Do you know the kind of work it takes to clear a field? The rocks that need hauling and stumps pulled?"

"Helen, why did you come here?" His smile slid off his face.

Suddenly the ghosts of the past were closing in, making it hard to breath, hard to focus.

I thrust out a palm as though I could hold them back. "I don't know why I bothered to come. I guess after all the hoopla over the remains, I... I don't know."

Joe balanced the bag on the other hip. "Carrie and I wanted to raise our kids in the country. We've got a pony now and more chickens coming next week. We have plans to fix things as we have the money for them. I was just hired at the Building and Supply as a carpenter, so money won't be so tight. Quality of life is what we were looking for here. Unfortunately, it came with a skeleton out back." He wiped his brow with the back of his free hand again. "This investigation can't be done fast enough for us. You either I suppose."

Why did I feel the need to berate him so?

"I am sorry I was rude. It's a bit hard to be here. And I'm sorry you've had to deal with this, these bones. After all, it was none of your affair." The yellow-ribboned forest was closing in. The past came marching forward with strong, steady strides.

"That's okay."

"I did the best I could." The words left my mouth without permission. A tremor began in my core and spread to my skinny, veiny limbs like wildfire.

"What are you talking about?" Joe was confused.

I nervously wrung my hands. "Nothing, nothing. This is all a bit much."

"Do you want to go back to where Dylan found the remains? Back to the river? Maybe see it for yourself? What's left anyway."

"NO! Hell no."

"Can I get you a glass of water?"

I shook my head and looked past him to the forest to where the river pulsed beyond the trees beyond what I could see, to where the awful tree once stood.

"I'm sorry. I shouldn't have come." The words spilled like bitter bile. I felt dizzy, unsteady. "I…" I began to turn away. "I…I'm sorry for what your child found. I hope it's not causing nightmares." I took a step but faltered feeling disoriented and a bit panicked.

Joe set the bag on the grass and quickly rushed to my side. He put an arm around my middle and one on my arm. Once steady, he said, "Maybe I should get you to a doctor."

"For heaven's sake, no." I grabbed onto his arm. "Absolutely not."

"What's wrong, Helen?" His eyes were so kind.

For the first time in years, tears wanted to seep out, but I stopped them in their tracks. "Our life here, was tough. I had a job, a farm, a sick parent to nurse and a child to raise. All by myself. My brother was gone. There wasn't time for anything frivolous. I had to be tough. I didn't have time to think about anything but plowing ahead, staying steady, taking care of us all. I'd have sold the place many years ago, but my mother wouldn't hear of it and asked me not to."

"That's a lot for any person. You must be a very strong woman."

"I didn't have a choice. It's what had to be done." I was embarrassed beyond belief at my weakness. I straightened, pulled away from him and regained my composure. "I really need to leave."

Joe angled his head.

"Would you join us for that squash bisque for supper? If Carrie were here, she'd insist."

"Oh, no." I stepped back. Curiously, the ghosts were gone.

Just then Carrie pulled into the yard in an older, rusted Jeep Cherokee.

I wished I'd gotten away before this. After making such a mess of things, I had no desire to stay any longer, to prolong this intrusion of mine.

"Why, Helen. It's so nice to see you." Carrie came forward, her chestnut hair down to mid-chest, silver hoops in her ears, a long skirt on her slender body and sandals.

I bobbed a hello.

"Helen brought us some of her canned goods and a large container of squash bisque." Joe picked up the bag and held it out for Carrie to see.

The girl smiled wide and peered inside. "You must stay and have supper with us." She had wide, doe-like eyes that exuded kindness.

"Told you." Joe grinned.

"I couldn't." How did this backfire so? Curiosity killed the cat, as they say.

"The bus will be dropping off the kids any minute. They'd love to hear about your growing up on the farm." Carrie nodded eagerly.

"Oh, I don't know about that. I'm not much of a storyteller." Good God, how did I find herself in this situation? The last thing I needed was to be plopped down in front of a group of children to tell stories.

"Don't worry about a thing. The three of them will keep you knee-deep in questions."

"I couldn't. Really. I need to get back. I will talk to Reed, the deputy, about taking down that yellow tape. It must upset the children."

"Helen, that would be a huge help. We've mentioned it, but it's still there. Anyway, please stay for supper. I think having you here may be healing for the kids. They need other memories, other stories about this place. We don't want to leave here. We want to create a happy home for all of us and you are part of the history of this farm. Please stay."

"Come on, Helen." Joe winked at her. "You don't want to miss out on this great soup."

It was mighty tempting. When was the last time I had experienced a family meal? Besides, Charlie would be so proud of me, being friendly and all. I took a deep, cleansing breath. "Yes, I would like that." Moving my gaze to the house, a new thought occurred to me, a happy family lived here.

I had the strangest sensation of a hand on my shoulder.

185

The Witness Tree

CHAPTER 22

Esther

I folded my body onto the back stoop alongside Luddie as he whittled a stick with his pocketknife, his skinny legs angled out from cut-off dungarees. He kept his head down, intent on the stick in hand.

Petey lay at his side showing his age. At thirteen, our good buddy was slowing down, spending most of his days lying in the cool grass on the north side of the house, or in his dog house by the barn. The children and I were thankful for every morning he showed up at the porch for his breakfast.

I touched the back of Luddie's sandy hair. My son was so innocent, so much of life ahead. I often wondered what the future would hold for him.

"What are you makin' there?"

"Nothin'." He bumped a shoulder and brought the corners of his

187

mouth down as he concentrated.

We sat for a few moments in silence while he worked. I watched his able hands move the knife back and forth, his long fingers brush away the shavings.

It was a beautiful morning. A stark contrast to the night before when Harlon blamed his son for a broken barn window. Of course, he had no proof, but it provided an opportunity to bring his wrath upon Luddie.

"You know, Luddie, you're nothing like him. I'm grateful for that."

The boy stopped his work for a moment. His gaze wandered beyond the barnyard. For a boy of eleven, he bore the weight of the world on his shoulders.

I watched his throat bob as he swallowed. Luddie was not one for words, except when the radio was on in the evenings. It was the only time I saw him truly come alive. He hummed along to the music, drummed with his fingers, kept time with his feet, and laughed at the jokes.

Soon he began to whittle on the stick again.

I leaned my shoulder into him and pointed.

"See that bird over there? The sparrow?"

Luddie raised his face, and his eyes focused on the bird hopping along the barn.

"That's a White Throated Sparrow. They've always been my favorite birds. Do you know why?"

Luddie simply shook his head.

"Mrs. Hegstrom, my sixth-grade teacher, loved sparrows too. She said whenever she saw a sparrow, she could put all her hopes and dreams on the wings of that bird. When it lifted into flight, it carried them into God's safekeepin'. I've never been very religious, but isn't that a beautiful thought?" I looked down at him and smiled. "I think that would work for our fears and our hardships as well."

Luddie was thoughtful a moment, then nodded. A corner of his mouth lifted briefly, and I knew he understood. We sat for a few more silent moments taking in the morning.

"I gotta muck out the stalls." He threw the stick aside, folded the knife, slipped it into his pocket, and sauntered toward the barn.

After a few pensive moments, I went back to fighting with the weeds between the flowers. Kneeling into the tiger lilies, I looked up to see Robert Sommers strolling into the yard. His arms wrapped around a bushel basket, Winifred panting alongside. I swear, I couldn't stop the excitement that bubbled from within.

Helen came running from the barn in a yellow cotton dress and bare feet, braids flapping behind. "Mama, cumpny's comin'." She stopped just short of the clotheslines and pointed. Petey struggled to his feet.

I nodded keeping my eyes on the approaching man. "I know. It's Mr. Sommers from up the road." My stomach flipped at the sight of him, so tall and handsome, the sun glinting off his glasses. I tucked a fly-away strand of hair into the red kerchief tied around my head.

"Good afternoon," he said with a wide grin and a wink. He boldly strode across the barnyard as I pushed up from weeding. His arms held a yellowed bushel basket trimmed in red and piled high with plump acorn squash. "I just picked these. Can you use some?"

"Why, Mr. Sommers. What a nice surprise," I couldn't wipe the smile from my face no matter how hard I might have tried.

 I brushed clippings from my dungarees and white sleeveless blouse, then went to inspect his offering. Helen followed close behind. Winifred came forward to sniff Petey, the latter barely acknowledging the other dog.

"I know you've got a garden, but if you could use some squash, here you go. I had some of it myself and it is quite delicious." His eyes met mine and held for longer than necessary. "Don't feel you have to take it all. If you take any, that is."

Helen came up and tipped the bushel to look inside.

"I love squash." Helen licked her lips in anticipation. Winifred came over and Helen gingerly touched his snout, then wrapped her arms around his neck and hugged.

"This is my daughter, Helen." I set a hand on Helen's shoulder. "Helen, this is Mr. Sommers."

"I 'member you from town." Helen piped up. "I sure like your dog."

"She likes you too. Her name is Winifred. That means 'peaceful friend'." Mr. Sommers squatted down to Helen's level. "Look at those beautiful braids. Why they're as golden as the corn."

"My Daddy likes 'em too. I think Winifred likes Petey, too. Maybe they could be doggie friends." Helen giggled.

"Petey doesn't get around much anymore," I said.

Robert touched Petey's head, but his eyes were squarely on me. "He has a lot of miles on him as they say."

Helen squatted on the ground between the two dogs, a hand on each furry head, and began a conversation while Robert set the bushel on the ground.

I crossed my arms and angled my face up to his. "I, ah, I found a few minutes of free time and have been trying to clean out my flower bed, scraggly as it is. I transplanted the tiger lilies last year and they are limpin' along trying to find their footing. Oh, you should have seen my peonies this year. They were gorgeous!"

"I wish I had. Unfortunately, I can always find something to fix on that old place of mine." His eyes twinkled. "My water pump has been acting up lately," he rubbed the back of his neck. "I don't know what's gotten into it. The days have been so dry. I thought I would start using it to water the garden, but I cannot get a thing out of it. Certainly, hope it hasn't dried up on me."

"You need to prime it," I said. "It probably hasn't been used in some time."

"Prime it? How do I go about that?" His eyes remained upon me and my heart quickened with the heat of it.

"Pour water into it. That will create suction and get it workin' again."

"You don't say. So, a little water will fix it all?"

I spread my hands apart, gesturing to the farm around me. "I've had to learn to fix quite a few things on my own."

"Well, thank you." A corner of his mouth turned up in the most pleasing way. "I'll try that as soon as I get back. Now about this squash, can you use it?"

"I would, but…" Pride kept me from saying I could not pay him for it unless I dipped into my freedom fund. It would take more than a bushel of squash to precipitate that.

"I'm giving it to you, Bess. Especially since you have given me such wonderful advice. I am more than happy to have you take it." I noticed the dimple in his right cheek. My heart longed for another dance and the feel of his arms around me. Instead, I bent to pick up the bushel of his generous bounty.

"Thank you very much, Robert. We will certainly enjoy these. I'll make some squash soup and send some over for you. Let me dump these in the porch and give you your bushel back."

Then Robert winked and my heart fluttered like the wings of a thousand butterflies.

"You've made my day by lightening my load."

"Can I please take Winifred to see Luddie?" Helen asked as she came to stand between us.

"You sure can," Robert said. Helen ran off toward the barn with Winifred bounding along behind. Petey simply lay back upon the grass for a nap.

"Looks like they have made fast friends." I was grateful to have

191

time alone with him. I lowered my voice and said, "There is something I want to tell you."

"And what would that be, Bess?" Oh, how I loved that he called me Bess.

I checked to make sure the children were not within earshot and leaned closer. He did as well, anticipating my confidence.

"I…ah…I went to see Judge Shadduck about a divorce." I rubbed my hands before me, attempting to stem the nerves.

"Did you now?" Robert's brows knit together with concern. "What did the judge tell you?"

"He said he would look into it." I swallowed the ball in my throat and spread my arms wide. "Can't imagine he would deny my request. After all, half the people in this county know about Harlon and his ways."

Robert studied me for a long moment. He wasn't brimming with excitement as I had imagined.

"That must have taken a good deal of courage."

"I won't deny I am a bit nervous, but it'll be for the best." I pursed my lips to stem the tremor of nervous anticipation that bubbled through me.

"What are your plans?" Robert asked.

"I have a bit of money I saved. Thought I would take an apartment in town for the children and I. Mr. Nelson offered me a job at the store. I mean to stay in Peeksville. Near my family."

"I don't know what to say. I wish you all the best." He took a step closer. I held my breath. "I am worried for your safety. Your husband doesn't strike me as the kind of man that will take this lying down."

"I can handle him." I stuck my nose in the air with confidence.

"What if you've misjudged him? I'm worried for you." Robert ran a hand through his hair, long fingers plowing the auburn hair like a rake through hay.

Of course, he remembered the day I'd returned his letter and the nasty bruise on my arm. How I wished I'd have worn longer sleeves that day. Or not. Maybe I wanted Robert to know the state of my life with Harlon.

"He'll be relieved to be rid of me, to have the burden of supportin' us lifted. If I can reason with him, he'll see the benefit of it." How desperately I longed for Robert to reach out, offer comfort. But this was not a time for weakness. "I know what I'm doin'. Trust me."

"I hope you're right." He let go of a ragged breath. "I'm just up the hill if you need me. I mean that."

"I know you are." I suddenly questioned my decision to tell him. The light I hoped to see in his eyes at the promise of my freedom had not been there. Not at all.

Helen and Winifred came running from the barn.

"I'll leave you to the work I've interrupted." Robert stepped back and I sensed a disconnect. I so wanted to reach for him, know the comfort and support of his arms around me.

"It was good to see you." Disappointment weighed heavily upon me.

He smiled, but it didn't quite reach his eyes. "Good luck to you."

I only nodded.

"Enjoy the squash. Don't worry about getting the bushel back to me. I found a stack of them in the grainery." He held out a hand to me, then thought better of it and pulled it back.

Robert and Winifred strolled from the yard leaving my heart to feel like a stone in my chest. Helen stood at my side and waved. When he reached the end of the drive Robert turned, waved, and disappeared behind the trees lining the road.

I felt so foolish. How could I have been so wrong?

***

The Witness Tree

Harlon failed to show for supper again that night.

Just after eight o'clock in the evening, the children and I were reading in the parlor when the growl of Harlon's truck broke the silence. This was early for him when he was on a bender. Something was wrong.

I went to the kitchen window.

He nearly leaped from his truck, stumbled, slammed the door and came toward the house in a drunken weave.

"Luddie, Helen, go upstairs." They quickly picked up their books and ran up the stairs. I glanced out the window once more. Harlon was almost to the house. I checked the stairs to see Helen peeking around the banister.

"Scoot!"

"Maybe we should go to the barn." Luddie suggested from the top of the stairs, his face pale.

I tried to stem the panic building within me. "It'll be fine." I hurried to the kitchen.

Harlon burst into the house, hair mussed, face red as a beet. I braced as he grabbed me by the arm.

"Harlon, what's wrong?" I fought to remain calm as his fingers dug into my skin.

He pulled me tight against him. His breath was hot upon my face and the stink of alcohol permeated the air. "A friend a yours came into Whitey's tonight. Never realized you had such high-falutin' friends there, Esther." He gave me a shake and I bit my tongue.

"I don't know who you're talking about?" I tasted blood and feared there would be more to come.

"Betcha you didn't know Otto Shadduck is a drinker. You know the *judge*, don't you, Esther?" He jerked me viciously this time and thrust his snarling face in front of mine. His breath hot. "You want a divorce, do you?"

194

"Harlon, I ..." I shook my head insistently. "No, I wasn't serious. I...I was just angry. The children, Harlon, they're right up the stairs. Please, let's not do this in front of them."

"Save your breath. I'm gonna fix you so you don't embarrass me like that ever again." The feral look in his eyes was terrifying.

"Harlon, please, think of the children." I put my hands on his meaty arms. "Let's go outside and talk about this."

"Talk?" He grabbed my blouse in his fist. The other hand came up to grip my jaw. "Seems the time for talkin' is over." He pulled the material of my blouse out and then popped my chest with his fist. The tender flesh bruised under his knuckles.

"Harlon," I fought to remain calm. "Please. Let's be reasonable. You don't want us. We're nothin' but a burden to you. You tell me that all the time." I had his attention now. He was listening. His grip released slightly. "What am I supposed to think? You don't love me, you never have. Sometimes I think you would be much happier if we were gone." I prayed he would see the common sense in my words. "You can have this place all to yourself. I won't ask you for a thing. I mean that. You would be free of us forever."

His hands released me. I was getting through to him. Freedom danced in the near distance.

Then his eyes narrowed, and I knew this wasn't over.

"No one makes a fool a me like this. I won't have every mouth in the county talkin' that Harlon Foley couldn't keep a wife. That Harlon Foley don't take care of his own. I ain't got much, but I got my pride."

"Your pride doesn't keep you from stumblin' through town in a drunken stupor and takin' up with every whore you can find. I'm not as stupid as you think," I said through gritted teeth.

The back of Harlon's hand came across my face. My head snapped back.

"There's no shame in a man that's a widower," he growled. "You got that, Esther. Ain't no shame at all." His threat was heard loud and clear. "Cost me a good deal a my paycheck to get the judge to drop your divorce. That asshole's nothin' but a thief."

Harlon shoved me against the dining room set. Chairs tumbled and the table scratched across the floor. He grabbed my arms and threw me toward the door. Hitting the frame, I felt the knob punch my lower back. I tried to duck his advance, but he caught me with one hand in my hair and the other by my blouse.

"You want out? You got it?" He kicked open the door and gave me a shove out onto the porch.

I tripped on a loose board, spun to the right and fell hard against a metal washtub at the bottom of the stairs. My forehead hit the top edge and I spiraled into the dirt.

Sitting up, blood trickled down the side of my face from a cut on my forehead. I tasted blood and raised fingers up to find a deep gash in my lower lip. My knees and palms were red and scratched. Tears mixed with the blood and the dirt on my face.

Harlon came out the door and looked down at me from the porch. With one hand on his hip, he rubbed his forehead with the other. "Christ sake, woman." He downed the steps and tried to help me to my feet.

"Leave me be!" I shrugged him off and slapped at his arms.

"You're bleedin' pretty steady, there. Let's get you to the house." He again offered me a hand.

"Stay away from me!" I pushed up, limped to the steps and found a seat on the top step.

"You know, I didn't mean for this to happen." Harlon went inside and returned with a wet cloth. He tried to dab at the cut on my forehead, but I grabbed the cloth from him. He took a seat next to me.

"But it did happen. All because you've been drinkin' again. Is it any wonder I don't want this life anymore? Do you ever think about what you're doin' to our children?"

"I know I ain't been the best husband." He hung his head, elbows on knees, fingers knit together. "Damn drink. I'm turnin' into my Pa."

"Damn right, but your Pa wasn't as bad as you. The drink got him in the end. You saw what it did to his insides, the cancer nearly ate his stomach out. You want to end up like that? Do you?"

"I know I gotta give it up, but I... I don't know what's wrong with me."

"You're weak, Harlon. You can't hold a job for long and the least little problem, you run to the tavern."

"I know. I don't want no divorce. Our family is the only thing I got worth spit. I never planned on bein' a farmer, yet here I am. 'Member when we talked of goin' to the city when we first got married? We could still do that."

"It's too late. I've lived this life as long as I care to. I'm not doin' it anymore. And as far as makin' a new life somewhere else, I don't want it. Not with you."

Harlon's face darkened. "I ain't all bad. I keep a roof over your heads and food on the table. What makes you think you can do that, a skinny little thing like you? I ain't gonna let you take my kids. The judge ain't givin' you no divorce. I took care of that." He stood, kicked the ground and stomped off toward the barn.

I watched him go. There was nothing about Harlon I wanted except his children and the children were what he wasn't about to let me have. I was sure of it.

Pulling up from the step, I went to the mirror hanging in the parlor. Bruises were already starting on my arms and right cheek. The cut to my forehead and lip had stopped bleeding. Anger welled in me with such force, I thought I would blow apart.

197

CHAPTER 23

Helen

I offered to help Carrie with the dishes, but the girl assured me she had it under control. Joe had gone to finish a few evening chores and the girls, Sierra and Luna, had gone to their rooms for homework. The boy, Dylan, was outside.

I sat at the dining table finishing my cup of coffee.

"You haven't changed much with the house," I swung my gaze around the room.

Carrie turned from the old farmhouse sink. "No, not really. I'd like a new kitchen, but I don't see that happening anytime soon. This one works just fine."

I merely pumped my head and took another sip. The house was still the same boxy rooms, same paneled doors painted white as were the moldings along the floors and ceilings, and the old-fashioned paned windows. I craned my neck to see into the living room. One of the windows still had a crack in the glass from a day

Ivy was playing baseball with apples in the orchard. Somehow the window continued to hold together and never cracked beyond the single line curving around the corner.

Of course, the furniture was different, more updated. The cream-colored wallpaper with the gold and pink flowers was gone and now covered with beige paint. There was a desk along one wall heaped with papers and books. No television. I suppose that was a good thing.

Then there was the staircase. That's where my nostalgia took a turn. I couldn't bear to think of the many times Luddie and I had run up those stairs in fear, and then there was the last time. The memory hit me with a force that made it hard to breathe, hard to stay upright in the chair.

Sweat beaded upon my upper lip and my heart fluttered. I braced against the table. The scene before me blurred. It was coming back to me. The sounds, the fear, fleeting ghostly visions, the feel of the stairs under my bare feet and the hardwood floor under my belly as I crawled across it.

I blinked trying to clear my vision. Breathed deeply to steady my heart. The memories left me exhausted.

"Helen, it seems a shame we haven't gotten you here before all this." Carrie kept her back to me.

"Oh, I... I don't get out much." I stared into the depths of the cup in my hand, breathing hard.

"Still," Carrie wiped her hands on a towel hanging from the stove handle, "we should have. After all, you gave us a good deal on the place, and we appreciate being here. Even with the ghost." She turned, her face creased in concern when she looked at me. "Helen are you all right? You look pale?"

"I'm fine." I wiped my lip before taking another sip of the now tepid coffee.

"You sure?"

"Just fine. What's this about a ghost?" I squared my shoulders and tried to focus.

"Has been here ever since we moved in. I've always meant to ask you about it."

"There's no ghost here." I pulled my shoulders up and looked to the ceiling.

"Oh, there sure is." Carrie took a seat across from me. "He or she is really harmless. Doors open and close, lights blink. We're used to it." She giggled. "There was one night, Joe and I were having an argument. I mean a dandy. I was screaming at him and he was screaming at me and suddenly, our cookie jar flew off the cupboard. I kid you not. Smashed all over the place. I looked at Joe and said, 'I think we've been told to behave.' We really don't argue much anymore. Worked like a charm."

I failed to see the amusement of such news. "This is the first I've heard of such a thing. I don't know what to think of it."

"Seriously, you had never experienced it?"

"Absolutely not." My skin prickled at the back of my neck. For some reason, I didn't doubt what Carrie was telling me.

"Anyway, the activity had been worse the week before the bones were found. We couldn't figure out what was up with that, and then Dylan found what he did, and the activity stopped. Freaky, huh?"

"I suppose." I stood, it was time to go.

"Deputy Bolton has been out here several times looking for answers, but we have no clue. I even took him up to the attic one day to search around for anything helpful that might have been left up there, but there was nothing."

This was too much. I couldn't take any more. "I really need to go." I set the coffee cup in the sink, allowing my eyes to slip around the perimeter of the room. Ghost? A friendly spirit was not in the wheelhouse of my father. *Mother, is that you?*

"Well, thank you for staying, Helen." Carrie stood as well. "We'll enjoy the goodies you brought. Let's do it again, shall we? You're certainly not a stranger here and I want you to feel welcome any time."

I nodded. "It was a real pleasure to...to be here." I hadn't been treated this kindly in forever. As I prepared to leave, Carrie threw her arms open wide and I stopped in my tracks. The girl wanted a hug. I bent forward and loosely embraced Carrie as she came forward.

With my purse hanging from an elbow, I bobbed my head and with one quick glance at the staircase, went out the back door. Dylan was sitting on the bottom step.

"I want to show you what I made," he said.

I navigated down the paint-bare wooden steps, around Dylan and stood in the grass before him. "What do you have there?"

His dirty hands produced a crude box. "It's a birdhouse for the sparrows."

"They'll be flying south before too long," I answered.

"That's what Dad said, but I thought if I made a nice house, they would stay." Dylan's eyes held a longing that spoke of more than birds flying south.

"The sparrows are leaving to survive the winter. Your house there wouldn't be enough to help them through." Maybe I was being a bit harsh with the boy. "Although, it'll give them a place to come back to in the spring." The boy suddenly reminded me so of Luddie. Something in his eyes and the curve of his mouth.

The boy nodded as though he understood. "Sure was scary to find those bones. Kinda like it was Halloween." He looked up at me with such innocence in his eyes.

I took in a deep breath. Reassurance, if that's what the boy was looking for, wasn't something I was much good at.

"Well, that happened a long time ago. Long before you moved

here. The...the people involved are long gone and won't be able to cause any more trouble. You know that don't you?"

Dylan nodded without looking up.

"Does that worry you, what happened across the field?"

Again, he nodded. Under the spent lilac bush along the house a sparrow landed, pecking at the end-of-season grass.

I took a seat next to him on the wooden step, setting my purse in the grass.

"See that bird." I pointed and the boy followed with his eyes. "I'll tell you what my mother told me. Put your troubles on the wings of that sparrow and let them go. Let them fly away with the bird." When he didn't seem comforted in the least, I added, "Life isn't always that simple, is it?"

"I guess not," Dylan brushed sawdust off his jeans. "Do you think the person in the tree had a mom and dad?"

My throat closed and my face grew warm. "I'm sure."

"They must have been scared when they couldn't find him."

"That's not any of your concern. You don't need to worry about things in the past. You just go about being a little boy. That person might not have been missed by anyone."

Dylan's brows squiggled together like two little worms as he pondered my words. "That's sad. I'm glad we found him."

I nodded, took up my purse and went to my car without a word and a large knot in my throat.

CHAPTER 24

Esther

I sat on the boulder by the river's edge. The deep cut to my lower lip was still raw and the one on my forehead taking its time to heal as well. I'd strained my pinky finger when I fell, and it was healing crookedly. My cheek still held a purple stain.

Closing my eyes, I listened to the sound of the Redemption's current rushing over the rocks. If only I could melt into the water and float away.

Freedom had been so close. Or had it?

The annoying caw of a crow broke my concentration, yet I didn't look up to seek its source. Instead, I allowed great, wracking sobs to fill me. I placed a hand on the boulder to steady myself, as a wail broke from my mouth and echoed through the forest.

I slid off the boulder and lay in a bed of fern. How I craved the comfort of loving arms but there were none. None at all.

The Witness Tree

The last of my tears fell salty upon the earth and exhaustion washed over me. My entire body ached, and I felt so broken. I needed this time to grieve over the life I had.

The children needed their dinner. Luddie's dungarees waited to be mended, and Helen asked me to bake a blackberry cobbler. For the sake of my children, I had to pull myself together, rise above this wallowing in misery. How could I have known that my attempt at divorce would go so horribly wrong? The judge wouldn't grant it, Harlon wouldn't allow it, and Robert seemed put off by it all.

Harlon would be home soon. He'd been kinder of late, even going so far as to take us into town for an ice cream at the Robin's Nest one evening.

My dress was wrinkled beyond help and errant strands of hair had loosed themselves from the pins at the back of my head.

"My word, Bess, are you all right?" I jerked, startled to see Robert Sommers toss aside his fishing pole and creel and run toward me. Winifred bounded behind him.

"I'm fine." I carefully pushed my body up along the boulder. Winifred sniffed at my ankle, her tongue cool upon my skin.

"You most certainly are not all right. Bess, what happened?" He offered a hand as I tried to settle against the rock for support. "I suppose I don't have to ask." He stood in front of me and gently took one of my hands in his. "Harlon did this. You asked him for the divorce."

I couldn't look him in the eye. This was so humiliating. Tears tumbled down my cheeks.

"I didn't have to ask. The judge told him my intention over a beer at the tavern. Harlon paid him off."

"Oh no." Robert dug into his pocket and handed me a handkerchief.

I dabbed at the corners of my eyes. "I won't be getting my

divorce if Harlon has anything to say about it. The judge promised Harlon it won't happen."

"Why, that's ludicrous! What kind of a judge is he? I'll speak to him."

"Absolutely not! Please, say you won't."

"He took his fists to you. What kind of man does that? This has to stop."

I hesitated for a moment. Was it awful of me to allow him to think the injuries came from Harlon's fist and not my stumble from the porch? Either way, Harlon was to blame.

"It's not usually this bad."

"This should *NEVER* happen, no matter the degree." Robert's face softened. He shook his head. "I don't know if I can keep quiet about this."

"You have to. For me." I put my hands on his arms and put my face in front of his. "It would only make my life more difficult. You haven't seen him when he drinks, and the law will do nothing to protect me."

"You can't be sure about that. Does he hurt your children?"

"He...he's cuffed Luddie from time to time, but never more than that." I wiped at my nose.

"Bess, leave him. Now."

How my heart ached for Robert and the life we could have with him. If only...

"He says there's no shame in his being a widower. If I pursue this and he follows through, then my children would be raised by him alone. I can't have that. The judge would never take them from him." I wiped my nose again, then began to hand the handkerchief back to him, thought better of it, and put it in my pocket. "I'll get that back to you." I tried to smile, but my lip hurt, and I winced.

"Widower? He'll kill you?" Robert's face morphed into one of horror.

"I don't know, sometimes," I ran my tongue over my split lip, "sometimes there's this look he gets in his eyes. It's as though he could tear me apart. I've always been able to talk him down from that degree of anger, but I always fear the day when I can't. I can't take the chance." From somewhere deep in my soul, strength bubbled forth, the depth of which I had not known was there. "I can handle Harlon."

"Obviously, you can't." He stepped back from me. "I've worried so ever since you told me you went to the judge. I thought I should stay away. I didn't want to be the cause of your putting yourself in danger."

I opened my mouth to argue the point, but had nothing.

Robert put his face in his hands and was quiet for a moment. Then he looked to me with renewed spirit.

"We'll sneak you away to a secret place. There are some old parishioners of mine who will take you and the children in. Your husband would have no idea where you've gone."

For a moment, I considered his plan. Could we do it? Robert was right, Harlon would have no idea where we'd gone. But then reality clawed through my optimism.

I shook my head. "No. I can't. Harlon would have the law after me. I won't endanger innocent people. I'll find a way to get through this. I need some time to think. As my mother said, I've made my bed and now …"

"Bess, my God, you've got the weight of the world on you. I wish I could carry that away." He gently touched the side of my face. I noticed a touch of gray at his temples. It only made him more handsome.

Without thinking, I reached up and covered his hand with my own, pressing his palm against my skin. I closed my eyes, breathed in the leathery scent of him, and turned my face into his palm.

206

How I ached to have his arms around me.

"Hold me," I whispered and dared a glance at his face.

Robert hesitated a moment, then gently put his arms around me. I sank into him, laying my head on his shoulder feeling his bones, his muscles and the breath move in and out of him.

Something passed between us, I knew. Something that reached beyond the Redemption and the farm and all of Peeksville. But, unfortunately, it didn't help me one bit now.

After a moment Robert leaned next to me on the boulder. He slid his arm across my shoulders and pulled me to him. I fit so perfectly in the crook of his arm and my head found his shoulder again. His other hand reached across and tenderly stroked my arm.

"I wish we could stay like this forever," I said.

"I wish I knew how to help you."

"I know you do."

For a long moment, we remained as we were with nothing but the flutter of the trees, birdsong, the rush of the river and the sweet smell of evergreen to soothe us. Despite my aching body, this comfort was as a drug to my battered soul. And I wanted more.

"There is one thing you could do for me."

"Yes?"

"Let's meet here at the river from time to time." I pulled back slightly and gazed up at him.

"I... I don't know." He was pulling away from me again. I could feel it.

His arm slipped off my shoulders. I was sorry to have broken the spell.

"I need this, Robert. I need something to look forward to. Even if only for a few minutes. Just to have a conversation. To have a friend."

"What if your husband finds out? Something so innocent could surely be construed into something more."

"Harlon is at work every afternoon and the children in school. If we meet, say once or twice a week, say one o'clock, that should work just fine." I nodded trying to convince him.

"I…I suppose. There may be days when I'm subbing at the school, although they've told me it will be mornings most of the time."

"There may be days when I can't as well, but let's try. If the other doesn't show, that's all right. We do have lives to live, but that would be something wonderful to look forward to. This Thursday? One o'clock?"

"One o'clock it is, beginning this Thursday. I'll see you then." Robert stood before me. "Please, take care, Bess."

Walking back to the farm, my world had brightened, if just a bit. Thursday would not come soon enough.

CHAPTER 25

Helen

I carefully navigated the cracked sidewalk on my way home from Habeck's Grocery, a brown bag in each arm. The heaves and cracks were hidden under a blanket of fallen leaves and the last thing I needed was to end up on my kiester in front of the whole town. So, I watched every step.

Neighbors had long since stopped offering me a ride. Turned them down every time. I had no desire to feed their do-gooderitis. I could drive but preferred the walk. It was a pleasant enough day. The October sky was the purest blue, the temperature still warm enough, and what leaves remained on the trees neared their peak fall color.

As I reached the First Congregational Church, the brick exterior and stained-glass windows in shades of green and blue, and its tall, white steeple, was one of my favorite buildings in town, despite that I held no regard for what went on inside. Still, the sight of a church was comforting somehow. On Sunday mornings I turn the radio down precisely at ten a.m. to hear the bell chime like clockwork and it gives me a sense of calm and I picture all the families gathering.

I glanced at the flower bed growing alongside the church parking lot. Whomever the gardener was, did a fair job in the summer, but now it all needed cutting back before winter. The north side could use some snow-on-the-mountain to dress it up and it wouldn't hurt to replace the planters of spent petunias with mums of yellow and rust, purple and white.

Just then, the massive wooden door carved with crosses and lilies opened, and Charlie stepped into my path.

"Well, as I live and breathe. If it isn't Miss Helen Foley in the flesh." He stood before me, arms cross over his chest and a stupid grin across his face. "It's been a few days."

"Charlie." I nodded and kept walking. Until he fell into step beside me. I stopped and stared at him.

"Your eyes look real pretty when you pull your brows down like that," he said.

"Like what?"

He waggled a finger at me. "Like that. You know, when you are trying to intimidate someone. You're very good at it. Except that you're scowling now." He did an imitation of me. I struggled to un-scowl.

With a tip of my head I indicated the church behind us. "You subscribe to that bunch of hooey?"

"Would do you good to try it sometime. Ever been inside?" His brows arched in challenge.

"Funerals and weddings when I have to. It's not Sunday, so what are you doing there?"

"I volunteer to fix what's broken from time to time. Today I refinished the banister leading to the choir loft." He puffed his chest and hung his thumbs from his belt loops.

"Sounds important." I deadpanned and continued walking.

He matched me stride for stride and reached out. "Let me take a bag for you."

"No." I kept my eyes focused on the sidewalk ahead. "Maybe you had better go back and find another job at the church. Some people buy their way into the great beyond. I guess you're working your way in."

"I have no doubt where I'll end up one day, Helen. Stroke of luck, isn't it, that I was leaving just as you were walking by? Maybe the good Lord put me in your path for a reason. I think it's because you could use a good friend. You've been avoiding me."

"I'm not avoiding you. The gardens need to be buttoned down for the winter and the screens taken off and put away. I've got canning to finish and windows to wash. Guess we're all working our way to the grave one way or another." I quickened my step. "Anyway, I've been busy." He hung right with me.

"Admit it. You saw me wave from my yard yesterday. And Tuesday, when you started out for a walk, you saw me and went the other way."

I ignored him and finally gained some ground on him.

"You running a race, or running from me?" Charlie called after me.

I stopped, clenched the bags and fought a powerful urge to throw them at him.

"Running from you, Charlie? Really? You have no idea!" The bitterness in my voice shocked me. My heart thumped with a powerful beat.

"Helen…what?" His natural smile slid off his face and I was glad.

"You ran from me! I tried to get you back but only ended up with egg on my face. You ran from me and right into the arms of your Beth." The corners of my eyes were moist, and I shook my head to clear them and gain control. What was wrong with me lately? Why was I dredging up the past? Didn't I have enough to deal with, with the remains, the deputy, and Ivy?

"You never tried to get me back. What on earth are you talking about?"

"Do you remember the day you came back from the service? Big hometown hero. Everybody made such a fuss over you. The whole town was there." I looked away from him trying to find the strength to go on. "I was there too."

Charlie took a step toward me. "You were?"

I tried to stop from trembling, but it was no use. "I was there. All gussied up and waiting for you to take me away from Peeksville. Me and Ivy, that is."

I remembered that day so long ago. The train brought Charlie Soderberg back from the war. The high school band waited at the depot in their red and gold uniforms along with the mayor and the city council. Banners hung from the businesses on Main Street and Tucker's General sold out of hand-held American flags.

I did a lot of soul-searching in the time he'd been gone. Charlie had every right to live his life as he chose. And he'd chosen an honorable path, serving his country with courage and dignity. I also knew my love for him had not faded one smidge.

Although now, there was one complication. A little red-haired girl named Ivy. But knowing Charlie as I had, I knew that he would welcome her with open arms.

The day of the grand homecoming I pulled out all the stops. I curled my golden hair to sit on my shoulders just so. I even bought makeup and dusted my cheeks and colored my lips. The blue dress I bought for Sally Kaminski's wedding, I knew, would bring out the blue of my eyes. I polished my black shoes and pulled white gloves over my work-worn hands.

The Witness Tree

Ivy was so pretty in a green dress I had sewed with lace on the collar, her hair in braids, green ribbons on the ends, and freckles across her nose.

I put Ivy in front of the long mirror in my bedroom and stood behind. We formed quite a lovely picture, the two of us.

"Now," I said to the girl, "You don't speak unless spoken to. Got it?"

Ivy nodded and didn't say a word all the way there, even when we passed the root beer stand.

I drove us to the depot just as the train was pulling in. The crowd cheered and the band struck up a lively rendition of *Stars and Stripes Forever.*

Taking Ivy by the hand, I pushed through the crowd until I was near enough to get a good view of Charlie as he disembarked.

He stepped off the train so tall and handsome in his blue uniform, his brown hair clipped short, his face rugged and tan. He was slimmer than when he'd left. Someone called, "There he is!" The crowd cheered wildly. He waved, smiling broadly, and his parents rushed forward crushing him in an embrace.

I brought a hand up to my neck, ready to wave when he looked my way. My heart was near to bursting and my head spinning with all the life that lay ahead of us, Charlie, Ivy and I.

Then, just as the Soderberg's released their son, a young woman stepped off the train. Charlie helped her down, slipped an arm around her waist and brought her forward.

My breath caught in my throat and bile churned in my stomach.

The young woman held her hand out and the sun caught the diamond on her finger.

I wished everyone would stop making so much noise so I could hear what they were saying.

Mrs. Soderberg threw her hands in the air and screamed as Mr. Soderberg bent to take the young woman's hand in his. The four of them wrapped arms around each other and the awful truth came through the crowd. Charlie had a wife.

I looked down at the little girl at my side and stemmed the urge to throw up.

That same feeling came through me now, all these years later, as I wondered what possessed me to accost him with this now and on a city sidewalk.

"I…I didn't know," Charlie said.

"Why would you?" I clutched the grocery bags tighter.

Charlie took a step toward me looking very solemn.

"Don't." I shook my head.

Charlie shoved his hands in the pockets of his pants and looked away. "I'm so sorry, Helen. You never wrote me. Not once. I had no idea where life had taken you."

I felt so foolish. "Well, it didn't take me very far. Never mind. I shouldn't have brought it up."

"Helen, I never meant to hurt you. I would never hurt you like that again."

"Yes, you would. We're old. No one knows how much time we have left except that God of yours." I breathed deeply and released my grip on the bags slightly. The loaf of bread was sufficiently crushed. And the eggs beneath? Who cares. My heart was once again, a cold, hard door with a heavy lock.

"I'd like to think I've got enough time left to make a cherished friendship, for us to experience life together," he said.

"Charlie, I want peace and quiet now. Just leave me alone." I turned, crossed the street and left him standing there.

CHAPTER 26

Esther

"Did your son tell you we've met?" Robert spread his lanky body on the grass along the Redemption, leaned on one elbow, and sipped lemonade from a small coffee cup.

"Luddie? No, he didn't." I poured myself a cup from a Mason jar cooling in the current.

"I was at my mailbox trying to shore it up when he came along with a fishing pole in his hand."

"Oh, yes." I took a seat upon the tablecloth on the ground. "He walked down to Dead Man's Slough. He'd heard the walleye were biting. They weren't." I smiled and took a sip of lemonade before reaching back into the basket I brought. "I made raspberry muffins." I handed him one.

"You baked in this heat? I'm impressed." He took a bite and closed his eyes. I enjoyed watching him savor the treat. He had a few crumbs at the corner of his mouth.

"I waited until evening when a pleasant breeze kicked up, and it wasn't so bad. So, you met my Luddie. Were you able to get a conversation out of him?" I handed him a napkin.

"By George, I did. I was having trouble holding the box in place, and he came along at just the right moment. He put down his pole and offered a hand before I could ask. He is quite the boy." Robert extended his cup. "Do you have more lemonade? Next time, I'll bring some bakery, although my talents in the kitchen are quite mediocre."

I refilled his cup. "Bring some of the apples off your tree." I offered him another muffin. "Those would be just fine."

"These are heaven." He took a bite of the muffin. "Luddie and I shared a few fish stories, and he took the time to give Winifred a rubdown. He's got a good heart."

"My Luddie has a heart of gold." I thought of the unhappiness I saw in my son's face so often.

"Tell me about this Dead Man's Slough." Robert pulled his knees up before him. "There must be a story behind that name."

"Years ago, the story goes, Omer Rasmussen came home from World War I to find his wife living with another man. In his grief, he ran to the river and hung himself from the bridge. His father found him the next mornin', swingin' o'er the water. Wasn't long after, his father suffered a heart attack and died. Such sadness. Ever since, it carried that name."

"That's too bad. It's actually a very scenic spot. The type of place that would inspire great poetry. I went fishing there for walleye a few weeks ago. Caught some dandies too."

I went to the edge of the river and knelt, put my hands into the cool water and rinsed them. The sun warmed my shoulders.

From behind Robert said, "You're very pretty with your hair swept up like that. The sun creates a bit of a golden aura around you."

The Witness Tree

I looked over my shoulder to see him grinning. "Oh stop. I'm a mess." I dried my hands on my skirt, then ran them over my hair, tucking stray strands into the twist at the back of my head. I then went back to our picnic, wrapped the leftover muffins in a cloth napkin, set them inside the basket, followed by the cups and the empty jar.

Robert stood and folded the tablecloth and handed it to me. He then picked up a twig and twirled it between his fingers as he leaned back against the boulder near the shore.

I held the tablecloth to my chest watching his graceful fingers work the twig. The gentle movement of his hand stirred a longing deep within me. He looked up and our eyes held.

"I have to go." I closed the basket.

Robert threw the twig into the water where it bobbed among the waves.

"This has been lovely, Bess. We'll do it again next week?" He brushed his hands on his pants.

"I don't see why not." The basket hung from my hands as I grinned at him. "This is the best part of my week."

"How is your life at home these days?"

I didn't want to talk about Harlon. "Fine."

He narrowed his gaze.

"Really, Robert. I can handle him. He's been calmer as of late. He even had the children laughing during supper last night. I think he's feeling guilty."

"You seem more peaceful as well." He angled his head and studied me. "Just be careful. I'll walk you to the edge of the forest."

"Why, thank you, sir." Yearning to touch him, I slipped an arm through his. He smiled down at me. I loved the deep creases on either side of his mouth.

We walked arm in arm along the path through the forest toward

217

the edge of our field. Robert asked about the local churches.

"I'm afraid I can't help much with that. I'm not a church-goer."

Robert stopped and looked at me. "That surprises me … and I don't know why."

I shrugged. "I guess I don't have much in the way of faith, although I've always thought it was a fine thing to have." I angled my head and asked, "Does that make me a bad person?"

"I'm not one to judge. I haven't stepped foot in a church since I lost Polly and Emily. But no, you are not a bad person, Bess. I'm privileged to call you my friend." His blue eyes sparkled like the burbling water of the Redemption. The sun dusted the angles of his face and a breeze moved a shock of his rusty hair onto his forehead. I fought the urge to reach up and push it back in place.

"I thought you were lookin' for a church and that's why you asked."

"I'm not certain why I asked. Knowing you these past weeks has made me question the importance of faith in our lives." He rubbed the back of his neck and looked off into the trees. "That day I met you at the river and you were crying I went home and picked up my Bible for the first time in years."

"So, the sorry state of my life has made you look to your religion. I suppose that's a good thing. I'm not certain if I should laugh or cry at that."

He studied me for a long moment as we walked. Instead of feeling uncomfortable, I welcomed his gaze.

"I've got a long way to go to return to my religion, but every person needs hope and faith. Otherwise, life would swallow us whole."

"How do you keep breathin' after losin' your family? The hopelessness of my situation doesn't compare to yours."

He took a deep breath and looked to the forest around us. "I suppose I find faith in the return of the rising sun by day and the light of the moon by night. The return of new growth in the spring and the beauty of the falling snow in winter. The Earth keeps spinning and we must keep going because, for whatever reason, we've been given life. That life needs to be respected and protected." He brought his gaze back to me. "I'm finally finding value in living again. Maybe it will lead me back to church, maybe it won't. But I want you to have faith, Bess, that life will be better."

"I...I appreciate that, Robert."

"I want you to be happy. It matters to me." He pursed his lips. "You matter to me."

I pushed up on my toes and kissed his cheek. "I am more hopeful than I've been in a long time." It had been an impulsive move, and he was startled, but in all honesty, I'd wanted to do that for a very long time, and it didn't feel unnatural in the least.

A slight breeze rustled the leaves and allowed the sun to skitter here and there.

I took his arm again. "We'd better go."

At the edge of the field, just before the tree line gave way to pasture, he bid me farewell and I left him.

The feel of his smooth skin still lingered against my lips. Meeting Robert was the best part of my week. The fact that it was only an hour or two didn't matter. It didn't matter that my work had to be done in less time to make room for our visits. He was my guilty pleasure, and all we did was talk.

Part way across the field I turned. He was still watching from a stand of birch, as I knew he would be.

CHAPTER 27

Esther

The sweet strains of a fiddle and a banjo danced on the warm evening air as Harlon and I and the children crossed the parking lot of the Greenfield Dancehall. The wedding couple, Mike and Jenny Gallagher, kissed as they hurried through the front door. Behind them, the happy throng followed into the reception as did we.

Inside, streamers hung between the rafters and joined in the center where a white paper bell swung over the crowd. Women bustled about the tables of steaming food while the band at the front of the hall played a lively jig. Couples twirled and children zigzagged among them. Harlon went straight to the bar where other men gathered in raucous laughter amid a cloud of cigarette smoke.

"Momma," Helen pulled on the skirt of my best dress, the pink

220

with the white collar and belt.

"Yes, deary."

"May I go by Daisy?" She pointed across the dance floor.

"Yes, you may, but we'll be eating soon, so I'll be looking for you."

"Okay." The girl skipped off toward her friend.

I turned to look for Luddie. He sat on a bench along the wall up front by the band. His feet tapping out the beat, head bobbing, his hands drumming the bench.

Harlon's booming laugh carried over the music. I crossed the dance floor to the gathering of women preparing the food.

"Esther, come here." Mary Jankowski called.

"Mary, hello." I joined the short, stocky woman in an orange flowery dress, her curly salt and pepper hair in a lopsided bun on top of her head.

"Beautiful wedding, no?" Mary waved a meaty arm.

"They're so in love." I watched as the groom tenderly kissed the blushing face of his bride. So young and full of hope for the future. I longed for that kind of innocent faith in love. Maybe I would see that in Helen and Luddie one day.

"Ya, well, enjoy it while it lasts, I say," Mary said. "We'll see how his Jenny likes sloppin' those pigs a his. Those shiny hands a hers won't last long once hayin' season comes, not to mention pullin' on a cows teat twice a day." Mary crossed her arms over her generous bosom and pumped her chins.

"Oh, come on now, Mary. She'll be busy with babies if they keep up with all that smoochin'." I chuckled and smoothed the front of my dress.

"I s'pose you're right at that. Still," Mary leaned toward me, "she's been a city girl all her life. I'd like to see her help birth a calf. Poor little girl will prob'ly drop at the first sight a blood."

Bertha Bishop banged on the bottom of a metal pot and

announced the meal was ready.

The band continued playing as the bride and groom led the line to the bountiful tables of fried chicken and slabs of ham, rolls, mashed potatoes and gravy, potato salad and various forms of vegetables. Helen came running. Luddie was nowhere in sight.

I left Helen with Mary and went to find Luddie. Outside the back-door children were racing between parked cars, men were smoking under a maple tree, teenage boys sipped stolen glasses of beer. I scanned the woods beyond and spied him.

He was visiting with Robert Sommers at the edge of the woods.

At the sight of me, Robert rose from the car bumper where he sat. Luddie followed the trajectory of his eyes. With a wave to Robert he sauntered toward me. Robert followed. I wished I'd had a better dress to wear.

"Time to eat." I put a hand on my son's shoulder. "Helen's waiting inside. Go find her while I say hello to Mr. Sommers." Luddie nodded and left.

My gaze met that of Robert. In the golden dust of early sundown and the backdrop of green forest, he was so handsome in his brown suit and white shirt. I moved toward him.

"Robert, you're here." I tried to stem the smile breaking across my face but could not. The sight of him was too welcoming. Too exciting.

"Bess, you look lovely." His voice was sweeter than the strains of a fiddle.

I brought a hand to the bodice of my dress and one to the twist of hair at the back of my head.

"You shouldn't say such things to me. Might go to my head." I grinned and batted my eyes.

"I speak the truth ma'am. Only the truth." His smile widened.

"It didn't occur to me that you would be here."

"It's a bit of a story. Mazie Lonblock is coordinating the

teaching schedule for the school year. She introduced me to Peter Rosenbloom, the math teacher. We struck up a friendship and he invited me to go fishing on Pike Lake. There, we met Sam Scribner, a fine fellow and father of the bride. He insisted I come today."

"I'm so happy he did." I clasped my hands in front of me.

"Pink is a wonderful color for you. Matches your cheeks."

"Now, Mr. Sommers, you are knee-deep. Better stop while you're ahead." I shook a finger at him.

Whether Robert was flirting with me, or simply being kind, I didn't know nor did I care.

"Listenin' to the music made me think of our dance at your house," I said. "I can't tell you how often I think of that day."

"I'm so happy you enjoyed that. I did too." The shadow of a dimple appeared on his right cheek. I wanted to run the pad of my thumb over it.

I clasped my hands behind me. How I longed to take him by the hand and lead him into the woods where we could dance along to the music coming from the hall and allow the rest of the world to fade away.

"Well…the food is ready and my children are waiting for me."

"Then we better skedaddle." He motioned for me to lead the way.

Once inside, I went one way, Robert the other. I glanced to the bar where Harlon was engrossed in conversation, beer in one hand, cigarette in the other. Luddie stood with two boys from his class and Helen danced with Daisy. I motioned for them to come get in line.

I watched Robert out of the corner of my eye. The band took a brief break and all that was heard was laughter and conversation amid the clinking of silverware.

Sissy Pardon leaned into Robert as though they were sharing a secret. A twinge of jealousy assailed me. I nearly dumped my own plate and came close to drowning all of Helen's in gravy.

While we ate, Harlon continued to drink. Robert somehow lost Sissy and took a seat with the Rosenblooms.

Every once in a while my gaze found him across the room.

After everyone finished eating, the tables were cleared away as the band resumed their places on the stage and struck up a lively rendition of *Chattanooga Choo Choo.* Luddie sat with a few boys at the front of the hall by the band while Helen and her friends danced among the adults. I sat with Mary on a side bench.

"Just look at that tart." Mary indicated Sissy on the opposite side of the room. "That girl has no shame whatsoever. She don't miss an opportunity, that one. She sees fresh meat and she's on it like a fly on manure."

I chuckled.

Sissy tried persuading Robert to follow her to the dance floor.

"Oh, she's harmless." I wished I believed that.

"The heck she is. Sissy's the one that caused the Warner breakup. She'll flop those tits in front of the wrong man one of these days, and if the wife has any gumption, she'll give her what for."

Robert followed Sissy to the dance floor. Jealousy bit hard as I watched them.

A more opposite comparison between Sissy and myself could not be found, with Sissy's jet-black hair and red lips. I couldn't tell whether Robert was enjoying the dance or embarrassed at Sissy's gyrations. When the song ended, Robert thanked her and turned away. Sissy captured his hand and pleaded her case for another. Robert gently extracted himself and went to speak to Sam Scribner.

I downcast my eyes and bit my lip to keep from grinning.

"Oh, lookey who cleaned up and pulled themselves outta the

tavern," Mary snickered. Whitey and Clarice Luder entered carrying a large gift neatly wrapped. Both were dressed to the nines, he in a dapper suit and tie, she in a gorgeous red dress with black buttons down the front, her black hair swept up in a neat chignon at the back, a matching red hat on her head, white gloves on her hands.

"I hear they're quite generous when it comes to weddin's and babies," I said as they came through the crowd.

"I heard that too. Although our husbands helped pay for them gifts and those fancy clothes a hers."

Bile rose in my stomach at the thought. Some husbands helped pay more than others and I knew Harlon had donated his share of the tavern's profits while the children and I went without. Clarice did, indeed, look quite stylish.

Whitey went off toward the bar and Clarice, after looking uncomfortable for a moment, made eye contact with me and came toward us.

"Hello, Mrs. Luder." I said. Mary grunted, turned abruptly, and left.

"Mrs. Foley," Clarice said. "Sorry I scared off your friend there, but that Jankowski woman is an old biddy anyway."

I smiled at that. I'd seen the way other women treated Clarice and couldn't help but feel compassion for her. After all, one never knows what circumstances takes a body down one path over another.

"If you're lookin' for the gift table it's over in the corner behind that group of men over there." I motioned toward the southern corner of the building.

"Thank you kindly. I don't make it to these kinds of shindigs often. Missed the church service, but then I always do. Feel like a caged cat at them places."

I leaned toward her and lowered my voice. "Me too."

"You? Figured you'd be up front and center." Clarice scrunched her face and looked me up and down.

"We're not church goers, although I did go to this one and it was very nice."

"Well, better get this here gift to the right spot. Nice talkin' to you Mrs. Foley."

"Esther. Please call me Esther."

"Clarice to you as well." Clarice gave a clipped nod and navigated through the throng.

The band began the next song. It was one I knew so well. *Sentimental Journey.* One of the tunes Robert and I danced to on that magical afternoon in his parlor.

Suddenly, I felt very bold. More than anything, I wanted to relive that moment where, in the arms of a gentleman, I felt alive again.

I crossed the floor to where Robert stood, my heart racing, palms damp. Harlon and his group of cronies were nowhere to be seen.

"Mr. Sommers, would you care to dance?" I asked and desperately hoped he wouldn't turn me down.

"Why Mrs. Foley, this is quite forward of you." He grinned. "That would be lovely."

Robert tucked my hand into the crook of his arm and led us deep into the dancing throng. I stepped into his arms and together we sashayed from side to side. I so wanted to press my breasts against his chest, pull him close, dance the way a husband and wife would. Instead, I needed to be content with an appropriate distance between us.

I breathed in the spiced scent of him, savored the feel of his palm against mine and the knowledge of his skin that lay just beneath the thin shirt he wore. How I longed to turn my face into the crook of his neck, lay my head on his shoulder, let my heart be

226

free against his own.

I looked up, and what I saw in his gaze told me that surely, he was having the same thoughts as I. I knew I must be blushing and turned my face to stare straight into the hard, unforgiving eyes of my husband as he sat at the bar watching.

For a moment I met Harlon's stare with defiance. Then reality set in.

I stopped moving. I don't know why. There was nothing wrong with a dance among friends.

"Is something wrong?" Robert asked.

"No, I..." I stepped back from him and dropped my hand from his shoulder. "It's suddenly very warm in here."

"Would you like to sit down?" Robert continued to hold my hand in his.

"I think that would be a good idea." I took my hand back.

Robert guided me to the bench. "Can I get you anything? A drink of water?"

"I'm fine. Truly." I glanced in Harlon's direction. He had turned his back. Sissy sidled up against him and he handed her a glass of beer.

"Are you sure you're all right?"

I needed to hold on to some measure of dignity. "I'm sorry. I have a bit of a headache."

"Why don't you sit for a while? You might feel better."

"I'm sure I will. Thank you for your concern." My stomach was in knots.

Robert nodded and strode across the dance floor where he was stopped by Einar and Cora Nelson. As truly as there was breath in my body, my soul had intertwined with his. I was sure of it. And now, I was an empty shell of emotion that belonged only to him.

CHAPTER 28

Helen

I peered around the doorway to see Clarice Luder lying in bed, gold blanket pulled up to her neck, eyes closed. Good grief, I hoped she wasn't dead.

"Clarice." I whispered.

Clarice's eyes opened to tiny slits. She looked like a little bird in that big bed.

"You again," the old woman said in a raspy voice.

"I have something for you." I held out a tiny box wrapped in pink paper with a white bow on top.

"A present?" Clarice's face brightened like a child's.

"Of sorts."

"Ack, I need to get these old bones movin' anyways." She shoved the blanket back. Underneath, she was fully dressed in a block house smock under a tattered white sweater, and her walking stick tucked in the bed alongside her. "I like to sleep with my stick. Reminds me of Whitey…if you know what I mean." Clarice cackled in delight.

"That's naughty, Clarice." I chuckled and helped her to sit by guiding her stick-skinny legs over the side of the bed. "I'm going to have to come visit you more often."

"Well, good. Now, what's this present for?" The old woman's white hair made a spikey halo around her head.

I sat beside her and set the box in her bony hands. She slipped a long fingernail under the wrapping and in one swift movement had it off. She opened the box to find the ring tucked into a bed of tissue paper. Recognition spread across Clarice's face.

"Well, I'll be jiggered." Gently, she took it from the paper. "It's my ring. Where did you find this?" Her voice a whisper.

"In the attic. In a Mason jar my mother used for her...for her egg money."

"How strange." Clarice held the ring up to the light as tears slid down her wrinkled cheeks.

"Whitey gave me this ring when I lost the fifth baby." Clarice held her hand out to admire it. "S'pose he thought I should have something for all the trouble."

"Five babies?" A knot the size of a fist stuck in my chest at hearing that.

"Five. I told him that was the last time. Wasn't gonna put us through it no more."

"I'm sorry."

Clarice sniffed and dried her eyes with the sleeve of her sweater. "Sweetest thing he ever done for me. Can't thank you

229

enough. Never thought I'd see this again."

"I'm happy to return it," I said as Clarice struggled to slip the ring past her arthritic knuckles, but finally got it into place.

"Those old farts in the TV room are gonna think I'm the Queen of Sheba when I walk in there with this on my hand. Hell, might get a few a those fellas after me. Well, I'll just tell 'em 'get the hell away, got my Whitey with me now for real'." She held her hand out again and smiled proudly.

An idea came to me, from where, who knows.

"Clarice, how would you like to go for a ride one of these days?"

"You gonna spring me from this joint? Hot damn!" Clarice's rheumy eyes lit up. "I'd give my right arm to see the countryside once again. Maybe go to where the tavern used to be. The house in town I bought after Whitey died should still be there. I'd like to see the apple tree I planted in the back yard. This must be my lucky day."

"I will speak with the nurse. Maybe on Sunday. A drive in the country might do us both some good." I stood. "Now, don't you be talking dirty to those old men in the lounge."

Clarice's hearty laugh filled the room, and I felt a sense of peace settle over me that I hadn't felt in a long while. Here I was making Clarice's day, being generous with Ivy. Maybe there was hope for me yet.

CHAPTER 29

Esther

"Point the goddamn gun and shoot." Harlon shouted at Luddie. The boy brought the gun up to his shoulder and pointed at our beloved dog, Petey, as the dog stood on trembling legs in the clearing behind the barn. The dog pulled its head up and looked at us with pitiful eyes. He'd been suffering for far too long.

"I don't wanna." Luddie allowed the gun to drop from his shoulder.

"Whatd'ya mean you don't wanna?" Harlon roared. His face getting redder by the second. Ever since the wedding, when he saw me dancing with Robert, he'd been different, angry.

"Harlon." I stepped forward. "Luddie doesn't feel comfortable with this."

"He needs to learn to shoot a gun." He glared at me, daring me to object. His meaty hands in knots at his sides.

"This is our family pet. It's not like he's aiming at fresh venison. This is Petey, for goodness sake. He's older than Luddie."

I was grateful Helen was in town visiting a friend. The girl would have been beside herself at what was happening.

"The dog's dyin'. It has to be done, and the boy needs to be a man about it. The dog needs to be put out of his misery." Harlon gritted his teeth in that way I knew there would be hell to pay if I interferred too much.

"Harlon, this isn't the way. Not by Luddie's hand."

Petey's mangy form wavered, and then dropped to the ground where he lay panting. His droopy eyes begged for mercy. I knew there was no hope. I went to the dog and cupped his snout in my hand.

"There, there my buddy." I turned so Luddie would not see my tears. I lowered next to the dog's ear and whispered. "I love you Petey."

"For chrissake, Esther, you're makin' this worse than it has to be."

I stood with my back to them, wiped my tears and went to stand alongside my son.

"This is our pet and if Luddie doesn't want to shoot him, he doesn't have to. This is a horrible way for him to learn to shoot a gun. Even you must understand that."

Luddie glanced up, fear in his eyes.

Harlon took me by the arm and pulled me close. "You should be glad I don't treat the boy like Pa treated me. My old man woulda left me bleeding in the dirt for not doin' like I was told."

"And your pa would have been wrong to be so cruel," I stood my ground before him.

Harlon grabbed the gun from the boy's hands and Luddie flinched, his skinny shoulders up around his ears.

Harlon turned the gun to the dog in the field and pulled the trigger. In one swift motion, Petey was gone. Luddie ran to the dog and dropped to the ground. Our beloved friend was nothing more than a pile of fur blowing in the wind.

Tears poured down Luddie's face and he and I knelt beside the carcass in the dirt.

Harlon stood over us, a look of pure disdain upon his face. With both hands, he threw the gun. It landed with a thud at Luddie's side. "You whiney little snot. You'll never be a man. Nothin' but a mommie's boy." Harlon started to stomp away but stopped and turned. "Now you can bury him yourself. And you," he pointed at me and came forward, "you think I didn't see you makin' eyes at the new neighbor that night?"

There it was. This was his way of making me pay for dancing with Robert at the wedding.

I rose and stood before him, eyes steady, waiting.

Harlon gave me a shove. "He's lucky I didn't clean his clock for him. That skinny pansy ain't worth my time. One swipe of this," he released an uppercut that nearly connected with my chin, "and he'd be done for."

"It was just a dance between friends, Harlon. That's all." My tone was even, strong.

"Are you sure, Esther? I got my suspicions."

"What do you mean by that?" Fear skittered up my spine.

With that Harlon kicked the ground. "I don't like it. The newcomer needs to know his place. Somebody needs to teach him a lesson. And if I ever catch you talkin' to him again, it'll be the last time." With a snarl, he turned and stomped away.

The breath rushed from my lungs at his threat.

Luddie sat in the dirt staring at Petey.

"I'll get the shovel," I said.

***

233

The Witness Tree

Two weeks had passed since I had boldly asked Robert to dance at the wedding. I hadn't returned to the Redemption since. I knew Robert would be wondering, but the feelings I had for him frightened me. I hadn't counted on that and I didn't want to make a fool of myself.

The air was heavy, and the threat of rain hung overhead. I walked to the end of our drive and as I was taking the mail from the box, Robert stepped out of the trees.

"Robert." I promptly dropped the mail. Three envelopes scattered at my feet. "What are you doing here?"

"I've missed our visits at the river, Bess. Where have you been? I've worried."

"I'm just fine. Please," I put up a hand to stop him from coming forward, although my heart pleaded for him to continue. He didn't.

"Did Harlon learn of our meetings?"

"No, that's not it."

"Then what? Is someone ill?" Behind his glasses his brows knit together with concern.

"We can't continue to meet. I can't take the chance that Harlon will find out. You've become a wonderful friend, but it really can't continue."

"That's it, we're just friends." The space between us seemed a million miles now. How could he not see the effect he had on me? Friends?

"You know, Robert, that a husband would never view a friendship between his wife and another man as just that. He would never understand."

"Does this have something to do with the dance at the wedding? If it is, I am so sorry." He ran his hands over his hair. "He hasn't hurt you, has he?"

"No, no." I shook my head. "That's not it."

234

"You wouldn't tell me if he had, would you?"

He knew me better than I thought.

Then Robert came forward and I held my breath afraid he would touch me, but he bent to pick up the letters lying at my feet. He straightened, tall and kind, and held them out to me.

Harlon and his threats be damned.

I took the letters from him, purposely allowing our fingers to touch. My skin prickled with desire and my heart thrummed happily. I pulled in my lower lip and tried to swallow the knot in my throat.

"In all these weeks since we've begun our friendship, Robert, my life has seemed...kinder. Why do you suppose that is?"

"Maybe I'm your lucky charm." He grinned. The sun broke through above and dusted his cheekbones and the curve of his chin.

"I have no doubt." I breathed deeply of the late summer air. "The truth is, I don't know how I'm goin' to get through my days without our visits. Mid-afternoon comes and I'm lookin' out the window toward the woods. Knowin' you are waitin' and I am not there. I feel like a bird that's flown in through a broken window and can't find a way out."

He looked off toward the woods, as though searching for the proper response.

"Let's meet this Tuesday," I said with defiance. "Same time as always. Although, no more dances in public. That was a bit reckless of me."

"No more dances in public, then."

"Agreed." Anticipation spread through me like wildfire. "'Till Tuesday."

"Till then, Bess." He smiled, turned, and walked back into the cover of the trees.

CHAPTER 30

Helen

Desperation pushed me across the street as fast as I could go. This was it. Something was terribly wrong. I could barely breathe, my chest was tight, it felt like someone was sticking a knife in my back, I was sweating buckets, and had to fight like the dickens to stay upright.

I was dying and rather than welcome the grim reaper, as I always thought I would, I was scared stiff. Stiffer than stiff.

I leaned against Charlie's front door and banged. He didn't answer so I hit it again. What in the world was I going to do if he wasn't home? The last thing I wanted was to die in his front yard. The humiliation would kill me all over again.

A spasm hit me, forcing the air from my lungs, and nearly dropped me to my knees. Squiggly lines danced in front of my eyes. I balled up my fist and beat on the door as hard as I could.

The door finally opened, and Charlie stood on the other side, a half-eaten pear in his hand.

"Helen?" His eyes were wide with concern. He threw the pear into the spirea bush along the stoop. "My God, what's wrong?" He took me in his arms.

"Finally! I need to get to the hospital, and I don't think I can drive."

"You're sweating and shaking like a leaf. Come in and sit."

"Sit? Did you not hear me? I need to get to the hospital. I can't breathe. It took all I had to cross the street. I think I'm having a heart attack, maybe a stroke. My face feels numb. Look at me. Am I droopy?" I brought my hands up to my face.

"No." He swung his head from side to side as he studied me. "Can you stick out your tongue?"

"Stick out my tongue?" I shrieked. "What's wrong with you?"

"Helen, that's a sign of a stroke, if you can stick your tongue out straight. If you can, it's not a stroke." He took my hand and tried to pull me inside, but I resisted.

"Oh, for God's sake." I stuck my tongue out at him feeling like an absolute fool as he leaned back and judged the trajectory.

"Looks good. I'm calling an ambulance." He started to turn away, but I grabbed his arm.

"No! There's no time for that. Drive me." My whole body shook now, and I was dizzy with lack of oxygen.

"Helen, I..."

"I said no ambulance, Charlie. Goddamn it, I mean it."

"Fine. You sit on the steps and let me get my car out. You're a stubborn old hag, you know that?" He hurried around me and went straight for the garage. In seconds, he had the car idling alongside me, jumped out, helped me inside and buckled me in. After which, I doubled over in pain.

"Helen, don't make me sorry I didn't call an ambulance!" He backed out and squealed the tires as we hurtled down the street.

At First and Main he ran the red light and swore a blue streak when a blue minivan pulled in front of him. I gripped the edges of my seat.

"Faster, Charlie, faster."

"For chrissake, I can't go any faster. You should have let me call an ambulance. I can't believe I listened to you."

"I can't either." I barely squeaked out the words. If I didn't a decent breath shortly, I was going to faint. Charlie's tires whined as we rounded into Linden Street and Murphy Memorial Hospital came into view.

At the emergency entrance, Charlie pulled in too fast and screeched to a halt as an aide with a wheelchair veered off the sidewalk in fright. Good thing the chair was empty.

Charlie ran into the entrance leaving his door wide open and returned with a nurse and a wheelchair. I was roughly stuffed into the chair and Charlie ran alongside as she whisked me in.

"What happening?" My heart was beating wildly in my chest and try as I might, could not get in a full breath. The sterile smell of the hospital made me want to vomit. "I can't stand this." Panic filled me so I wanted to pass out.

"I'm sorry sir," The nurse addressed Charlie. "You'll have to wait out here."

"No, I want him to come in with me." I gripped the yellow blouse I had on to stem the pain in my chest.

"Is he family?" The nurse, who's name tag read Alice, didn't have the look of someone worth trying to bullshit.

"He's my...friend." I looked to Charlie with pleading.

Charlie took my hand and gripped tightly.

"I'm sorry, but he'll have to wait in the waiting room. Hospital policy."

The nurse pushed the doors to the ER open, followed by a receptionist with a clipboard, and Charlie was left on his own. I

238

was certain that was the last I'd see of him, and he of me.

Four hours later, many tests and a bill, I was sure, would eclipse the national debt, I was wheeled out, defeated, exhausted. Charlie was still waiting. He looked like he'd been through the wringer. In fact, he looked as though he'd wrung the last bit of strength he had from his body as he nervously waited. He jumped from his seat and quickly came to my side.

"I'm fine. All this damn hoopla only to be told its stress. Stress! The doctor ordered some test for next week and a prescription for a pill for anxiety. I don't like this one bit. Where's my purse?"

"Thank, God. Helen, I haven't prayed this hard in a long time." He took my hand again. "I have your purse in the car."

"The doctor says I'm not dying yet. I don't know if I should hope she knows what she's talking about or not. At this age, who knows? Could be any minute now."

The nurse chuckled. "Mrs. Foley, the prescription has been called into the pharmacy. You should start taking it today." She patted my shoulder. Normally, I would have corrected her. I'd never been a Mrs. and never would be. "You're going to be just fine. You need to follow the doctor's orders to take it easy. I have some brochures on stress reduction for you along with some deep breathing exercises and stretches to help if you feel an anxiety attack coming on."

"Anxiety, my ass!" This was embarrassing and it all played out in front of Charlie.

"Helen be nice to the young lady. Please?" Charlie was grinning from ear to ear. "I'll make sure she follows orders."

"Good luck," Alice said.

"I can take it from here," Charlie said.

"Oh no, I have to take her out to the car. Hospital policy."

"Oh, for pities sake, I can certainly get into a car on my own." I started to get up, but Charlie put a hand on my shoulder.

"Helen, don't make me get crabby with you." Charlie gave me a mock frown. "Don't be so cantankerous. You're much prettier when you smile."

"Oh! Fine." I had to look away to hide the smile pushing my wrinkled cheeks apart.

Charlie spent the rest of the day at my house making tea and heating up chicken soup. He made me put my feet up and draped an afghan over my legs. Together we watched a movie on the television and later I beat the pants off him in cribbage. Well, not literally.

I'd never been fussed over this much ever in my entire life. And it wasn't half bad.

He offered to stay the night in the spare room, but I wouldn't have any of it. As he left for his side of the street, he kissed my forehead. He'd caught me off-guard with that. I gave a start and he chuckled as he went out the front door, closing it tightly behind him.

I waited a full thirty seconds before I pushed the drapes aside just enough to watch Charlie cross the street. Maybe, just maybe, it wouldn't be so bad if history repeated itself just a tad.

CHAPTER 31

Esther

Robert closed the book he had been reading aloud and set it on his long legs, his bare feet stretched out before him from rolled up dungarees. I grinned at him from over the quilt block I pieced together as the Redemption flowed lazily by. It had been an absolutely perfect afternoon.

"I like that poem. What is it called again?" My fingers deftly moved the needle in and out of the cotton fabric.

"Written in March by William Wordsworth." He took his glasses off and cleaned them with a handkerchief. I had never seen him without his glasses. I liked what I saw.

"Those words describe how I feel when I come to the river," I said, "*The rain, of my life, is over and gone*. Silly, isn't it?" Our eyes met briefly.

"Absolutely not." Robert set his book aside, scooted over to my side of the blanket. "What are you working on?" He angled his head over my busy hands.

"I'm experimentin' with a new design. It's a baby quilt. A gift for Minnie Hannigan's daughter." His face was so close to mine. I wondered what it would be like to lean in, just a bit, and kiss him.

"You have a wonderful eye for color. May I see it?" Robert slipped a hand under the material of sunflower yellow and pea green. Never once had Harlon been interested in anything I created.

Without thinking, I did it. I leaned forward and kissed his cheek, lingering a moment to take in the leathery scent of him, to feel the smoothness of his skin against my lips. It was an action that surprised him as much as me for even though I'd kissed his cheek once as he walked me out of the woods, this seemed more intimate somehow.

He pulled back, eyes wide.

"You must know, Robert," I touched his arm, "how I feel about you."

"If circumstances were different, Bess..." He stared at the ground.

"I don't care anymore." I pushed my handiwork aside, folded my legs beneath me and knelt before him. "You are the man I thought I would find someday. Not Harlon." I touched the side of his face. "Is friendship all you feel for me?"

He closed his eyes. "No, in all honesty, it's not. Not anymore."

"Are you ashamed of what you feel for me? I will never be ashamed of what I feel for you."

"Bess, we aren't in a place in our lives where we can give in to those feelings. You and I have been over that. And frankly, putting my feelings aside, this is against all I stood for in the past."

"Now you're concerned about your past. Your past is gone,

242

Robert. That past was ripped from you in the blink of an eye. You didn't deserve that any more than I deserve Harlon."

"The past is with me in every breath I take." He pushed away from me. "I can't do this."

"Then what have we been doin' here? Playin' house? Are you pretendin' I'm Polly?"

"Of course not!"

"We come here and slip into this easy way we have with each other. Why do I have to sneak away with another man to have that? To have happiness? I want that life, Robert. I want you."

"Bess, I…"

I cut him off with a clumsy kiss, my lips on his, my hands on his knees. He didn't resist, but he didn't gather me in his arms as I'd hoped. After a moment, I pulled away. Had I dreadfully misjudged the situation? We were nose to nose.

"I have very deep feelings for you, Bess."

"Then show me." Harlon and propriety be damned.

Robert slipped an arm around me and pulled me to him, kissing me as a woman should be kissed, deep, passionate, and loving.

Hunger raged within me as fierce as any storm and I pulled him tight against me.

"Bess, oh Bess," he whispered. "I haven't kissed another woman since..."

"Kiss me again." My entire body trembled with anticipation. If I could have pulled him into my very body, I would have.

The taste of lemonade lingered on his lips. To me it was the sweetest of summer wine, and I was thirsty with a need that wouldn't stop. I needed to drink of him until there was no more, until I was filled and complete.

"I've wanted to do that for so long." His voice had a desperate tone. "Bess, I wake in the morning and my first thought is of you. My greatest desire is for what we have just done." He bent his head

243

and continued. "I have built my whole life around the principles of honor, integrity, goodness, love and … and God. Yes, I have turned from serving God, but those ideals are ingrained in me. How can I reconcile what I feel for you with the values I hold?"

"Not too long ago you begged me to run off with you."

"That was to save you from your husband. We never went as far as professing our feelings for one another."

I cupped his face in my hands and searched his eyes. "You cannot turn away from me now. I love you, Robert." I gulped back a sob. "If I could walk away from Harlon I would, but the consequences are too great. All we have is now. Can't we at least have that?"

His voice was barely a whisper. "God help me, I've fallen in love with you as well."

With those words, he sent my heart soaring. I laughed and looked to the sky above as a flock of sparrows lifted heavenward.

His lips brushed the base of my throat.

"You make me feel as light and free as those birds." I laughed again—a musical sound that danced off the trees and skittered over the rushing waters. A sound bubbling free from my body that I hadn't heard in a very long time.

He put his gentle hands on either side of my face. "I need you in my life, but the future frightens me."

"Then let's not dwell on things we can't change," I pleaded.

"I worry for your safety, Bess." His hands rest on my arms. "

"Harlon would never allow us a life here. And he most certainly wouldn't allow me the children." Reality slapped hard. "And I can't live without them."

"Then we'll take the children and go somewhere he could never find us. California or Canada. I don't care."

"The depth of Harlon's rage has no bounds." I fought for control.

"We'll find some little town or get lost in a big city." Such hope I saw on his face.

"Stop it, Robert!" Tears dripped onto my dress. I pressed my forehead against his. "The time may come when circumstances change, but until then, let's enjoy today. Make this our special place and our special time. Promise me."

He sighed and nodded in agreement. We sat, forehead to forehead, a while before I whispered, "Love me, Robert."

"Are you sure?"

I nodded and in the shadow of the rotting basswood, Robert pulled me into him. Together, mouth to mouth, body to body, we melted onto the blanket beneath us.

***

I nestled in the crook of Robert's arm, the blanket covering the bumpy earth beneath. I tried to smooth my rumpled slip. Robert, clad only in his boxers, kissed the top of my head. The sun edged closer to the western sky and a cooling breeze released the heat from our bodies.

"When soul meets soul on lover's lips." Robert wove his fingers with mine and kissed the back of my hand. "That's Percy Bysche Shelley."

"Hmm." I could not remember feeling so satisfied, so complete. So loved. "When soul meets soul."

"Have you read the Book of Esther in the Bible?" Robert asked.

"There's a Book of Esther?"

"A queen of great beauty that summons the courage to save the Jews. You are my Queen Esther." He pecked my cheek. "Good Queen Bess."

"You'll have to lend me one of your Bibles so I can read about her."

The Witness Tree

The Redemption continued to slip past and leaves rustled overhead. The sun created a lacy pattern on the ground. A busy chipmunk skittered from tree to tree.

My gaze settled on the rotted remains of the Witness Tree jutting from the earth. Laughter bubbled from me as as I looked upon it. Of all that the things it has witnessed over the years, I'd lay money on it never having witnessed what it had this afternoon.

"What's so funny?"

"That," I pointed, "is a sorry monument to the place we professed our love, don't you think?"

Robert chuckled. "You're right. But we can fix that." He grabbed his pants and rummaged in the pockets.

"What are you doing?" I lay back.

"I always wanted to do this." With a pocketknife in his hand, he went to the trunk of the tree and began to carve.

I brought a crooked arm up under my head, giggling.

Robert stopped his carving and asked, "What's so amusing?"

"You cut quite the picture in your skivvys there Mr. Sommers."

He chuckled, then returned to his project. "There, now this old piece of wood has become a proper monument to us and us alone."

Robert had carved a perfect heart with 'R-n-B' in the middle.

"Do you like it?" he asked.

"I love it." Tears filled my eyes.

"What's wrong?" He rushed to my side.

I tasted the tears on my lips. "No man has ever wanted to carve my initials in a tree before. A silly thing to cry over, I know, but it means so much." I touched his cheek. "You mean so much to me. I couldn't bear to lose you."

"Oh, Bess," he wrapped his arms around me and held me tight, "you'll never lose me. I promise."

A nudge deep inside told me that fate had other plans.

CHAPTER 32

Helen

It was a cool day, and I pulled a sweater tight about my bony shoulders as I crossed the barnyard. I may be sorry for this trek back to the Redemption, to where the Witness Tree once stood, but confronting the awful truth was the only way I knew to rid myself of the weight of it all, keeping me awake at night, blinding my thoughts every minute of the day. I had to shed this albatross and come to grips with the truth that had come back to me, bit by bit, every day.

The doctor said I'd had a panic attack, that I had to deal with the stress in my life. Normally I would have told her to file that bunch of hooey where the sun doesn't shine, but deep down, I knew it was true.

Dr. Peters gave me something to calm me down in the emergency room, but most importantly, she held my hand and we talked long and hard about life. Drained from the certainty that

247

death was finally banging on my door, I let the words flow. I told her about the remains and the farm, my worries for Ivy, the return of Charlie, and my frustrations with nearly every part of daily life. And I learned something, I was lonely and had been for most of my life. Then she asked about the past and that was where I felt the walls rise again, and I knew she could tell. I told her some, about the fear we all bore when my father was at home, how his disappearance affected our lives, about the stresses of managing a business and a farm on my own, about being an unexpected parent. But I most pointedly did not mention that awful night. That was something I needed to deal with on my own.

But in the days since, I came to realize the good doctor was right when she said I needed to make peace with my life, reconcile those things that robbed me of going about my day with a measure of happiness. And honestly, I had to admit, I wasn't ready to open that door when death finally did come for me.

Charlie continued to call every day, but I rebuffed his invitations to lunch or for coffee, to a movie or a ride in the country. I was grateful for his help that day, but my life at the moment was in flux. I knew sooner or later I had to begin to confront the past, but where to begin?

The first step came to me as I was eating a liver sausage sandwich for lunch one day. My father loved liver sausage. It was just a flash of an idea, but it felt, in my heart, the right thing to do. I needed to go back to the river.

After the okay from Carrie and Joe, I parked by the barn and walked across the field. Joe had offered to accompany me, but this was something I needed to do alone.

Upon reaching the edge of the field, I looked back toward the house that sat on the rise, the barn off to the right, the paddock where a pony fed, the garden plot already tilled for spring. This was my home for the bulk of my life. I knew it well, yet I didn't know it at all. The unknown lay down the path through the woods.

I shoved aside the offensive yellow crime scene tape and followed the uneven path, broken here and there by exposed roots, fallen branches, and blanketed with autumn leaves. I was mindful to watch my step. It would be damn inconvenient to twist or break an ankle way back here.

Soon, I reached the place where the landscape sloped down to meet the Redemption and my heart nearly stopped beating as I stood there staring, afraid see where the tree had been.

The river carried on as it always had, pooling to the east, sluicing through a set of rapids to the west before meeting the Flambeau River and eventually making its way to the upper Mississippi, the rocky shores still graced with conifers and birch, maple and balsam. This place, so beautiful it could make the heart ache, was also a graveyard.

I touched a hand to my chest as my eyes took it all in. It seemed time had suddenly ceased, and the place was eerily silent. No birds, no rustle of leaves, no burble of water.

It was time to address the reason for my visit and I set my eyes upon the indentation in the earth.

What lay before me was nothing more than the grotesque remains of the trunk, an upended stump with roots clawing deep, gnarly fingers into the earth where it found purchase, and where it didn't, the roots looked like fingers clawing out of a grave.

The Witness Tree was no more. It would no longer see what we humans brought upon this land, upon this family. When I thought of all it had seen—Luddie and I swimming in the river, my mother enjoying time alone, her liasons with Mr. Sommers, and the final hiding place of my father's body.

I heard, rather than felt, the sob escape me and I covered my mouth. Tears began and I feared they'd never stop. The salty stream of them raced down my face and neck, catching in the weave of my gray sweater. These were tears that needed to be shed, memories that needed confronting. I understood this and welcomed the unburdening.

Where the log once lay, I knelt to the ground and put my hands on the flat blades of grass. The bones of my father once lay here. There was no doubt in my mind that it was him. Then I looked up to the wooly sky overhead. This is where they put him. This is where he'd spent the past seventy-two years. Rotting, decaying. Did he deserve that? He was not an upstanding fellow, he was brutal and cruel. But did he deserve this?

He was a human being. There had to be underlying reasons for such unhappiness, such cruelty.

This was my Daddy after all. I had loved him at one time. I had crawled into his lap and felt safe, until he changed, and I no longer sought the security of him. I had wished with all my might that he would stop the drinking and end the anguish he brought my mother and brother. I wanted us to be a happy family. Why didn't he love us enough to be happy?

I reached into the grass and pulled out some with each hand and put it to my face. I wanted to feel him, smell him, something.

After a time, I went to the boulder by the river, plopped my butt against it, feeling the stony cold on my behind, and looked around at this place, his final place, until now, of course. His bones were being carefully removed from the trunk in some lab. They would be cleaned and catalogued and tested for DNA.

Would this have been his end, had I not done what I had? Would he have had to answer to the Pukalls for the pain he caused their daughter? Would he have had to pay for the hurt he caused Clarice, or the trouble he caused at the mill, or the people he owed money? It was hard to know what might have been. For me, I didn't feel absolved just yet. I had more work to do.

CHAPTER 33

Esther

Mother Nature had been kind to the farmers this year. As a result, the time came to harvest a second crop of hay. I struggled to guide the fork loaded with hay to be hauled up to the mow and stored for winter feed.

"Get the lead out, Esther. I can't do this alone," Harlon barked from his seat on the tractor.

"I'm doing the best I can." But I knew that was a lie. Late August heat bore down ferociously upon us. Perspiration ran down my back and through my hair, drained the last ounce of energy and left me dizzy with it. Every chance I had, I sought relief inside the barn and the cool of the cement floor.

The sky above refused to offer any clouds to break the torture. I wiped my forehead with the backside of a glove. The golden mass of hay before me beckoned with the promise of a soft place to collapse, if only I could.

I pulled myself up into the wagon, filled the pitchfork and pushed the hay forward. Suddenly the barnyard spun, and my knees buckled. I braced one hand against the wooden rail and sunk to the floor of the wagon.

"Christ, what the hell's the matter?" Harlon bellowed.

I pulled myself up and sat on the hay. Let Harlon rant and rave, I simply couldn't do it. "I think its heat stroke." I put my head in my hands. The air was heavy with the scent of newly cut hay baking in the heat. My stomach lurched with the pungent aroma.

I covered my mouth and glanced over to see Harlon jumping from the tractor and coming toward me.

"Harlon, I don't know...I'm feelin' a little woozy. It has to be the heat." I fanned my face with my gloves.

"It ain't that hot. Get yourself to the house." He flung an arm in the air. "Send Henny out."

"She's too young to handle this." I wanted to add that he'd gathered the crop too soon. As a result, the hay was heavier than normal. It was no use explaining his miscalculation, as he'd never admit it. It was too late now anyway.

"It's time Henny learned. Go on, get her out here." Harlon was making a point—the point being that if I could not work, Helen would pay the price. Although he would never work Helen as hard.

"Pa," Luddie called from the mow, "can I get a drink of water?"

"Might as well. You're about as much help as your mother today," Harlon said.

To me he added, "Get yourself a drink. I gotta check the hitch on this piece a shit." He indicated the tractor and stomped off toward the garage.

I went to the pump and worked the handle until water ran cool on the ground.

"Must be a scorcher in the mow." I handed Luddie a cup and

252

watched as he drank.

He finished gulping. "You sick, Ma?"

I took the cup and filled it for myself. "Just the heat." I drank deeply, feeling the coolness spread through me. "This hits the spot."

"Don't you pay attention to what your father says, you've been a big help today." I touched his hair, a little darker than the hue of the hay. "Your Pa doesn't know how to show it."

Luddie shrugged, clearly not buying it.

"Son-of-a-bitch!" Harlon screamed from the tractor.

Luddie and I whirled around to see Harlon, wrench in one hand, the other covering his forehead.

"What's wrong?" I asked.

"Wrench slipped. What does it look like?" He threw the wrench into the side of the barn where it banged with a hollow slap and clattered to the ground.

"Are you all right?" I gulped and moved toward him.

"Does it look like I'm all right?" A purple bump was beginning to pop just above his brow.

"A cool compress will help." I took the kerchief from around my hair and turned toward the pump.

Harlon shoved me out of the way. I spun and nearly lost my footing. He grabbed the pump handle and brought it down against the shaft with a mighty clang until water gushed forth. First, he stuck his dirty hands underneath and then his whole head, sending water spraying.

The farm began to spin, and I dropped to my knees in the dirt. With a hand, I steadied myself and looked to see if Harlon noticed. He had.

"What's the matter with you?" He straightened and chased the water from his head. "We don't got time for you to be sick. Feels like rain'll be comin' tomorrow."

253

I opened my mouth to respond, but nausea hit me in a sickening wave. I closed my eyes and concentrated on breathing. Unsteadily, I rose to my feet and clutched my stomach.

"I…I just need a moment inside." My head swam, the blood in my veins pulsed in my ears. As I neared Luddie I gave him a reassuring smile. "I'll be right back."

"You sure you're okay?" Luddie asked.

I nodded and focused on making it to the back door without vomiting. Once there, I changed my mind. Rounding the corner of the house, I knelt in the grass next to a spent peonie and wretched.

A sparrow landed under a wild rose bush.

"Shoo!" I whispered, then wiped my mouth with the kerchief, dabbed at the sweat on my chest, and leaned back against the house. The truth could no longer be denied.

I was pregnant.

I was pregnant with Robert's child.

At that moment, I wished the ground would open and swallow me whole. Harlon would kill me if he realized the secret growing within me.

For the first time in my life, I wished I knew how to pray. For if there was a God, divine intervention would be my only salvation.

I sat there, hands covering my belly, eyes closed.

"Esther!" Harlon hollered from the barnyard.

The sparrow 'seep, seeped' and flew off. Had I loaded my troubles upon it's wings, the poor thing would have done a swift nose-dive to the earth.

Willing my stomach to still, I pushed to my feet. For as long as I could, I would keep this to myself. Not even Robert could know, for if he did, he would never give me the time I needed to plan an easy solution. He would demand I leave Harlon and, of course, I would, but I had to be smart about it. It was the only way to keep us all safe. And by the time I could no longer hide the pregnancy, a plan would come to me. It had to.

CHAPTER 34

Helen

A pounding on the back door startled me at nearly eight thirty at night. I was knitting a winter scarf in shades of purple for Maudie's birthday in November. Who in the world would bother me so late?

I set aside my work, and wrapped in a robe and slippers, went to the door.

Ivy's face was illuminated in the porch light.

"What in the world?" I opened the door and saw Maudie and Evan waiting behind their mother looking sleepy and a bit unsettled. "It's nearly nine o'clock."

"Helen, is the offer of a place to stay still open?" Ivy's face was pale and hard as steel.

I pushed the door open wide for the three of them to enter. The children had clearly been sleeping in the car. They each carried a backpack and a pillow.

"It's late, but of course, you can stay as long as you like." I put a hand under Maudie's chin. The girl's blue eyes raised up to me. "You're growing up, girl. Won't be long and you'll be as tall as your mother." I admired Maudie's shoulder length chestnut hair. "I miss those long braids of yours, but this cut is fine."

Turning to Evan I put a hand on his ginger cap of hair. "And you're still cute as a button. Got a girlfriend yet?"

Evan grinned up at me. "I'm only eight."

"You both take your things into the bedroom and I'll get you a glass of milk and some of the oatmeal cookies I baked yesterday." I watched them pass through the kitchen and dining room, then turned to Ivy.

It was then I noticed the purple bruise along her jaw. Putting a hand under Ivy's chin I asked, "What's this?"

"Just what it looks like." Ivy pursed her lips and closed her brown eyes, clearly trying to keep her emotions in check.

"That useless..."

"He looks worse." Ivy had that same steely look again. It was with this certain set of her jaw, the determination in her eyes, that Ivy didn't resemble her mother one bit. The girl had a backbone as tough as nails.

I looked her in the eye. "Does he now?" Violence was a piss-poor way to solve anything but backing down wasn't worth snot either.

"I'm not taking his shit one more minute." Ivy put her overnight bag on the dining room table. Anger and frustration clearly coursed through her body like electricity.

"Has this happened before?" Had I been so blind not to see it all these years? Images of the past swirled before me. Was history repeating itself? Not if I could help it.

"Not the physical stuff until recently. We had one hell of a fight tonight and he hit me. I punched him back so hard he fell down the basement stairs." Ivy took a seat on the step stool in the corner of the kitchen. She was pretending to be cool, but the tremor in her jaw told the tale. "You should have seen him lying there in his boxers. That's all he had on."

Just then, Maudie and Evan came in to ask for that snack.

Grateful for the momentary interruption, I set the kids up with their milk and cookies in the living room and tuned the television to some kids show.

Back in the kitchen I said, "Violence is no way to solve anything."

Ivy took a cookie out of the jar and bit off a corner. "I know, but it sure felt good."

"Did they witness any of this?" I looked to make sure the kids had not overheard.

"No, they think I walked into the car door." She sat back down on the stool. "They have no idea what happened between Brad and I other than another argument. They think this is an impromptu trip to visit you. It's a long time coming, you know that. I can't be in this marriage any longer. I won't."

"I'm surprised he ran around on you. That would require some ambition." I picked off some fuzz on my pink nightgown. "How did you find out?"

"The husband called me. Brad admitted it. He was actually grinning about it. He wanted to be caught. That's when I let him have it. Now I feel like I can finally move on with no regrets. I gave it all I had and now I can be free to live as I see fit, without the weight of him hanging over me." She grew pensive for a moment. "He'll always be in my life because of the kids, and I hope we can get along for their sake. But I've learned never to count on him for anything."

I pulled a chair into the kitchen and sat, looking down at my old hands clasp in my lap. "I wish my mother would have had the opportunity to live her life. To have all she deserved and more." I wiped at a drippy eye. "Oh, I think she was happy to be free, but it was a hard life."

"You've never shared anything with me about your childhood. I'm sure it was hard for a woman, a widow, back then. Having to grieve her husband and at the same time figure out how she was going to feed her kids."

I was startled by how little I'd allowed Ivy to know. The girl didn't have a clue.

"Times have changed." Ivy dusted cookie crumbs from her hands and came to me, kneeling before me. "We'll be fine, Helen. I know it won't be a piece of cake, but I want life on my terms. I'm going to start over here, in Peeksville. That's if we can stay with you for a short period of time until I find a house and a job. Next week I'll enroll the kids in school."

"What about the house in Amery?"

"I had already called a realtor, but Brad needs to agree. I don't see that as a problem as he's going to need the money as much as I."

This was so much to absorb. Ivy and the kids here, in Peeksville.

"Then you're certain this is the best course. Moving here, I mean? What about custody and visitation and all that?"

Ivy bit her lower lip, then said, "He never was all that interested in being a parent, but I thought that would change especially as the kids got older. It hasn't. Although he says he loves them, he's never shown it. My beautiful babies deserve more."

"He's a damn fool. Does he know you're here?"

"No. He was so angry with me after the fight, he threw on some clothes and went to his brother's house. I'm sure they're sitting around a fire in the back yard, knocking down beer after beer and

259

complaining about the old ball and chain. He has no clue we're gone yet." Ivy stood and with hands on her hips looked to make sure the kids were engaged in the television. "Once he finds out we're gone, oh, there will be hell to pay. Maybe he'll calm down after a bit and we can discuss this rationally, but until then..."

"What if he comes here looking? What are you going to do?" Panic skittered up my spine. This was all too familiar territory. It brought me right back to hiding in the barn from my own father, only to finally spend a night at the river.

"It will be a lot of yelling and false accusations, but I refuse to be afraid of him."

"I think you're being foolish. If he could abuse you this way once, he'll do it again. Maybe worse." I wrung my hands together to stem my fear and gain control. Memories of the past hung heavy before me.

"I can handle him."

"No, you can't!" I grabbed her by the arm. "Don't you see how this could escalate?"

"Helen," Ivy covered my hand with her own, "don't worry. I won't let anything more happen. Please, trust me on this. Brad likes to throw his tantrums when he's drunk, but it's nothing more than that."

"He struck you!"

"That's the only time. I promise. I can handle him."

I covered my face with my long, weathered hands, took a deep breath, pushed the hair back from my face and nodded. These were words I'd heard my mother say.

"So," Ivy sat before me, "are you sure it's okay that we're here?"

"Of course." This was all the family I had in the world. I could never be that much of a shrew to send them away in their time of need.

"Hey, don't worry."

"Of course, I will."

"By the way, can you teach my kids to cook?" Ivy grinned at me. I knew she was trying to lighten the mood. "You know I'm not much for that and actually, Maudie's really good in the kitchen."

"Damn straight, I can." I smiled, but I had a bad feeling about Ivy and her situation. This would not be so easy. Something more was going to happen before all was said and done. I could feel it.

Still, never had I expected to have family close to me ever again. Ivy and her children were moving back. We would all be together for birthdays and holidays, I'd see Maudie's artwork in school and Evan in Little League. My life had taken a dramatic turn by simply opening my door.

Outside the wind chimes sang sweetly against the night wind.

CHAPTER 35

Esther

I waited for Robert by the Witness Tree that bore our initials. It was not lost on me that this tree, or what was left of it, witnessed the extraordinary love between Robert and myself, the miracle of the baby within me, and now, the heartbreak I must bring upon him.

I'd worn my best everyday dress of blue and swept my hair up the way he liked it, leaving a few wavy tendrils free along my neck. The press of heavy gray clouds mirrored the weight of the secret I bore. Robert could not know of this child just yet. If Harlon knew I was carrying another man's child, we would never have the life I dreamed we could have. All I needed was time, and the hope that Harlon would accept that the child was his.

Once the baby was born safe and sound, I would tell Robert and we could gather the children one day while Harlon was out and be gone. We would take the train to Seattle by Ruby and Eldon, buy a house and have our little family. Harlon would have no idea where to begin to look and I was certain Hattie and Vee would keep the secret safe. There was no reason Robert and I couldn't pretend that we were a married couple and half the country away, who would be the wiser? Maybe, from a distance, I could get that divorce.

I was willing to chance it for the sake of the little one growing within me.

The forest was damp, and the oppressive moisture seeped into into my bones. I went to the basswood that bore our initials and waited for him. I closed my eyes and lay my forehead against Robert's rough carving of our initials in the wood of the topless tree trunk. What bark remained smelled earthy, musty.

I would need every ounce of strength I could garner today.

Suddenly I felt his presence and turned.

There he was, standing amid the mist, the man I loved with all my heart, the man that offered all I craved in this life, dressed in brown pants and suspenders over his white shirt, just like I'd seen him that first time.

"I've missed you." I went to him, wrapped my arms around his middle and held on tight. His arms went about me, warm and secure.

I buried my face in his shoulder and in my memory traced the feel of his flesh and bones against me, the scent of him, the whisper of his breath in my hair, the gentle brush of his lips.

"What is it? What has he done?" Robert asked, his lips touching my ear, his embrace tightening.

I simply shook my head and held on.

"Bess?"

I stepped away from him and his questioning eyes, turned to face the river, running my hands up and down my upper arms as much to calm my nerves as to stem the chill of this day.

263

"What's wrong, Bess?"

"I have somethin' to say." I faced him, covered my mouth as I thought how to proceed, then pushed away the hair blowing over my face.

Tiny raindrops dotted Robert's white shirt.

Pulling my sweater tighter about me, I began. "We need to stop this, Robert." The words spilled from me more forcibly than I'd planned.

"The sky is going to open up on us before long. We need to find shelter under one of these trees." He reached for my hand.

"No, I...you're not hearin' me."

"Let's head for that maple over there." He tipped his chin to indicate a tree a few yards away.

"Robert! No. I don't care about the rain." My voice cracked with emotion. The weight of what I needed him to understand was a massive boulder upon my chest, crushing every ounce of the life I'd come to cherish.

"What's wrong, Bess?" Rain dotted his glasses.

"We can't see each other anymore." There, I'd said it. He had to believe it was over, for how would I explain that after the long months ahead we could be together again? That after the baby was born, we could resume our relationship. That once I safely delivered his child, we could take all the children and run away together?

If he knew the truth, Robert would never stay away for the remainder of the pregnancy, never allow me to be pregnant and living in Harlon's house. I firmly believed that if Harlon found out I was carrying Robert's child, he would kill all three of us. I couldn't trust that he wouldn't, and I wanted this baby with everything in me. As long as Harlon knew I was pregnant, he would take care not to inflict physical harm. Once I delivered the baby, I would tell Robert the truth and we could spirit ourselves away. To do it now would only be taking a risk I wasn't willing to take.

"Has something changed?" His face was pinched. "You're scaring me."

How could I convey the magnitude of the situation to him? That I was carrying his child, yet he could not be a part of this child's life until I was certain it was safe. He'd already lost one child. He would move heaven and earth to have the chance to love another. That's why he couldn't know. Not yet.

"I've come to my senses, is all. This is too dangerous. Too many people would be hurt should we be caught."

"You mean at the hands of your husband if he finds out? We've always known that was a risk we were willing to face."

"It's become more clearly apparent that Harlon would ruin us all and take my children." Harlon would beat me to an inch of my life if he knew the child was Robert's.

"We wouldn't let that happen. We'd disappear into the landscape. Bess, isn't it worth a try?"

"Just as I was denied my divorce, I'd be denied my children. We've been over this. There's only one solution and it's to stop this now, you and I, before anyone gets hurt." There was still the chance Harlon would take Luddie and Helen from me, but if we could steal away and blend into an out-of-the way corner of America, we'd be okay. If we went far enough, I didn't think he'd look too long. Keep breathing. Stay strong.

"What's changed?" he asked, his face reddening, eyes narrowing upon me.

"Nothing." I struggled to keep the plains of my face calm.

"It darned sure has. Is he hurting you or threatening you?" He stepped forward, but I stopped him.

"The threat has always been there, I chose to ignore it. Now I can't." As soon as those words left my mouth, I was sorry.

"Now? What does that mean?"

"It's just a word, that's all. I …I…this has been bothering me for a while. You know my husband. He would never stand for us to make a life together here or anywhere. And Luddie and Helen. I have to think of them first." I silently added this new little life to the list.

"Trust me. Please?"

"I love you, Bess." Before I could stop him again, he wrapped me in his arms and held tight.

Emotion bubbled up from deep within me. I buried my face in his shirt and wept. This was more difficult than I'd thought. I wasn't as strong as I needed to be. Shaking my head, I pushed away. Somehow, I had to find the strength.

"Listen to me," rain pelted my face as I curved my fingers into the fabric of his shirt, "this needs to stop. We can't meet anymore."

"Don't you see? This love of ours is a gift from God." Tears glistened in his eyes. "We can't simply toss it aside for any amount time. There has to be a way. It was meant to be. I believe that."

"I believe that too. It's been very precious to me, you know that, but it's time to call it a day. For now."

Robert looked at me as though I were speaking a foreign language.

"Don't do this to us." His voice was low in his throat.

"It's just for a time."

Robert ran a hand over his hair, his chin trembling. "This is crazy. We need to get you out of that house."

"My goodness, Robert. You're making too much of this. I know my life there. I know what triggers his anger. I can handle him."

"Judging from the way I found you here, sitting on this very rock, after he beat you because you wanted a divorce, I would say no. You can't handle him at all." His face creased in pain, and anger.

The Witness Tree

Robert sat on the boulder and put his head in his hands. "Please don't do this, Bess. I beg of you. I need to know you're safe."

I went to him, knelt in the very bed of ferns where we professed our love the first time. The breeze picked up around us and the forest came to life.

"This is what's best, Robert." I took his hands.

"How can I lay my head down at night without knowing you're safe? At least with the arrangement we've had, I could give you happiness and love. I couldn't protect my Polly and now I can't do anything for you as well." The thin line of his mouth turned down at the corners and his eyes watered.

The choke of grief held me in a steely grip. I had to stay strong.

"If his temper gets the best of him, I'll send one of the children up the road to fetch you. I promise."

"It's not enough. Oh, Lord, it's not enough." His gentle face grew from sadness to panic.

The rain began in earnest and pelted us as we knelt before the ragged basswood with our initials carved inside of a heart. I released his hands and stood.

Robert stood as well and reached for me. I held up a hand to stop him.

"Please, Robert, this is what I ask of you. I have to go." I backed away from him.

"No, Bess. There must be a way." Robert's tears mixed with the rain. "I need assurance. There has to be a way. I can't simply let you go." He swung his gaze one way and then another as if an answer to this horrible situation would appear. "I know. Let's write to each other."

"How? We could never send them by mail."

Robert searched, then his eyes brightened. "This old, sorry excuse for a tree. The Witness Tree. How perfect."

"What?" Was he crazy?

"See here." He bent and put his hand at the base of the trunk and the hollow opening there. "We can exchange letters here. Every few days we could leave a message."

I studied the hollow. How could I deny him this one small favor? "This might work. Once the snow flies, it will be too difficult to make it back here. What then?"

"I don't know. We'll cross that path when we get to it."

I had to admit that letters from Robert would provide a lifeline in the difficult months ahead. My resolve was crumbling just a tad and it worried me something fierce.

"We'll do it, for now," I agreed, feeling ashamed that I'd not been stronger.

"Oh Bess, I will take whatever I can get of you. Just maybe I can change that stubborn mind of yours. We'll check the tree every few days. And I will change your mind. I promise you."

I opened my mouth to speak but could not. My heart was breaking and the knot in my throat was making it difficult to breathe. My face was wet, and I wasn't sure the measure of tears to rain.

As I turned for home, the baby inside me fluttered for the very first time, like a rose petal fighting against the breeze.

CHAPTER 36

Helen

Ivy and the children were sleeping soundly, but I couldn't. I was still in shock that Ivy had come to me for help, that she'd brought the children here, that my little house was full of family. At last.

Clad in the pink flannel nightgown and in bare feet, my white hair hanging about my shoulders, I went to the thermostat and bumped it up a degree. The nights were bringing with them a whisper of winter lately. On the way back I stopped in the moon-washed kitchen and looked out toward the gardens bathed in silvery light. A ghostly shroud descended upon the yard spreading sparkles upon the grass and the leaves. A light frost was upon them.

Turning from the window. I knew I wouldn't sleep this night.

269

The situation with Ivy brought back too much of the past. And after I had visited the site of the discovery at the river, I needed to continue to keep the past in the present until I could make peace and put it away for good.

The letters.

The box of my mother's letters called to me from the shelf in the closet. I pulled it from the shelf taking care not to make noise, switched on a lamp, and sat back on the bed. In the buttery glow of the lamp, I gingerly lifted the lid.

The novel, *How Green was my Valley*, lay snuggled inside. The book fit perfectly as though the box was custom made for it. With a finger I wedged the old book from the box. The smell of musty paper and age filled the room. Several sheets of paper, inconsistent with the pages of the book, lay tucked inside.

The binding cracked as I opened it.

Yellowing and brittle, I slipped the first sheet from between the pages.

My dearest Bess,

I am writing this in hopes that you will return to our Witness Tree, to where we confessed our love for one another. It has only been one day since you ended our time together, but I feel I have been separated from you for days. I thank God for the brief time we had together. Yes, you heard right. I thank God. In these past, painful years, I have pushed faith from my life. It has returned, and you are to thank for that. Especially now. I need guidance in all this. I want you to have faith in the future and I want us to have faith that our lives will work out in the end.

Do you miss me as I miss you, my beautiful Bess? It seems as I sit here at my table listening to the sparrows outside my window, it is your voice I hear. Your face I see. How will I survive without you? The completeness I had hoped to discover in moving to

The Witness Tree

Peeksville has found a home within my love for you.

Bess, you know I worry for your safety and that of your children. I wish you would allow me to take us all away. We could have a wonderful life. I would love your children as my own. Please, my darling, reconsider your decision.
Yours eternally,
Robert

My heart ached at Robert's words. How all our lives would have been different had our mother allowed him to steal us away in the night, to create a new life in a new town. Never had I considered my mother's decisions as wrong, but I had to wonder. What if?

Would we have had a little house in another city with a picket fence around the yard, a more plentiful life and not simply of things, but of affection and familial happiness? Would our father have allowed us that happiness in the house of another man?

I set the first letter aside and took out the second.

My Lovely Bess,

I am overjoyed that you found my letter and I cherish your reply. I would like very much for our communication to continue. I need to know that you are all right. It would be a glorious day to meet as we hide our letters in the tree. The birds would sing, and the sun chase all the clouds away. I know I am being silly, but I would be so happy.

I think often of the first day I saw you at the river. Redemption River. A fitting name don't you think? You had gone for a swim and stood there barefoot, your hair in wet waves around your face afresh from the cool water, a light cotton dress with pink flowers. The sun that day shown down upon your features and you looked like an angel from heaven.

271

The Witness Tree

That picture of you sustains me.

Bess, it breaks my heart not to be there for you. If Harlon lays one finger on you or the children, I am only one cornfield away.

Please assure me, dear Bess, that you will contact me if you need help.
Forever,
Robert

How humiliating that their situation was so desperately felt by Robert, yet our mother would not allow him to help. Was it pride? What else could it be? Did Mama care the effect her pride had on her children? I bristled at that. Or was it simply fear that our father would do something horrible? I strained to remember what I'd seen as a child. What I'd heard.

I closed my eyes. I could still remember the fear of those nights when he came home in the wee hours, the house smelling of beer, his bumbling in the dark, furniture shifting, his boots clomping on the stairs, the sounds of anger and slurring words from my parents' bedroom. The occasional sound of the slap of a hand against skin.

I opened my eyes to the next letter.

I had long ago recovered from the shock that our mother'd had an affair. That Annabelle had a different father. Auntie Vee told me the truth after Mama's death. It explained the far-off gaze, sometimes pained, always wistful, expression whenever Mama looked at Annabelle with her auburn hair and brown eyes. The intense closeness between the two was hard to watch at times. I felt abandoned by Mama during those growing up years. Was it punishment for the havoc my actions caused that night? I never did understand Mama's sudden interest in church for Annabelle, but there was so much I never really knew.

Annabelle never knew. What would she have thought of it all?

I could never blame Mama for seeking the love of another man

272

when her own husband clearly did not have any love to give. Yet, anger was brewing within me. Anger for what had been and what could have been.

Mama's secrets. The weight of it all must have been so difficult yet for me, so maddening.

I unfolded the third letter and noticed a thumbprint, dark and smudged, in one corner. Had it always been there?

I placed my thumb over what I assumed was Mama's print, but it was too large. This was Robert's. A feeling went through me I can't describe. As though he and I were reaching through history, a tether from one moment in time to the next.

The poor man had no idea he had a daughter on the way.

My darling girl,

As I sit on my porch and watch the full moon kiss the world around me, I want to be kissing you. I wonder if you are at your window seeing the same moon as I and feeling the same. In my mind you are with me, under the spell of the silvery light.

Do you think of me as I you? I would gander our Witness Ttree is lonely without us. I want to see you.
Forever Yours,
Robert

I thought back to when Charlie and I were in the throes of new love, every waking hour consumed in yearning for the other—the touch of his skin, the smell of his hair, the way his mouth lifted on one side when he smiled.

I couldn't imagine being so desperately in love and the only expression for that love being limited to words on paper.

How I missed those two young people that were Charlie and I.

I refolded the letter, closed the book.

CHAPTER 37

Esther

It was October the eighteenth. Outside the parlor window, I watched as the wind swung from the north and with it, pulled a blanket of woolly gray across the sky. Barely a leaf hung on the trees because of the raw wind and unrelenting rain of the past week. Even though the rain had subsided for now, the ground was saturated and spongy. Redemption River rose to record levels with the over-abundance, already washing out a few roads. The Sheriff's department kept a watchful eye on the bridge over Dead Man's Slough as it struggled to hold its own against the force of the river.

Because of this damn weather, it had been days since I had exchanged letters with Robert. I worried what we'd do it if the waters permanently swallowed the ground around the basswood. It was nearly at flood level as it was.

I had to find a way. His letters were all that kept me sane.

Moving from the window, I curled into my rocking chair and concentrated on finishing a quilted runner for my mother's birthday. Helen lay on the sofa with her reader from school and Luddie on the floor, drumming to Ernest Tubb on the radio singing *Walkin' the Floor over You*. A warm glow filled the room from the stove in the corner where I'd built a small fire.

A thump against the window startled us all. Helen set her book aside, ran to the window and pressed her little nose tight against the glass creating a sphere of fog.

"A birdie hit the window," she said as Luddie joined her at the glass.

"It's a sparrow," he said angling his head over hers. "Prob'ly just stunned itself."

"Should we go get it?" The way Helen scrunched her face in concern made me want to gather those cheeks in my hands and kiss them until they were rosy.

"Luddie may be right. Just wait a bit. Sparrows are tougher than they look. We'll check on it again in a few minutes." I returned to my stitching. The pink and yellow flowered runner was turning out nicely. Rose rarely gushed over gifts, but I was certain she'd like this, even if she didn't let on.

Luddie turned up the radio and took his seat on the floor.

"It's okay! The sparrow flew away!" Helen clapped her hands, her face wreathed in delight.

I grinned. These calm, cozy evenings when Harlon was out, would never be taken for granted.

Not long after, dusk gave way to darkness and from far off, a storm rumbled. As my needle went in and out of the pretty pink fabric, I thought of Robert. *Is he thinking of me?*

Headlights cut through the lace curtains covering the long

275

windows of the parlor. The familiar pall of disappointment settled on us as we waited. If he had drunk his supper at the tavern, this was early for him to be home. I heard the tinny slam of the truck door and set the runner aside.

In minutes Harlon banged through the back door unkempt and unsteady with a vicious look in his eye. The stench of beer and cigarettes spewed from every pore of him. His green work shirt was open halfway down his chest and his brown pants were stained with grease and dirt.

I quickly stood. "I'll get you some supper."

"I don't want any goddamn supper. Goddamn woman!" Harlon's mouth twisted, his black eyes glowing hot with anger. I had seen this too many times. It never ended well.

My hands at once settled over the slight mound of my belly. From the corner of my eye, I saw Luddie brace against the sofa. Helen went to the stairs and crouched behind the wooden banister. Her small fingers curved around the rungs.

"Harlon, what's wrong?"

Harlon grabbed my wrist. "You want to know what's wrong?" His voice ricocheted off the walls. "You want to goddamn know what's wrong?" The air was thick with the warning of worse to come.

"Stop it." I said as calmly as I could and placed my hand over his.

With a shove he sent me back against the over-stuffed rocking chair. I landed in the softness of the cushions, my head jerked backwards.

Harlon went toward Luddie. The boy cringed into the gold cushions of the sofa.

"You little coward. You ain't never gonna learn to be a man." He turned at the sound of the radio. "This all you got to do all damn day?" He lifted his booted foot and kicked the radio from the short table where it sat. It flew into the wall with a crash.

"Harlon!" I braced.

"There. That takes care of that foolishness." He faked a punch in Luddie's direction. The boy had tears in his eyes just waiting to spill.

"Luddie, take Helen upstairs." I tried to convey calm, but I knew the children understood the graveness of the situation.

"You stay right where you are, boy." He rounded on me. "I work my ass off all day, and I come home to you all lollygaggin' around that damn radio. There's work to be done goddammit." Spit flew from his mouth. "You all need to earn your keep!"

Helen scuttled up the stairs.

My eyes moved from Harlon, and, with a slight tip of my head, motioned for Luddie to move upstairs. He obeyed quietly and quickly.

"Harlon, it's getting' dark outside. We've got our work done for the day. You need some supper in you. I have a roast with potatoes and gravy waitin'." I moved toward the kitchen, but Harlon's thick fingers wound into my hair and held me in place. I put my hands to my hair. "I'll have somethin' for you in just a few minutes."

He pulled me back and with his mouth next to my ear and said, "You think a little food will fix what's wrong here? Huh? Do ya?"

"Whatever's wrong, we can fix it. Can't we? We always do."

Harlon shoved me into the wall. I caught herself with my hands.

"I lost my job today. Supper's the least of my worries."

"How could they do that to you? Why, you've been with them for nearly two years now." I tried with all that was within me to show concern. How many jobs would he have to lose before no one in the area would hire him?

He took a step toward me, sweat beaded on his brow, hands balled into fists. "Ain't that just great? Some cockamamie story about my drinkin' on the job. They say I caused Ned Ryberg to

277

lose two of his fingers in the saw. Ain't one bit a truth to it. Not one bit." He stabbed a finger at me and grit his teeth.

Lightning flashed, sending a single strobe of white through the house.

I knew in my heart the accusation was true. "Is Ned all right?"

"You're worried about that wimpy bastard? It was just two fingers, not like he cut off an arm." Harlon's bloodshot eyes narrowed on me like a target. "You don't believe me. A good wife would be more upset."

I swallowed hard. "I am upset, Harlon." I touched his arm and steadied my voice. "I'm tryin' to be calm for you. There're other jobs out there. You could call Willis Bleimel tomorrow? I hear he's just lost one of his sawyers and they're startin' a job out on Hay Creek."

Harlon threw my arm off and leaned in toward me. "That'd be the day I'd work for a cheapskate like him." He stepped back and ran his thick fingers through his hair. "I need a break. Maybe I'll farm for a while."

I crossed my arms in front of me, pressing them to my body to stem the anger churning within. Being dragged through life by Harlon was more than I could take. How would I get through my days with Harlon watching my every move?

"You said yourself the tractor isn't going to make it much longer and we don't have the money to buy another. Milk prices have dropped, and this year's corn crop was shoddy at best. Farming isn't going to get us very far if it's the only source of income we have."

The look in his eyes was feral. I'd made a terrible mistake.

"All you care about is sittin' around here all day with your goddamn quiltin'." He went to the chair and picked up the runner. "I'll show you what I think of that."

"Harlon, that's a gift for my mother's birthday. Put it down."

He grinned as he held it in his fist.

"Happy Birthday, Rose." He opened the door to the wood stove and shoved it in. The small fire puffed then lit the fabric. Harlon slammed the door.

I turned away from the stove, my hands curled into fists, eyes closed. How much longer could I do this?

"Time you stopped with all that nonsense that don't mean a thing." His mouth twisted with satisfaction at his cruelty.

"Mister Nelson offered me a job in his store. I'm going to take it." I pushed my chin in the air in defiance.

"A man doesn't send his wife out to work." He came at me again. "A man works to feed his own. You tryin' to tell me I ain't done a good enough job?" Red rimmed his small eyes and spit gathered in the corners of his mouth.

"What do want from me, Harlon? You want me to work, but only here. What is it that's not done? What is it that makes you so angry with us?"

He simply glared, searching for an answer.

I turned my back to him and went to the kitchen.

"I would never say you don't take care of us." I answered him with the emotionless composure I'd practiced for years as I set about slicing the beef. The knife handle fit so neatly into my hand. Like they were one and the same. How easy would it be to turn around and thrust one quick jab to his middle? That's all it would take.

"You're lyin' to me!" He kicked a cupboard door and it cracked with the impact.

The sound of small feet caused both of us to turn.

Helen stood before us, a pair of scissors in her hand and a look of pure steel upon her face.

"I hate drinking!" She held the scissors high and with her other hand, brought a braid forward.

279

I switched hands with the knife.

Harlon looked down on his daughter, hands on his hips.

"What do ya think you're doin' there, Henny?"

"I said I would cut off my braids if you got drunk again." She brought the scissors nearer the flaxen braid.

"You wouldn't do that. You know how your daddy likes them braids."

Helen looked him straight in the eye and in one swift movement, snipped the braid in half.

"Helen!" I gasped and dropped the knife to the floor as the girl held the remnant in her hand while the shorn locks fell to her shoulder. This daughter of mine had more courage than all of Peeksville combined.

But then Harlon leaned over her like a giant thunderstorm.

"You shouldn't a done that, little girl. Now you're gonna look like your brother."

"I don't care." The girl was old beyond her years. She took the other and cut it with one quick snip.

I could see the storm building within him. Helen's plan backfired. I knew that as clearly as I felt the baby kicking again.

"So, you've turned on me too." Harlon's nostrils flared. The scissors in Helen's hand began to quiver. The girl pulled in her chin, her eyes glassy with fear, her courage fleeing. "Get yourself upstairs. I don't want to look at you." When the girl failed to move, he barked, "Go!"

She turned, braids in hand, and fled as I bent for the knife.

"The hell." He whirled on me with a fist held in the air. His face was just inches from mine. "You're raisin' a brat, there. You're nothin' but a stinkin' burden to me, Esther. You always have been. If you coulda kept yourself from getting' pregnant all them years ago, I wouldn't be in this mess."

"I didn't do it alone." My voice was quiet for fear Luddie just

280

heard what his father said. Deep within me, anger spread like wildfire, leaping, singeing, burning.

"Now you're blamin' me. You wanted it. You know it. Every time I turned around, there you were." Harlon shoved me against the ice box. "I wouldn't a had to marry you if Rose hadn't a gone to my Pa. You ruined my life, Esther." One hand loosely curled around my throat. His thumb stroked along my windpipe and panic seized me.

My hand closed in tighter around the handle of the knife. I didn't want to use it, but...

"Harlon stop it. Calm down and eat your supper. You need some food in you."

Just as thunder cracked outside, his fist smashed into the wall next to my head. I flinched and only thought of the baby growing inside me, and the two hiding upstairs. What would become of them if I went to prison?

Harlon gripped me by the bodice of my dress and tossed me about the narrow kitchen. I had to drop the knife and grab his forearms to keep from falling, my fingernails digging into his flesh. "Stop it right now!" I smacked the wall just inches from a window and sank to the floor.

He came at me, drew back a foot, aiming for my middle.

I held out a hand. "Harlon, STOP! THE BABY!"

CHAPTER 38

Helen

In the depths of my slumber, I heard the ring of the cell. Prying my eyes open, I looked at the clock on the nightstand. Twelve forty-five in the morning.

There was a rush of feet, then a hushed voice. Ivy's.

I rolled over, my body wanting more sleep, but intuition told me something wasn't right.

Just then, Ivy came quietly into my room and knelt beside the bed.

"Helen," she whispered and touched my arm.

I stretched. "I'm awake."

"He's coming. Brad's on his way here." Ivy's long hair hung in loose waves around her pretty face. Night shadows highlighted her cheekbones. Her eyes were glassy as though she'd been crying.

"How do you know? Was that him on the phone?" I sat up, pushed my feet over the side of the mattress and slipped on my tattered old moccasins. Standing, I pulled on the robe at the end of my bed.

Ivy went to the bedroom door searching for any sign of him.

"It was Justine on the phone. He just left her apartment." Ivy moved into the darkened living room with me right behind her. "He's really drunk."

"We need to call the authorities." I went to the phone in the kitchen.

"No, Helen, I don't want to do that."

"For heaven's sake, why not? What's wrong with you?" I gestured toward the back bedroom. "You've got children here. You don't know what he's going to do."

"I don't think it's necessary." Ivy ran a shaking hand through her hair. "That will only add fuel to the fire. And what if the kids wake up? That will only scare them."

"I don't give a crap. He's drunk."

Just then, the back door flew open with the impact of a boot. Brad stood, dark and menacing, filling the doorway.

He stomped through the kitchen. His eyes narrowed on Ivy.

"You're not ruining my life this way. I don't want a divorce. You can't take my kids." He advanced on her. "I loved you Ivy. You know that. You ruined it by being such a bitch."

"That's enough." I had seen that look before and moved between them.

"Calm down, you'll wake the kids," Ivy put a hand on his arm and with her free hand pushed me out of the way.

"They need to hear that their mom is planning to rip their daddy from their lives. If you think you're getting child support, you can kiss my ass. That's not happening. I'll make sure I never work again."

"Afraid you'll lose your meal ticket? That's all I am to you."

At that, Brad pulled back his fist, but Ivy ducked and spilled backwards onto the dining room table. I quickly went to secure the door to the bedroom where the children slept, but they were sitting on the bed wide awake and all I saw were Luddie and I so long ago. Two frightened children not knowing what would become of their world next.

I slipped inside the room. "Everything will be fine. You two lay back down." At first, neither moved. Then I nudged them back down and pulled the covers up. "Just go to sleep. Your parents are having a disagreement, but it will be over soon, and all will be fine."

Maudie looked up at me, serious as a judge. "Everyone always says that. It will be fine. But it never is. I wish people wouldn't say that."

That did it. Something had to be done. Someone had to stop this from escalating. I was not going to allow these children to go through any more pain. I tucked them in and slid out the door.

Brad was trying to wrest the phone from Ivy's hand and nearly had her on the ground.

I slipped past him and ran to the back porch where I found the garden pitchfork leaning against the wall next to the back door.

CHAPTER 39

Esther

For a moment time slowed, then Harlon's foot found the floor and I let out a ragged breath. The rage on his face washed away into disbelief.

"Baby?" His shoulders slumped, his face slack.

Swallowing hard, I leaned against the wall, knees to my chest and waited for whatever would come next.

"What baby? You're pregnant? Again?" He shook his head, his body released.

I placed my hands on my belly and looked up at him. "I was going to tell you after supper tonight." My mouth was so dry and I was cold to my bones.

"How the hell did you let that happen?" He pulled out a chair from the dining set and took a seat, forehead resting in his hands.

"I'm due in the spring."

"The last thing I need is another mouth to feed." The room was silent but for the tick, tick of the clock on the credenza. "We ain't got no money. I ain't got a job. This can't happen."

"Harlon, it's a baby. It might be another little girl, just like Helen, or a little boy we could name after your brother Leo. You lost him so young, this would be a way to keep his memory alive," I said quite proud of my quick thinking.

"No, no," he said, shaking his head. Then his eyes narrowed on me. "We ain't been..."

My heart picked up speed and pulsed in my ears. I had to distract him.

"We'll work it out. If it's a girl, we could name her after your mama. Evelyn. What a pretty name. Think of it, Harlon. This is the good news among the bad." I cautiously eased myself up along the wall, praying for strength.

"No, Esther, we ain't been together in a long time. How'd this happen?" His thick brows came together. The silence between us was deafening.

"Harlon, please. We shouldn't discuss this. The children are right upstairs." I reached out with a shaking hand and touched his forearm.

Harlon looked down at my hand on his arm. I was certain he would welcome the news. He pushed my hand away, stood, hands on hips, and kicked the chair.

"Don't you tell me what to say in my own home." His voice was frigteningly quiet. "I ain't slept with you in months. You ain't even got a bump yet. You messin' around on me, woman?"

Terror raced through me as I stood before him. "That's insulting. I did no such thing." I kept my eyes on him in a hard stare. "I would never. But look," I placed my hands on my abdoman, "see? It's just starting to show."

He was studying me, his eyes unreadable. "I ain't been sleepin'

286

with you, Esther. I know it."

"Yes, you have." I lowered my voice. "Don't you remember? It wasn't all that long ago. You were drunk after a night at Whitey's. It was the night you were all celebrating Ray Hertlen's new little boy and he was passing out cigars. And now, soon, it will be your turn."

He was speechless for a moment. I had a fierce need for fresh air but didn't dare walk away now. I watched for any small sign that I was getting through to him,

Harlon moved closer, backed me up against the wall, and placed his hands on either side of my head. "I know I ain't been with you because I..."

"Because you've been chasing after Martha Pukall?" Immediately I knew that was a stupid thing to say, but it had been biting at me ever since the sheriff had been at our door and just maybe I could shame him into being reasonable. "I know all about that. I hear the gossip in this town."

"You believe everything you hear?"

"It's all over town, Harlon." I was breathing hard and fast. "Do you honestly think I haven't heard of the things you've done? But that's the past. This baby gives us another chance. Think of it."

My ruse wasn't working. I could see it in his eyes. His anger was building again. His breathing was deeper, nostrils flaring.

"I might a been a better husband if you'd been a better wife. But that baby there," he flicked my stomach with his fingers, "ain't mine." He put his hand over the tiny rise in my stomach and roughly kneaded. "Maybe this baby is his." He leaned in and nipped my ear lobe with his teeth. Into my ear he whispered. "Mr. Sommers your boyfriend, Esther? I seen the way you looked at him at the weddin'. I ain't stupid. You're accusin' me, but you...you're no different."

"Harlon don't be silly. Where would I find the time?" A violent tremor crawled through me.

"I seen you about a month ago comin' home through the field. You was smilin' and singin' as you went. I thought I saw someone back in the trees watchin' you go, but the sun was in my eyes."

"That's ridiculous. I would never do such a thing." I was shaking with fear.

"I watched you after that. Noticed you been findin' more reasons to sneak away to the river. You're dressin' up better and wearin' your hair up. You been a lot happier. And now this." He placed his hand over the seed growing within me and his fingers dug into me. "I thought there was somethin' goin' on with you. And I thought to myself, 'do I care?' Mostly I don't, but you ain't gonna make a fool outta me. I don't want this baby and he ain't getting' it either."

"Oh, dear God, Harlon. Don't talk that way." I could barely get the words out. "I've been happy about the baby and waitin' to find the best time to tell you."

"Bullshit! You ain't makin' a fool a me." His rage returned full-blown. He slapped me hard and I went sprawling against the sofa.

Pain exploded in my jaw and right ear. I shielded my belly as I landed on the floor. Harlon reached for me, but I pushed away, slapping and kicking as he tried to pull me to my feet. My fingernails connected with his face and blood beaded down his cheek.

"This is your last night on this Earth, Esther, and you got nobody to blame but yourself." He came at me, his hands reached for my throat.

Thunder boomed, shaking the house, followed by a deafening bang.

Harlon stopped, his eyes bulged, then glazed over, he opened his mouth, but no words came out. He fell to the floor as loose-jointed as a rag doll, landing face down, arms and legs out to the sides.

At first, I didn't understand. What happened? Then I saw the red mark on his back that sprouted fingers and spread across his shirt.

I looked beyond the lifeless body of my husband on the floor.

Luddie lowered the gun to his side. Blue haze hung in the air between us.

"Luddie!" I screamed and clutched at my throat. "Oh, sweet boy, what have you done?"

I stepped over Harlon, having to cover my mouth not to vomit, gathered my son in my arms and held tight. "Oh, sweet boy." I kissed his forehead and rocked him in my arms. His arms remained at his sides. He didn't seem to know I was there.

I released him and gathered his face in my hands. "You saved me, Luddie. You saved us all." I kissed him again. The boy stared off into the distance.

I looked up. Helen cowered behind the rails of the banister. She was shaking, her shorn locks on her shoulders in a jagged line. I motioned for her to come.

I clutched my children to my chest and tried to shield them from the horrific sight of their father.

Luddie then sank to the floor next to the gun.

I kissed the top of Helen's head.

"What are we going to do?" I asked of no one. I shifted my gaze to Harlon. Blood pooled at the site of the bullet hole and onto the floor. "We need to get help." I couldn't call the authorities. What would they do to my son? No one can know what happened here this night.

Still holding Helen, I turned to Luddie.

"You did the right thing, Luddie. You did." The room was so warm.

Rain pinged the windows.

I brought a fist to my forehead. What to do, what to do? I eased

Helen from my lap and stood, staring down at the body of what was once my husband. I quickly grabbed an afghan and covered him.

I needed Robert. Besides my sisters, he was the only other person I could trust. Hattie and Vee were too far away, but Robert was right up the hill.

"I need to go for help," I told Luddie and Helen. I pulled Luddie to his feet. "Luddie, look at me. I want you to take Helen upstairs and stay there until I return. Do you understand?" Luddie nodded. I guided them to the stairs and watched them go up. "I'll be back in a few minutes. Don't come back down until I say it's all right."

I grabbed a jacket from the hook by the back door, ran out into the rain and into Harlon's truck. It was there, that the reality of the situation hit full force. I gripped the wheel and screamed, a deep, guttural sound so consuming I didn't know from where it had come. The sky rumbled above me.

There was no time for pity, I had to act, and act quickly. I fired the truck to life, backed up, and drove down the drive as rain lashed the windshield. In less than a minute I was in Robert's yard and on his porch.

Robert met me at the door.

"Bess, what in the world? Come out of the rain." Winifred was at his side.

"There's no time. We need help. You need to come with me." I grabbed his arm, but he resisted and panic set in.

"Please, Robert, Luddie has killed Harlon and I don't know what to do." I wiped the wet from my face.

It took a moment for Robert to recover, he then pushed Winifred back into the porch and followed me to the truck without another word.

As he drove us, I explained what happened, leaving out any mention of the baby. That was a discussion for another time.

The Witness Tree

We ran for the house as a crack of lightning lit the yard.

"We're back," I called as we ran into the house, and the children came slowly down the stairs, Helen holding Luddie's hand, their eyes careful not to look upon their father. "Mr. Sommers is going to help us. No one can find out about this, and no one will if none of us breathes a word. Do you understand? Helen?"

Luddie nodded as did Helen.

"I mean it, you can't tell a soul. Not Grandma, not the Aunties or the Uncles and certainly not any of your friends. This needs to stay between us." What a thing to expect of your children.

Then I turned to see Robert, his back against the wall, sliding toward the floor. He crouched there, shaking, his face a sickly gray.

"Robert," I bent over him.

"I... I can't do this. He's dead." His eyes were wide with fright. This was not a time for cowardice.

"He was going kill me. Luddie saved us. Now we need to protect Luddie. I'm counting on you to help me. I can't do this alone."

Robert pulled in his chin and shook his head. He opened his mouth to speak, but nothing came out.

I put my hands on his shoulders and shook him hard. "Robert! I don't have time for you to be afraid or sick or whatever you're feelin'. We need to act." I shook him again. "Do you hear me?"

He nodded and took a deep breath. "Okay, okay. What do we do?"

I looked to the children. Helen clung to Luddie at the foot of the stairs. I turned back to Robert and said, "We need to hide his body."

"My God, Bess, that's illegal. I'm sure the justice system would go easy on a boy protecting his mother."

"I refuse to take that chance."

"Where in the world would we hide a body that won't be found?"

I put a palm to my forehead. "I don't know." In my brain I raced looking for anyplace to tuck a body. The barn, the outhouse, the well, a grave out back.

Robert took my arm. "We could take him to the river. It wouldn't be that hard to think he'd driven in there with the storm we're having."

"He's got a bullet hole in him. No, that wouldn't work." Then it came to me. "What about...yes...the tree."

"What tree?"

"The Witness Tree. Robert, it's perfect."

"Yes, but..." Robert said.

"It's a big tree trunk. A big, hollow trunk."

"It's got to be eight feet high. How would we get him in there?" Robert held his palms out. His hands trembled.

"If we use Harlon's pickup, we could drive in through your land, and reach the top of the stump using the bed of the truck."

"I don't know, Bess."

"It would work, Robert. I'm sure of it." My voice was sharp with urgency. "We can run his truck into the river then. Anyone who knows him will never question that it was a drunken accident. What other alternative is there?"

"I can help," Luddie said standing at the foot of the stairs. Robert and I turned to face the boy. He'd suddenly gained a maturity about him I'd never seen. Helen came to me and wrapped her arms around my middle. I gave her a squeeze and kept a hand on the top of her head.

"Sure you're up to this, son?" I asked.

Luddie nodded. "I can do it, Ma."

"Well, let's go." I went to Harlon's head and looked down upon him. His features, what I could see, were slack in death, the one

292

eye, cloudy and unseeing. Perhaps there should be some kind words spoken, a few tears shed, but there wasn't time and the emotion simply wasn't there.

I bent over him, sliding my hands under his shoulders. His body, still warm, was limp as a wet rag.

Robert stepped forward. "Let me take him there. Luddie, we'll turn him over and you grab him from between his knees."

The two of them turned Harlon and carried him through the war zone that had been the parlor. A trail of red smeared across the floor. I followed with an arm around Helen and a hand shielding her eyes.

Outside the storm raged as though it had found second wind.

Robert stopped as he backed out the door and raised his gaze to me. There was something in the depths of Robert's eyes that cut right through me. There was going to be more, but how? Then he backed out the door with my dead husband in his hands.

"Be careful," I called after them, but my voice was lost in the maelstrom of wind and rain. As the truck left the yard, I closed the door.

Harlon would not be able to hurt us any longer.

And yet … I was afraid. There was something more to come. I could feel it.

I went to the sofa and rocked back and forth, hands pressed over my mouth. Helen put a hand on my back, patting with her small fingers to offer comfort.

Together we stared at the bloodstain on the living room floor.

"I can clean it up, Mama."

I turned tear-filled eyes to my daughter. "Oh, no, sweetheart."

"It's okay," Helen said and patted my shoulder again.

Boom, boom, boom! We both jumped at the sound. Someone was at the back door.

I leaped off the sofa. Helen ran to the window.

"There's a car in the yard," Helen said.

"Oh, my word." I rushed to the window, unable to see beyond the glare of headlights and rain.

"Stay calm," I said, trying to sound reassuring.

The gun. I slid it under the sofa with my foot. Then there was the matter of the stain on the floor. I quickly threw a rug over the top.

Boom, boom, boom.

"Don't say a word, Helen."

I opened the door a crack. Helen stood close behind me, one hand clutching my skirt. Clarence Pukall was on the porch, rain dripping off his hat, his face twisted with rage.

"What do you want, Clarence?" With my body, I secured my hold on the door.

"I want that old man a yours. He and I got some business to discuss," Clarence growled.

"He's not here. He didn't come home." The shrillness of my voice alarmed me. I had to calm down.

"How do I know you ain't coverin' for 'im?" He pushed at the door with his shoulder.

"You see his truck? He's not here." I tightened my grip on the doorknob and leaned into it. "What's going on? What did he do?"

"It's my Martha." He stepped back from the door and pulled a hand over his face, rain dripped down his face like a thousand tears. "He was in Whitey's tonight shootin' off his mouth about my girl."

I eased my grip on the door. "He's not here. I wouldn't lie to you, Clarence. Try Cocky's Bar. He might be there."

"That son-of-a-bitch is gonna pay this time." Clarence pointed a finger. "He's gonna pay!" He kicked the side of the house before running back to his car. His tires spun in the mud as he raced from the yard.

I collapsed against the door. Fear and exhaustion wrapped around me like a vise making it hard to breathe. Helen put her arms around my neck. We stayed like that for a moment or two.

I removed her arms, took a bar of soap from the cupboard, and filled a bucket of water. With an old rag I wiped at the blood, scrubbing in the lines in the floor. Helen sat on the bottom step clutching her knees.

"Is Daddy dead?"

I stopped what I was doing and sat back on my ankles. "Yes, deary, he is."

"But I don't want him to be dead." Her lower lip bulged forward, and her eyes squeezed shut. Tiny tears trickled down her cheeks.

All I could do was go to her and hold her tight.

Twenty minutes later, Luddie showed up at the back door soaking wet and muddy. Helen was on the sofa, arms tight around her favorite blanket.

"Luddie, did you get...did you...?"

Luddie pursed his lips and nodded. "It was awful hard, but we did."

I looked beyond him to the black of the night. "Where's Mr. Sommers?"

"He took Pa's truck to the river. He dropped me off on the road. Said he'd be back in a while." His gaze went to the floor of the parlor.

"It's all better now," I said. "Everything is cleaned up. Everything is fine. We can never speak of this again. We just can't. Not to anyone. You understand?"

Luddie nodded determinedly. He seemed taller somehow.

"Let's get you up to bed. Why don't we all sleep together in our, my bed tonight?" I touched Luddie's arm and cupped Helen's chin.

Both children nodded and I ushered them upstairs. Together we cuddled, me between my two children. Helen fell asleep first, but Luddie took some time.

I eased my body from between them, wrapped in a blanket and went downstairs. The storm abated and the world outside was all cried out. Nothing left but a slight breeze coaxing the rain from the leaves of the trees in big, heavy blobs.

The baby fluttered in my belly.

Where was Robert?

***

The *Peeksville Herald* carried the story the following week regarding the bizarre set of events that took place the night of the big storm. Lightning struck a barn by Cedar Springs and burned to the ground killing a fair portion of the cattle inside. Flooding carried away the new flower boxes in Triangle Park and tore up many a culvert. And the hundred-year-old maple by First Congregational Church fell victim to the wind, now cut and stacked on Pastor John's woodpile.

Of course, those storm stories paled in comparison to the two tragedies that stunned the community.

Long-time resident Harlon Foley went missing. His truck was found under the bridge at Dead Man's Slough. Mr. Foley lost his job that day and it was not clear whether the accident was intentional or not. As yet, the body has not been recovered. The way the Redemption River was gushing, authorities worried Mr. Foley's body is somewhere deep in the flowage by now.

Despite the outpouring of support, Mrs. Foley is nearly out of her mind with grief.

In a strange coincidence, newcomer Robert Sommers, a neighbor of the Foley's, was struck and killed by Clarence Pukall as Clarence was cresting Jankowski's Hill north of Sommers' property. Mr. Pukall didn't see Mr. Sommers in the blinding rain. Sheriff Bergey deduced Sommers was out in the storm trying to find his dog, which was standing over her owner as authorities arrived.

CHAPTER 40

Helen

Ivy and her friend Justine took the kids for a hike up north along Lake Superior and I used the time to set my life straight. For the first time in forever, I felt a measure of peace and knew that the past could now stay right where it was. I'd sat Ivy down and told her the truth, about the Foley family, my father's battle with the bottle, his abuse, and about Ivy's true grandfather, Robert Sommers. Together we read the letters Robert wrote and spoke of the horror of the night that changed everything.

Ivy was miffed she hadn't known the truth sooner, she pointed out, this was her DNA and that of her children. I understood and apologized for that, for everything. The girl was grateful to know it all and, in the end, I came away feeling we were closer than we had ever been.

There was one more piece of business. There was one more

person to tell.

I invited Reed Bolton to stop by. It was his day off, but he had some time in the afternoon.

"I have to hand it to you, Helen," Reed said as he took a seat at the bistro set in the garden dressed in jeans, a denim jacket, and a white button-down shirt. His blond hair was neatly combed back with a bit of a stubble on his chin. "You saved Ivy and her kids. You're a hero."

"Oh, go on with you." I waved away his compliment. "I did what had to be done." I pulled my green canvas jacket tighter about my shoulders.

"Ivy had quite the black eye. I hope she's all right."

"She is. She's a toughie, that girl."

"Good thing you had that pitchfork handy. Who knows what would have happened?"

"A couple of holes in Brad's backside did him some good, I think, along with the night in jail." I put a hand to my mouth briefly as I remembered Brad shrieking in terror as I pricked his fleshy backside, then held the pitchfork at the ready as Ivy called 911. "Good thing he was up to date on his tetanus shot. Although, you'd think a butt would bleed more than that."

The two of us burst into laughter.

"The important thing is, he agreed to leave Ivy be. He went back to Amery and moved in with his brother. He's getting help with the drink and has a new job. Ivy is hopeful they can parent together in peace."

"I got the impression you wanted to talk about the farm. About the bones." Reed's face was full of compassion and kindness, and it was time. The riot of color that were my zinnias leaned forward to hear. It took me a moment to find the words.

"I started something I couldn't stop." I tasted bitterness as the words left my mouth. Never before had I said that aloud. Not to our mother, not to Auntie Hat or Auntie Vee. And not to Luddie, but my brother knew.

And he paid the price trying to keep it all inside.

"I don't understand," said Reed. I told him the whole sad story of my family that night, taking my time to let it all out.

It was time to lay it bare. Time to rid myself of the demons of the past and let the shattered pieces lay where they may.

"What could you have done? You were so young."

"That night I was consumed with fear. He was going to kill our mother. I was sure of it. I scrambled up the stairs and down the hall to my parent's bedroom. I was desperate. I knew my mother kept a shotgun under their bed." I covered my forehead with a hand as the scene played out before me. I could still feel the smooth hardwood of the floor on my hands and knees, see the glint of the barrel from the light in the hall as I pulled back the quilt smelling the lavender Mama used on the bedding.

"Someone needed to do something. I didn't know much about guns, but I could point and pull a trigger. I heard a crash downstairs and knew there wasn't much time." My voice cracked and my hands trembled.

"Take your time." Reed patted my hand and I allowed it.

"I can see it all so clearly. Luddie was standing at the door behind me. Lightning lit the room around us as I pushed the gun across the floor to him. 'Take it,' I said. We both knew that life would never be the same again."

"I was such a coward. I curled into a ball and covered my ears until it was over. Life was hard for so many years. Mama worked in town while Luddie and I kept the farm going. There never was enough money. Old man Michaels offered to buy the farm at one point, but our mother refused. We never understood, but I do now. She had to protect our secret."

I brushed at a fly that landed on the table.

"Luddie, well, he was never really the same. He took up the bottle, just like our father and one day, he was gone. We heard from him once in a while. It was so lonely without him. And then early one morning after a night of drinking, he pulled out a gun and shot himself in his apartment in Nashville."

"I know. I did a search on him. I'm sorry."

"Maybe Luddie wouldn't have shot our father if I wouldn't have pushed the gun on him. Maybe he wouldn't have been so tortured all his life. That one act changed so many lives."

"You might all be dead if you hadn't." A kind, compassionate smile graced Reed's face. "It was survival, pure and simple. You saved everyone. It was an act of remarkable courage."

"Doesn't feel like it." I took a shaky breath. "Now I understand why Mama held onto the farm despite all the troubles that came with it. She needed to keep the world away from the Witness Tree. I can't quite come to terms with the fact that I never knew where they'd put him. Never questioned it. It simply never was spoken of again."

"It's over now. You are a genuine hero, Helen. I want you to know that. Nothing else matters now."

"Am I? It's hard to reconcile any pride in that in the face of so much pain." I knew he was only saying those things to make me feel better. To be able to face the future with hope.

We sat in silence for a time. Autumn leaves drifted and danced in the slight breeze. Mums, in bursts of rust, yellow and white, nodded along to the silent tune.

"Are you mad at me for leading you on so?"

"Never. You're one tough lady, Helen. I admire you." The sunflowers by the back fence nodded in agreement.

"I want this behind me for the last time. Ivy now knows that Harlon is not her grandfather. She doesn't hate me for keeping my secrets. Robert Sommers would have been a wonderful father to

Annabelle and grandfather to Ivy and those children of hers. At least I can only imagine. It's Robert from whom she got that auburn hair, you know. But her temperament, I supposed the credit for that remains with me." Then a thought occurred to me. "Would you like her phone number? She's going to be single now."

Reed's booming laughter filled the garden. "I would. And, Helen, you know I'm here if you need me."

"I do. And now, Mr. Deputy, this pity-party is done."

As I watched him go, I distinctly heard my mother's voice. *"I love you, deary."*

***

"Wipe that goofy grin off your face, Charlie. I brought you something." I stood on his porch, shoulders square, determined to set life right-side up. "Are you going to let me in or not?"

"By all means, come in." He stood back, still grinning, and I entered with a plate in my hands. Stepping into his home was a comfort. Everything about Charlie spoke of comfort, and peace.

"I baked a Lemon-Vanilla Tea Loaf. It's very good. You have tea, don't you? I'm not really in the mood for coffee." I held the soft buttery loaf out to him on one of my best plates, still a bit warm from the oven.

"Is this an attempt to be nice, or should I worry that you're trying to poison me?" His bushy brows arched over his blue eyes like snowdrifts.

"Poison? Trust me, Charlie, if I wanted to do you in, I could be more creative than this. Besides, I wouldn't sully one of my tea loaves with poison."

"I saw you take that bucket of toys over to the neighbor kids. They sure were happy to have them back. And now you're here. So, you're being nice. Is the world coming to an end?"

"Oh, I don't know. Maybe I'm having a stroke." Then I laughed. It was only a brief, 'Ha'.

"That's not funny. I'll make us that tea." He motioned me to the dining room table as he went to the kitchen.

"This is my way of saying thank you for hauling me to the ER that day." I removed the plastic wrap from the plate.

"Could it be that Helen Foley's heart is softening just a tad? Maybe I should alert the media."

"Oh, shut up and make the tea." I turned so he couldn't see the smile breaking across my face.

Then he was there by my side, knife, forks and plates in hand.

The curves at the corners of his mouth melted my heart something fierce.

"Helen, Helen. You are still as beautiful as you always were." His old eyes softened. "I'm very happy you're here."

Suddenly I was nervous. My heart thrummed in my chest and my palms grew slick.

Charlie Soderberg was the last person to have ever told me I was beautiful, and that was so many years ago. Where had the time gone? How sad to think there had been no one else in all that time.

"Now who has the goofy look on her face?" He set the knife and plates on the table and put his hands on my arms.

The room was suddenly very warm.

"I mean it, Helen. You will always be that beautiful young girl to me."

I cleared my throat. "I…I just needed to thank you for the ride to the hospital and listening to my sad story. That's all. No need to turn it into something it's not." Silently, I wanted to kick myself in the behind for that last sentence. I didn't want him thinking I was pursuing him like a teenager. Good God, at my age?

Charlie touched my forehead with his lips and the hard, cold center of me melted like butter, running to the far reaches of my body.

I gently pulled back. This was most definitely not in my plans. How could tea and tea loaf go so awry?

"It's okay, Helen. I'm not going to hurt you again. You have my word on that."

"Yes, you will. You're going to die." I waved a hand in front of me to chase away the awful thought. "We're old. That's the way it is."

"Aren't you the chipper one?"

"Charlie, I...I want to start over. You and I." I held up a palm to him. "Not those young and foolish days, but now. I want to start a friendship. I'll warn you, I'm not good at it, but I'll try. I'm afraid I didn't quite know how to behave before and, well, I want to do better."

He took one of my hands in his. "We will be wonderful friends." I liked the way his palm felt against mine, warm, safe, and infused with kindness.

I nodded and blinked back tears. "I've never liked a crybaby. I don't know what's happening to me."

"I'll make us the tea while you cut that delicious looking bread." He winked and disappeared into the kitchen.

Tears spilled down my cheeks as the years of anger and bitterness washed away. I wiped them with the backs of my hands and fought the urge to sink to my knees and let the dam burst.

"Charlie, I need a better knife than this if I'm to cut this bread. A butter knife simply won't do. And I hope you have some honey to go with that tea."

"Yes, dear," he called from the kitchen, then I heard him chuckle.

Outside the window a sparrow took flight carrying all my bitterness and loneliness away upon its wings.

The Witness Tree

Terri Morrison Kaiser resides in northern Wisconsin with her husband. She writes a newspaper column and a blog, both titled Letters from Musky Falls. When not writing, she can be found gardening, enjoying a good glass of wine, traveling, trying new recipes and pestering her kids.